# DOCTOR GLASS

## GLASS MINDS, BOOK 1

## LOUISE WORTHINGTON

TCK PUBLISHING.COM

ISBN:
**978-1-63161-179-7**

Sign up for Louise Worthington's newsletter at
**www.louiseworthington.co.uk/newsletter**

Published by TCK Publishing
**www.TCKpublishing.com**

Get discounts and special deals on our best selling books at
**www.TCKpublishing.com/bookdeals**

Check out additional discounts for bulk orders at
**www.TCKpublishing.com/bulk-book-orders**

A CIP catalogue record of this book is available from the
British Library.

'To love at all is to be vulnerable.'
**C. S. Lewis**

# PROLOGUE

*A meal prepared with love, seasoned and softened, slides out of the oven.*

*Time has made it tender, tastier. It is hastily moved onto a ceramic dish to keep it hot. The stove walls drip with condensation, steam hovers, and the kitchen window sweats. The table is laid with a cloth as white as a lullaby, sharp knives, and a spoon shaped like a cupped hand. This meal isn't finger food: forks rather than an ink pen to write the words of love. Love is written in letters in the steam on the window, in the vapours in the air. It is in the calligraphy of the meat and vegetables, then the fruit dessert of blackberries, which gleam like glass.*

*The butter is at a perfect room temperature. It submits to the knife, lingering on cutlery like the yellow wax of a burnt candle. A thimbleful of salt and pepper to season—a merest suggestion, a hint, like a batting of an eyelash. There is love in the home-made pastry; flakes linger on the rolling pin. There is love in the harmony of flavours in the sauce of wild mushrooms to go with the beef en croûte, and on the glossy wetness of the green leeks. Love is even in the water jug, in those floating slices of lemons and in the tinkling of ice cubes, which bump against each other like flirtatious dodgems. It's in the mint peas, the thickness of the sauce and the delicacy of the beef, which falls noiselessly and dissolves like sleeping pills in a wine glass of claret. This food of longing belongs on pink, hungry tongues, between teeth, in the dark of the digestive system.*

*Not just one mouth, two lips, one tongue with its beaded*

*taste buds, but several, feeding and tasting to the sound of scraping forks and knives, to the slurping and sipping of civilised wolves. Is this a form of savagery masquerading as appetite? An aperitif to satiate a desire—an urge—to eat, and then fuck one final time?*

*Let's be civilised about it. Let's eat first, then dab each corner of our mouths with a white linen napkin. Then, and only then, talk dirty with our hands and our tongues. Indulge rapacious taste buds then squeeze the life out of a hungry groin, like all those lemons.*

*Ask the wolves what gives them pleasure and they'll say feeding. Is feeding better than touch?*

Love me. *The food speaks quieter now, for the plate is almost empty. Is anyone listening, or are the ripping incisors too loud to hear it?*

*Everyone needs feeding to fill the emptiness. Tuck into this last supper.*

*Dine before death.*

# 1

Under the canopy of a sycamore tree, the world is a kinder place.

Between the Cumbrian hills, a woman and child are in a hollow, a gentle curve where the roots of the sycamore tree laid its foundations. She sees them in a paradise, a garden of Eden, a place where they will return to innocence.

The finely spun shadows under her eyes hint at this deranged truth, as does her unblinking gaze across the grass and thistle, all the way to an exposed section of Hadrian's wall.

The sycamore tree creaks. *Is the sap rising?* she wonders, and the not knowing unsettles her. The muted tones of the landscape give her no clue as to the season.

*Mother Nature's kind. She knows we are good.*

'What are you staring at?' she suddenly shouts at the blank stare of a ewe. It bleats and runs in the opposite direction, trailing pieces of candyfloss-fleece wrapped in thistles. She moves further under the sycamore tree like a wild creature seeking camouflage and places a hand on its reassuring trunk.

*The canopy of the sycamore is a perfect roof for us.* Her shoulders drop a little, reassured now that she has done the right thing.

Desperately trying to recall something about the long journey from home, she pushes her hair away from her face. Then a smile washes over her pinched features.

3

Little Bear pointed out the lorries on the motorway. He said which colour they were and how their wheels were like huge grapefruits. The smaller ones, he said, were like tangerines. His favourite fruit of all.

It was only last year when Little Bear said each word like he was peeling an apple or unwrapping a conker from its protective case. Each new word was a poem. All those objects he's named—she sees them lined up on a shelf stretching out along Hadrian's Wall, running like a stitch through the open wound of the earth.

*Rope. Tree. Daddy.*

When she wraps an arm around Little Bear's legs and rubs a cheek against his thigh, the smell of washing powder—always jasmine and lavender—pulls at something in her insides.

A hand clamps to her mouth to stifle a sob as she recalls how he had needed the toilet during the journey, and she had refused to stop. He had wet himself on the back seat and sobbed.

*I made him cry. How could I do such a thing?*

She makes a fist and hits herself hard in the face. A twig snaps underfoot as she stumbles backwards, knocking Little Bear and making his legs swing.

'I'm sorry, love. Sorry. My beautiful, brave boy.'

She brought his hand to her face, soft fingers on her cheek, and recalls the lotions applied to his skin to stop the sun from burning his tender flesh; the moisturiser in the winter when it became dry; the calamine lotion when he had chicken pox; and ointment to grazes.

His hand fits perfectly inside hers, like a jigsaw piece.

She sees herself back in the kitchen telling Little Bear to put on his shoes, stained a little with mud now. She had tried so hard to be a wonderful mother. Did she put the milk back in the fridge? It was the rushing that made her forget. They had to get out of the house quickly. Someone had upset her. A woman. A messenger from hell. Was there blood?

*No.*

Just pain.

Little Bear had fallen towards the earth's floor.

His last words weren't goodbye.

He knew the word for rope. But not noose.

A noose. A snake coiled into a ring.

She told him to enter the noose. To step inside, like stepping into a new world, a magic world where the sky is pink and the grass is blue and where they will be together forever. A place where the stars will love them, butterflies too, and moths and birds will sing a lullaby just for them. He stood there patiently, so trusting on the stepladder, waiting for the colours to change. She told him that everything will sparkle and twinkle like Santa's grotto. There will be no shadows. It will be a bright gouache painting come to life.

A hand-print painting like they have made on the kitchen table.

As she said those things to her darling son, the birds kept singing. Not one dropped from the sky, nor a branch from the beautiful tree. So that proved it. She had done the right thing. The only thing a loving mother could do in her position.

'Don't let the coffin flies come,' she whispers. 'Or the birds' beaks.' She peers at the sky. 'Or flesh-eating beetles.'

*How wide the sky is. Or is it just that Little Bear is so small?*

Don't even think about how he will never grow an inch taller. How those white sneakers on his feet will be his last pair of shoes. All those trips to shoe shops over the years. His favourite pair, kept beside the fridge in the kitchen, always with the laces still tied because he hadn't learned to tie them yet. Now she remembers there is tomato pasta sauce splattered on the side of one of those shoes.

The rope swings in the breeze. The shadow of him is still alive, a smudge on the earth, moving closer to her, then further away. A swinging bell. They had bells at their wedding, yes; the peals went on for a long time.

She puts her hand in her mouth and bites down until the skin gives way to the taste of iron.

There was a time before this—a time before the messenger came and told her what she had to do—before marriage, before motherhood—but so long ago—like a different self—

'What day is it, Little Bear?' It feels important to know. She visualises the calendar hanging on the kitchen wall, where she records important dates and where ticks mark that she has taken her medication. 'Wednesday,' she says, pleased with herself for remembering.

*And the date?*

Her jaw clenches in frustration at her failing memory.

Little Bear looks as though a white wax candle has dripped down his angelic face. So, she lightly runs her hand over his eyes, closing the lids on the blood inside. The trunk is sturdy, so unlike her own weariness, her withered core.

*The sycamore tree is breathing. But he is not. Sad to think tomorrow and the day after, the grass under our feet will keep growing.*

She must rush now, so he isn't alone any longer.

The rope is rough in her hands. After placing it around her neck, she touches Little Bear's small hand one last time and looks to his face for all the answers to all the questions she has ever had. A look like water to a plant.

The ewe bleats, and in its pitiful sound, she hears kinship and understanding of a fellow mother. Her blank stare meets the horizon, one impervious to everything except the corpse dangling on her right. The beauty of the wild landscape is out of focus as the pain of confused thought and penitence takes hold.

She licks her dry lips. There is nowhere else to go now except down.

Little Bear's white trainers point back to the way they came from, where there is no return. He is nothing now but a target and a shadow to fall into.

And fall she did.

# 2

Emma-Jane gets up from the kitchen table to turn the radio on and then pours herself a glass of water. Her hand is still shaking when she brings the glass to her lips.

A door bangs upstairs. She accidentally drops the glass, and it smashes on the tiled floor. She kneels to collect the largest fragments, hating the mess and the adrenaline surging through her. A shard cuts her middle finger, so she sucks the blood and swallows it, grimacing at the copper taste in her mouth.

Sunlight streams through the kitchen window, and the clock reminds her she has the entire weekend ahead of her in her lovely home, where she is free. Her dry cleaning can wait, and she can always read the newspaper online to save a trip to the newsagents.

Stay inside. Stay safe.

*I'm safe,* she reassures herself, staring at the hate letter clutched in her trembling hand, a letter penned by a nameless enemy. The arrival of this letter has transformed the place.

*Dr Glass. Or bitch. Dr Bitch . . . Abominable woman. How amused I am by your name. Apt for a woman. A woman like you.*

*Your business is my business now.*

*How many more are going to die before you stop meddling? One, two, ten, Dr Death?*

The poisonous writer has gone to the trouble of finding out her personal address, presumably so the letter has more of a knife-edge when opened in the comfort and privacy of her home, rather than the impersonal space of her office and consulting room.

The words blur through panicked tears. She blinks. Taking a deep breath, she focuses on the white walls in the pristine kitchen, on the shine of the chrome taps at the sink, but the letter has thrown a lasso around her head, yanking her gaze back where it wants it.

This time she reads the letter forensically, as a scientist is trained to do. As a psychologist, she must not forget that she is first and foremost a scientist and devoted to her work.

*You like a test. I hope you're listening. Can you hear glass smashing? Those sharp little pieces will be your only legacy. No family. Just shards of glass. Sharp and pointed. You don't have children. You are not a mother, nor a rational human being. Merely satiated by ignorance.*
*How can you write garbage like this?*

Stapled to the letter is a copy of her article published in *The Clinical Psychology and Counselling Review* entitled 'Altruistic Violence in Maternal Filicide.' It reads:

'Mothers who commit maternal filicide are women lost in a personal darkness. These women are not aberrations. They are mothers lost in an untreated, deep despair, trapped in silence because of the taboo impulse to hurt their own child. With Angela Lamb, who took her own and her son, Teddy's life, the media have perpetuated the myth of an 'inhumane and barbaric mother-monster', ignoring the tragedy of a woman coping with depression and raising an unwanted child who was causing considerable distress to herself and her beloved daughter through his hyper-aggression. Angela's motive was altruistic, most likely to protect her daughter. Poor mental health stemming from having an unwanted second child is understated in this tragedy. A combination of complex and interwoven factors causes suicide and murder.'

*My favourite word in your article is 'altruistic.' Altruistic like Mother Teresa, like Gandhi! Woman, that gave me the biggest laugh. Do you know what that word means? You have a lot to learn, so I will teach you and train you. You could be teacher's pet. I am getting ready to handle you, so you better get ready for me. It's going to be so satisfying.*

*Have you started looking over your shoulder yet? When you see that bloke at the bus stop, that kid in a hoody sitting on a swing, that woman pushing a pram down the street outside your office. Think of me. Who am I? Which one? I will watch and wait because you can guarantee you will hear from me again, Dr Glass, your very own foe. I am looking forward to cutting to the chase and getting to know your insides better.*

*Be a good girl now. Wait for me.*

To the imaginary sound of fingers on a keyboard, she drops the letter. Dr Celia Dome, her respected supervisor, was right. There is a backlash to her article because she ignored Celia's words of warning about expressing views on a highly emotive subject.

Instead of lying low for a time after the published article, on local radio she asserted that society underestimates the prevalence of murderous thoughts because of the pressure society places on women to enjoy motherhood. 'The taboo nature of the thoughts prevents early intervention. We all have a role to play in failing these families.' It needed to be said, she'd thought. That, and how tragic the deaths were, and how suffering mothers should come forward and seek help without shame.

Now grime and threats have entered the sanctity of her house. Her home. Her life.

She washes her hands, but the sensation of ants crawling around her wrists remains. Have foreign bodies transferred to her skin from the paper? It feels like the bitter author is in her house, intruding on this very moment in the kitchen, on the weekend, a person unwelcome. Spiteful. Nasty. But violent?

Many of her clients or ex-clients could have penned it.

Out of respect for Celia, she had thought again—and decided she felt too strongly on the subject to pass on the publicity. It was a rare opportunity. The subject of women murdering their children is typically too horrible to be aired, which perpetuates the ignorance and taboo nature of maternal filicide. Too many people brand the mothers as evil, warped, because they don't understand the mental health problems, or the sad context in which something so terrible and upsetting as murdering your own child occurs. It seemed to Emma-Jane that she owed mothers and their dead children a chance for their voices to be heard. For a woman to have killed her child, she must have called for help and not received it. Not just once, but many times.

No, I am not a mother, she thinks, glaring at the letter. I am a professional and I firmly believe the causes of these deaths are over-simplified. They think I'm some kind of dog that needs handling, for Pete's sake!

'Yes, I'm listening,' she says to the letter. 'You have my full attention. So, you know a bit about me then? You like that. It makes you feel powerful, but I know something about you. I know you feel powerless, and threatening me makes you feel better, but only for a short time. I know that you've thought about hurting me.'

She swallows, and the sound is louder than usual. Perhaps the radio interview broadcast four weeks ago wasn't such a good idea. So far, she has received no feedback or reaction from colleagues in the profession which, she concedes to herself, speaks volumes. Emma-Jane paces, full of nervous energy.

*Let them take a step back from associating with me,* she thinks. *If that's what they want to do. It can't seriously harm my career. Or me.*

Or can it?

It was easy to be brave then, to give Angela Lamb a voice, but now? Suffering mothers hadn't contacted her as she thought they might, but perhaps they will when the time is right. Someone was listening because the repercussions of her actions were visible on her own kitchen table and in her trembling hands. She looks over her shoulder.

*Come on, think like a scientist. It's not personal. It's not addressed to Emma-Jane. Perhaps they don't know my Christian name. It is a professional attack. Everyone is entitled to their own opinion and reaction. Not everyone can engage in open discussion about emotional subjects. It's weak, a kind of bullying to send me this. They want to keep me guessing.*

*Don't be frightened.*

Pleased with her critique, she relaxes her shoulders

a little. The pulsing in her temples quietens. 'Well done,' she whispers.

The writer is reasonably well-educated, judging by the technical accuracy of the content, and careful enough to type both the letter and address label. There's no postmark on the envelope. Was it hand-delivered? If so, why the stamp? Is the front door locked?

She runs to check, then knowing it's probably pointless, she runs to the kitchen window, looking out onto the drive to see if anyone is there. Now that she thinks about it, it's strange that she didn't hear the crunch of gravel underfoot when the post was delivered. Or did she?

*Think like a scientist. Keep calm. Think.*

Somewhere out there, the author is perhaps walking, or driving, sitting on a bus, mixing with people, looking like they are just getting on with their normal business. This person is playing mind games.

'Damn you!' she curses at the letter.

*Should I call Celia, or report it to the police?* If she keeps the letter, then the option to report it to the police at a later date remains open; if she receives more letters, or feels harassed, truly frightened, that will be the time to report it.

*Do nothing. Try to forget it. At least, for now.*

The paper smacks of quality but it is without scent. It slides neatly between two books in the bookcase in the living room, ironically between 'Mastering Emotional Intelligence' and another on personality disorders written by the same author. The bookcase is almost full of non-fiction, arranged alphabetically in a room defined by straight lines and right angles. Most of the books are about psychology or counselling, and a few are on specialist topics she has taken an interest in over the years, such as grief and loss. Perfectly concealed yet still, there is an audible sound in her mind of fingers typing at speed, firmly pushing down the keys.

She turns up the radio and classical music plays from high-end speakers. A glass coffee table holds a stack of travel books. Not that she has travelled any further than Europe, but one day, when the time is right, when she is proud of her career, she would like to travel to Egypt and swim in the Red Sea, stay in the most luxurious hotels and be looked after twenty-four-seven. The adrenaline wearing off, she feels wrung out like she's been playing chess for days on end. She'd kill for a plush hotel room and room service right now.

Early on Monday morning, wearing blusher, eyeshadow, lipstick, too, and a tailored suit, she will lock the front door behind her, leaving this ugly moment behind. Then the hateful letter will travel from the privacy of her home to live in a spotless office, where the good doctor works, where the professional slur belongs.

She goes over to the mirror above the electric stove. In the glass, she is unblinking. She gently touches her neck. A strained reflection greets her in the gilt edge mirror. A kaleidoscope of shadows plays under her eyes at the sound of typing on a keyboard. Nothing shatters. Nothing breaks. She keeps looking at her reflection. She is Emma-Jane. Not just a doctor. Not made from glass. Not fragile.

*Or am I?*

# 3

The Farmhouse at Cleave, on the outskirts of Shrewsbury, is owned by Drew Rogers. It is a sturdy, sandstone building with a yard, several outbuildings, and half an acre of garden. At the point of sale, the land and large sheds were sold to a neighbouring owner.

Drew, a savvy property developer, had moved himself, his wife, Evie, and their son, James, into the property, knowing it would make a wonderful family home—and a packet when he sold it, developed to its full potential.

Like most farmhouses untouched by developers, it has retained its character in many of its features, like the dark wooden beams in the kitchen and the chunky chimney, which climbs up from the roof to enjoy a view of the Shropshire and Welsh hills.

It is such a waste for Drew's labourers, Pete and AJ, to work indoors on such a fine summer day, but they do it to keep the boss happy, especially as he has given them a steady stream of work on his various rental properties, and now on the farmhouse. Today it's painting and decorating and a spot of clearing.

AJ looks at his workmate, astonished to see a skip half-full of what looks like women's clothes and accessories in Drew's yard. Pink towels and chunky plastic jewellery, feminine bed linen and underwear; it's all on show. There's also a full-length mirror, dressing table, stool, and a rocking horse, plus other bits and pieces worth a bob or two.

Pete has an uncanny habit of raising one eyebrow in such situations. In this case, AJ concluded he must be thinking about selling the stuff for themselves. As Drew is rarely at home between nine and five and hasn't, for the last few days, swerved by in his Range Rover Sport to check up on them, AJ doesn't feel the need to be so discreet about nosing into Drew's discarded belongings and making a few easy quid.

'There's some decent stuff in here,' AJ says, as he climbs inside the skip. His workman's boots make a satisfying thud when he lands inside. He hitches up his jeans so he can bend over without them sliding down any further and exposing his crack.

'What do you think it's worth?' Pete asks, scratching his two-day stubble.

'Must be a few hundred quid here, at least for the rocking horse and those leather bar stools. We'd be doing Drew a favour by making more room in the skip. I'll ask Hannah to eBay it. Split sixty-forty with you.'

'Fifty-fifty, mate. You know this goes no further.'

'Sounds fair to me.'

AJ passes Pete the objects to load into his van. 'How is Hannah?'

'Good. Set up qualifying as an accountant, which suits me!'

'I bet,' Pete says, chuckling. Labouring isn't a bad job, but the physical nature of the work has a limited life expectancy; not like bean counting, which you can do into your seventies if you have to.

Half an hour later, with the contents of the skip safely stored in the back of his van, AJ carries the step ladders into the farmhouse and up to the second floor. He and Pete are tasked with painting the walls and ceiling of the master bedroom, which Drew has vacated. Refurbishment to the farmhouse is restricted to a certain number of rooms that Drew isn't using for the time being, as he continues to live in parts of the property. The place doesn't exactly feel lived in, now that Drew's wife and son aren't living there.

'Has Drew said when he plans to put this place on the market?' Pete asks.

'Not to me. I haven't seen or heard from him much, except for a text to say what to get on with.'

Pete washes down the walls of the master bedroom before giving them a fresh lick of paint, while AJ looks inside the other bedrooms, of which there are four, to find out where his boss sleeps these days. He shouldn't, but AJ can't help himself.

Drew Rogers is a decent bloke to work for, but it is clear from the farmhouse in which he is living that life is getting on top of him. No wonder, really.

AJ opens the door with an ornate sign on it that reads James. It surprises him to feel a fleeting sense of pity for Drew, knowing that he sleeps in his absent son's bedroom. A multi-millionaire, choosing to kip on a bottom bunk bed in a farmhouse with four other bedrooms. Who'd have guessed that? Sleeping in the same room as all those glass-eyed teddies and pieces of Lego still strewn on the floor would give him the creeps. He closes one of the wardrobe doors, which is ajar, before joining Pete in the master bedroom.

They simultaneously turn their heads to the windows at the sound of a sports car grumbling into the yard. Sunlight bounces off the windscreen and catches the red hair of the driver, like a match to paper.

'Kat,' AJ says with a sigh, immediately recognising the owner of the red car and the red hair within it. 'Again.'

Pete tuts when he sees the battered red MX-5 make a wide circle in the courtyard before disappearing from view.

'She doesn't give up easily, does she?' Pete says. 'Wasn't she here yesterday?'

AJ nods. 'And the day before that. Drew's given her the brush off.'

Apart from that raspy, sexy voice of hers and her tight little ass, AJ can't understand what Drew ever saw in her when he had Evie, who was gorgeous and simply adored him. Having worked for Drew for the last few years, he'd had the pleasure of sharing the odd brew with Evie when she'd turned up at one of Drew's rental properties they were doing up. He appreciated it. Some wives with money are stuck-up and don't show workmen like him the time of day.

But not Evie.

He looks out the window as Kat pulls out of the yard. It must have been convenience that took Drew to her bed, perhaps, as Kat is a tenant of his. Still is, as far as AJ knows. One thing he does know is that you don't mix business with pleasure if you want a good night's sleep and a quiet life.

'Do you think we should say something to Drew about her coming here all the time?' Pete asks. 'She should have taken the hint by now, if he's not talking to her.'

AJ opens a window in the master bedroom now that the car is out of sight. 'You can if you want, but I won't. Drew might think we're meddling in his business.'

Pete makes a start on painting the walls magnolia. 'You're probably right. He'll shoot the messenger, I guess. What's he hoping to get for this place anyway?'

'Drew reckons he's already got a buyer. Six or seven

hundred thousand.' Pete whistles at the sum of money. 'It could be worth a lot more if he developed the outbuildings like he was going to.'

'True enough. Plans change. What do you think he'll buy next? He could buy three or four at auction, maybe more if they need serious work. That's what I would do if I were Drew.'

'Yeah, me too. The bloke doesn't know how lucky he is,' AJ says, then hesitates. He was about to share his concern with Pete that they could be out of a job if Drew sold all his properties, as he suspected he was. It's fragments of information he's pieced together. Perhaps wrongly, because AJ knows himself well enough to accept he isn't a bright bloke. He knew that, long before his teachers told him so. He is not good with numbers or facts, unlike his girlfriend, Hannah, but he's usually pretty good with people. 'I do know he wants Evie's darkroom cleared of furniture and her photography equipment and the summer house taken down before the end of the day. We'd better get a move on with the first coat in here.'

'I'll crack on here, mate, if you want to see to that other stuff,' Pete says amicably. 'Then we might be in for an early finish. Day like today, I fancy a pint in the garden.'

Up until yesterday, the farmhouse landing and hall had looked like a gallery, with one framed photograph after another, all taken by Evie, who divided her time between their son and her passion for photography. The memory of the pictures is in the grubby marks on the wall, which AJ follows downstairs like a map to the darkroom.

Inside, he flicks on the single red bulb and the light is weak, like watercolour. The room has retained her scent, an expensive perfume. The familiar floral aroma is also in the wardrobe in the master bedroom. Judging by the number of unwashed mugs and wine glasses on the desk, she had spent a fair bit of time inside this room until recently. The desk is almost entirely covered with photographs, mostly monochrome shots of landscapes, plus a few portraits.

He shivers, and nervously looks over his shoulder. It's as though Evie is in the room with him, following his every move with wide and piercing eyes. All those photographs left disordered on the desk make AJ feel angry. Why hasn't Drew put them safely away?

He shakes his head. It's none of his business what Drew wants to do with his wife's photographs, but if it were him, he'd keep them in an album. A smart leatherbound one. There are a few shots on the desk of their son, James, and her. She's a good-looking woman, he muses, while taking a closer look into her eyes. That blonde hair, and the fancy engagement ring on her finger. A rock of a gem. Money, it buys beauty alright. He sniffs the photograph, as if expecting even that to smell of money.

The instruction from Drew is to bin the lot, but AJ puts the photos in a black box with a lid. The bloke might change his mind one day and thank him. When the plyboard comes off the window, the space immediately feels less oppressive, and the sun is still shining outside.

'Pete!' he shouts up the stairs, over the sound of Radio One. 'I'm going to make a start on the summer house while it's still dry.' AJ loves being outside, especially in pleasant weather, and away from the shadows and corners of the farmhouse. As a builder during the summer, getting a tan while you work is a real perk of the job. He rolls up his sleeves, exposing hairy arms, both tattooed in darkgreen Maori-style silver ferns.

'Alright, mate!' Pete replies cheerfully over the tones of Oasis' "Wonderwall".

The summer house is only a few months old. AJ knows this because he and Pete had erected it for James on his third birthday. Drew had said to chop it down for firewood, but he thinks it's too good for that. Way too good. Another young family could get joy from it, so he decides to dismantle it piece by piece and load it into his van with all the other stuff.

Drew needn't know. He just wants it out of sight. Hannah is a dab hand at selling stuff on eBay. They need the money more than Drew does because he's loaded, while they're skint and who knows how much longer AJ will be earning a decent wage. The thought adds fury to the strike of the hammer as he brings it down on the children's bunk bed.

*Why destroy something so perfect? What's the rich prat hiding?*

# 4

Pity the woman whose mother abandoned her, whose father disowned her and then died, leaving her an orphan all those years ago.

A contract is made between her brain and her face to keep the snake of secrets firmly within her mouth. Her expression shows no emotion; it's a smooth road recently laid, perfectly made, without flaw or lump. Whatever jealousy or fury she may have felt at one time, her polite, clay face doesn't betray her.

Except, no one does pity Kat Stiles. Just like Mary Lennox from *The Secret Garden*—only Kat is a twisted, nasty little version with a pert pair of tits and a pierced tongue. Hell, Kat doesn't even pity herself. Why should she? A young, confident woman who fears nothing and no one. Someone who knows herself and her sex drive, and the weapon of her sexual allure, better than anyone.

Without a family to take care of her, and men like Drew Rogers coming in and out of her life, Kat had made her own family. Stan, her Burmese python, is like a little brother to her. Luckily, there are always men around for company or entertainment. Some she plays like a marionette, moving their randy arms and legs this way and that, a nod of their head, a jiggle of their body. Sex is a play in a travelling theatre. Sweet, hungry Kat with red, fiery hair, a living devil, breathing and moving with all the other blackened souls.

Drew loved her for these things. For a time, at least.

Though, he'd turned out to be just like all the rest.

Today, Kat is a quiet and menacing figure, humming as she strolls along Welsh Bridge into Shrewsbury's town centre. She shops for fruit and veg (organic only), saying 'please' and 'thank you' to the staff before paying the bill, presenting as a charming woman enjoying a simple pleasure. Though, she knows full well she will return home to feed Stan live hamsters, mice, and rats, squirming and squeaking in her hand, all of which she breeds herself.

From a small table at the back of a vegan café, she sips a coffee before making her way to the last of the pawnbrokers, a place called D & R. A smile is etched on her face because she can walk among the other shoppers without heads turning in horror while she holds the darkest secret of all in her handbag.

Inside is a valuable engagement ring. But not hers.

D & R is tucked away down a narrow street, next to a charity shop. A bell above the door jingles as she opens it and steps inside. The shop is smaller than it looks on the outside, with an impressive window of stock under glistening white lights. Two soft chairs covered in a garish print add some bling to an otherwise functional space, and framed posters on the walls specify all manner of clauses and codes of conduct, which no one ever reads, but are a good piece of arse-covering by the pawnbroker. The man has made a mint in the most upmarket of the pawnshops in the vicinity by not asking too many questions.

Kat feels her presence is acknowledged before he speaks, so she corrects her posture and paints on a warm smile.

'How can I help you, madam?' the pawnbroker asks from behind the leather-topped antique desk. He is well-practised at not overtly looking customers up and down before seeing their goods. Kat knows he has been in the job for fifteen years and outlasted two recessions. He has probably seen all sorts in his time.

The pawnbroker adjusts his tortoise-shell spectacles, and a wider smile creeps across Kat's lips as she delves into her handbag and opens the ring box. It's a slow-moving smile, a slither, revealing teeth so white they could have been cleaned with Ajax. She shows him the precious item in the palm of her hand.

'Feast your eyes on that!'

It's a sapphire and diamond engagement ring, which should be on someone else's finger right now, only the rightful owner doesn't need it anymore.

The pawnbroker raises his eyebrows and looks at the ring, then fleetingly at Kat's clay face. His eyes are misty. Is he waiting for Kat to come out with a story which might explain how she is in possession of such an exquisite and valuable ring? It's bound to be one of the finest engagement rings he has seen in his career.

'May I?' he asks, and when she nods, he carefully places it on the desk.

He takes a closer look at a tiny inscription on the band, only visible with a magnifying glass. Kat does not attempt to conjure a tale; she just looks at it with her head to one side, like a mother doting on a newborn.

'Well?' she asks.

He hears her impatience and gives Kat an encouraging smile. His name badge says Dominic in a swirling cursive. It's a wonder the greedy bloke isn't rubbing his hands together right now.

'Lovely,' he mutters.

In a steely tone, she says, 'I want the cash, not a loan.'

'I see.' Dominic places the ring on his scales. 'Well,

it's a good weight,' he confirms with an eagerness that suggests he has never seen such a large sapphire before. 'And in good condition, for an antique ring.'

'Excellent condition,' she corrects him.

He places the loupe in his left eye to take a closer look and is silent for several minutes, before putting the ring and the loupe back on the counter. Between approving murmurs, he looks directly at her. 'Blue sapphire is said to be a stone of truth, wisdom, and . . .'

'Strength. Yes, I know. I've called in at a couple of other pawnshops. I like to do my research first.'

'Right,' Dominic says, trying to hide his disappointment that she isn't as ignorant as he would like. 'Well, the clarity of the diamonds is excellent.'

'Flawless. I know. The diamonds are three carats apiece.'

'Do you have identification or certification with you? We have certain protocols.'

'What's it worth to you?' Kat snaps.

'I can't—'

'Look, I'm not stupid, and neither are you. That ring there is worth a lot of money. Make me an offer,' she says impatiently, putting one hand on a skinny hip.

'As you want cash today, I'll give you five thousand pounds for it.'

Kat laughs, tossing her head back, her mouth wide. 'Pass it over. It's all of my divorce settlement, that is. Let's not waste any more of each other's time,' she says, her voice like flint.

'Settlement, you say? May I at least take a name?'

'Kat Jones.'

'Alright,' he says a little breathlessly, clearly wanting the ring to be his and not questioning the authenticity of her surname. One which couldn't be more common, but it's the best she could think of on the spot.

'It's worth around thirty thousand, possibly more,' she says.

'It's certainly incredible. Ten thousand.' He sees a flicker of interest in her eyes before they close. She puts her hand out for the ring to be returned. 'Oh, alright. Twelve thousand, and that's my final and best offer. That's all the cash I have available.'

'I know it's worth at least double that, so I'll want the money in cash, now, with no questions. Then we have a deal.'

'Sign here.'

A version of pleasure changes the expression of her face, a softening around the hard edges of her eyes. She sighs and then snatches the cash the way a cat claws at a warm blanket for a night off the streets, remembering the taste of its mother's teats.

They both stare at the shop window at the same time, hearing a noise on the street outside: two men laughing and chatting. The speech of one of them is slurred and loud, a trail of nonsense about a 'bloke who had it coming'. It's a vernacular familiar to her, having grown up on the rough side of Shrewsbury. She knows the types of sounds and voices to avoid, the way a wild animal knows when one of its own kind is injured and dying.

Once the men pass, Kat shoves the paperwork in her handbag and pulls it high on her shoulder. 'Good doing business with you,' she says. The bell jingles as she closes the door behind her.

It's a sunlit June afternoon as she pauses by the window of a shop selling stationery. The shop, called 'Adore,' sells cards and sentimental tat, like fluffy keyrings and teddy bears with 'Happy birthday' or 'I love you' stitched across a belly hanging as low as a hen's stuffed crop. Sneering at the emotional drivel, she strides away to the butchers, then the pet shop for a few extra special morsels for Stan, and finally to the Co-op for a bottle of cheap fizz to celebrate her recent windfall.

Kat takes a shortcut across Salop College's football pitch onto Dawson's Rough. The route winds into Hartlepool Estate, where her terraced house sits nestled at the end of the road. It's a far cry from Drew's farmhouse, but it's home, and the rent he charges is cheap.

After showering with a rose-scented soap, she dresses in clean clothes and applies mascara and eyeshadow. In the full-length mirror on the door of a single wardrobe, she toasts her reflection with a glass of sparkling wine. The blue jeans fit well, and the T-shirt is suitably tight to show off her ample bosom. She runs her fingers through her long, red hair and lies down on the double bed. Dirty clothes and several pairs of shoes are strewn on the floor. The sheets haven't been changed for months. There's no need to these days, without Drew coming by.

Above the bed, there is a framed print of a nude woman with a colossal snake coiled around her peach flesh, its head resting in her palm next to her head. Her long, fiery red hair drapes down her back like a waterfall. Kat likes to gaze up at it, imagining herself in the picture.

Beneath it, there is another print of a nude male snake charmer. She calls him Drew.

Opposite the bed is a terrarium for Stan, right where she can see him, and he can see her. A lot of people take issue with having a pet snake in the bedroom, but Drew didn't. He liked the way Stan and Kat seemed to communicate by protruding their tongues in synchronised flickers. He would have readily allowed Stan in bed with them if she'd let him, only Kat wouldn't want Stan to get squashed when one of them rolled over, as they liked to do, taking turns on top.

When Stan was just a few years old, he liked to curl up around her naked body at night and move around her, slowly sizing her up. It was a sensual time when they bonded, until Stan started to fast in readiness for a big meal . . . Kat herself.

Stan is happy enough and well fed in his enclosure. Only the two of them know that inside his long, thin belly is a golden wedding ring. Lucky its previous owner was washing up at the same time Kat made an uninvited visit to the farmhouse. The citrus smell of washing-up liquid had never smelt so good.

Kat takes a slurp of fizzy wine and burps. That fat gold band of a wedding ring is her pension, stored in the safest, most loyal, customer-focused bank she knows. The Bank of Stan.

A secret, illicit marriage of sorts, hidden away between flesh and snakeskin.

# 5

The clock on the coffee table sat in the middle of the room, angled for both Dr Glass and Drew Rogers to see its black and white circular face. In a room furnished to a minimum, every object has an obvious purpose. It is twenty past three and a thin rain is falling outside.

'Money isn't important to me, Dr Glass,' Drew Rogers says curtly. His expression, previously avuncular, hardens to stone.

'I understand that,' she replies, mirroring his precise way of speaking.

'Then why must we stop?' he asks, the lines deepening on his forehead.

'For the last two sessions, we ran over into a second hour, which was the right thing to do then.'

There is a long silence that's blanket-thick. 'Now it's not?' he asks.

'I have another client coming, otherwise we could continue,' she says gently. 'I'm glad you're talking. It's all positive, but we have to finish on time today.'

'How very patronising! Still, a change from your usual judgment.' He smiles, but it drops quickly.

'That's not my intention. I don't judge. I am not here for that.'

'For all your talking, do you even know what is important to me? No, I don't believe you do, Dr Glass,' he scoffs. 'You can't help me.'

'I think I can. And I will.'

'And if you can't, you'll be a failure. Right? If I fail, you fail.' He sighs, then glances at his expensive watch like she'd never spoken of the time. 'Time's up. I have to be somewhere else.' Drew slides out of the chair before she has time to stand up, then outstretches his hand to shake. His whole body is a statement of restrained strength while his eyes lightly brush hers. 'So long, Doctor. I will see you next week.'

The office door closes behind him and the sound of his footsteps fades, but the smell of spicy aftershave lingers in the room. She has another forty minutes before her next client is due and she doesn't know why she ended the session when she did, or why she lied. It was out of character. She feels a need for air, but decides against stepping outside.

Her feeling of discomfort diminishes in the office kitchen as she fills up the biscuit tin with chocolate digestives. She opens a new packet of Hobnobs, which she starts consuming without restraint. Mostly she is enjoying the knowledge that she is finally breaking through the layers of Drew's reserve and discovering the man beneath. At first, her job felt like treading water in the ocean at night when you don't know what swims beneath your feet.

But you must keep moving to keep yourself from drowning.

A strange, lonesome feeling washes over her, despite knowing more now about what lurks beneath the deep waters of Drew Rogers.

The kettle boils and begins to sing. The kitchen is just big enough for her and Lucy, her best friend and colleague, to stand and sip their tea or coffee. It has everything she needs, including a small fridge and a microwave to make lunch and, sometimes, dinner in, for those special evening appointments offered to clients who work long hours. She wipes down the surfaces and closes the door behind her. Where there are things she can control, Emma-Jane Glass likes them to be orderly.

She pours her coffee into what she calls 'Lucy's mug.' It is one of Lucy's favourites, with a chunky handle and a picture of Hadrian's Wall on the side. The Roman wall is dear to Lucy, as she grew up in nearby Carlisle; her elderly parents remain there. Between sips of coffee, Emma-Jane continues eating the chocolate Hobnobs. Unconscious eating.

With half a biscuit left, she places it on the table and looks at it.

*I'm not hungry. Why am I stuffing my face? And why am I so uptight?*

The hateful letter has left a bad taste in her mouth. Her eyes feel gritty. It could be the immense caseload, which is more demanding than it had been in previous months. She is treating two clients who loathe members of their family: one young man, a twenty-five-year-old journalist, claims his mother had been cruel to him as a child, while the other client, Melanie, has unresolved anger around her sister's sexually provocative nature. She no longer feels the need to see Dr Glass.

Perhaps Melanie channelled her anger through that hateful letter.

Emma-Jane's job doesn't rewrite the past for people, but it can improve their daily lives. Unfortunately, when she challenged Melanie about her thoughts and feelings to a point she felt Melanie could cope with, Melanie kicked off, stormed out of the office and hadn't returned since. Emma-Jane believes in the principle of respect for the dignity, rights, and choices of others, and therefore hasn't chased Melanie to return. That decision is Melanie's to make. If a client doesn't have trust in her as a psychologist, she isn't of use to them. Trust and honesty are fundamental to progress.

Drew is learning to trust her. She feels that more and more, but he's right, she doesn't know what is important to him, and so she makes a mental note to ask him next time.

Whether he tells her is another matter.

Leaning against the sink, she sips her coffee and reads the information on one poster Lucy has recently hung in the kitchen. The marketing messages about their practice promote holistic health, with Emma-Jane handling the mental, emotional, and social needs of clients as a qualified clinical psychologist. Lucy covers their physical well-being as a nutritionist. So far, it's been a mutually beneficial partnership, and one Emma-Jane is enjoying immensely after working alone for so long. For one thing, it's a comfort to have someone else in the office, especially late at night.

Four months ago, she had readily offered Lucy an office at her new premises in town, rent-free for the first three months, while Lucy got on her feet as a self-employed nutritionist. Having a friend and a professional in the same building is a great boost, worth the financial loss for a short period. They share a kitchen, an entrance, and all the difficulties of working for oneself in a person-centred business.

Sipping the dregs of her coffee at her desk, she checks her inbox. An email from the British Psychological Society reminds her to undertake a training course—an update to an online therapy session—before the end of August, and a short course on exercise and nature for stress and anxiety management. Some of her colleagues offer an online service to clients, which is popular, but so far she has resisted, while others meet with clients in the great outdoors, believing in the remedial benefits of nature. There is also an email from Dr Celia Domes, asking if they can rearrange their appointment on Tuesday, as she has an abscess requiring a dentist's urgent attention. Emma-Jane replies to Celia with a sympathetic message and alternative times.

There's a light tap at the door which makes Emma-Jane jump, then Lucy's smiling face appears.

'Oh, Lucy! You're a sight for sore eyes.'

'How are you? Ah, I see you've demolished the packet of Hobnobs. No need to answer that.'

'You?'

'Pretty well. Was that the very handsome Drew Rogers I saw leaving the building?' Emma-Jane nods. 'You don't look too happy about it.'

'Poor man. He was almost in tears again. You know he's recently divorced? I can't say too much, but he's devastated. Misses his family terribly.' She stretches her aching back after too many hours sitting in her chair, then decides not to say any more. There's a fine line to walk between supporting one another and protecting the confidentiality of clients. 'Anyway, how did your date go? I'm gathering from your continued interest in Drew Rogers, not that well.'

Lucy shrugs. 'Not really. The bloke talked at me the whole time, and I could hardly get a word in edgeways. I couldn't wait to finish my drink and get the hell out of there. Next time I'll order a half.'

'At least it wasn't a three-course meal.'

'God, no way would I agree to that on a first date.

A drink and a packet of crisps took long enough. I've got another date on Saturday night. We've emailed and spoken on the phone. He enjoys running and has a dog. Two big ticks from me.'

'There you go then. It's a good start. What's his name?'

Lucy hesitates. 'Martin.'

'How do you feel about that?' Emma-Jane asks carefully. Lucy's ex-boyfriend, the love of her life, was also named Martin. He died in a car accident two years earlier.

'It's okay. He's probably got a middle name I can use, like Herbert or Dick. Or there's always a nickname.'

'Does he smoke?'

Lucy shakes her head.

'Good.'

'I won't date smokers. I don't have many rules, but that's one.' She checks her watch. 'Better go. New client!' she says excitedly.

'Business is really picking up. Are you feeling more confident? You look it.'

'Definitely. The parrot on my shoulder is mostly silent, thanks to you,' she says, blowing Emma-Jane a kiss. 'I would have tossed the towel in weeks ago without your help, let alone got out of the starting blocks. Usually, with a new client on the way, I'd be sat on the loo with palpitations!'

Emma-Jane smiles warmly at Lucy, but wishes she could share some of her own troubles . . .

Appearing on local radio. The vicious words of the hate letter whispering in her ear. Still, hindsight can't change the past. As a kind of mentor and weathervane to Lucy, it wouldn't be right to show vulnerability, especially when she is finding her own feet. A few years on, Emma-Jane imagines she will share far more, and that it will be an evenly supportive professional partnership.

But for now, Emma-Jane must remain a stone pillar.

Self-confidence has never been Lucy's strong point. But by having an office directly opposite Emma-Jane's, and by meeting with her most days after work to debrief, Emma-Jane knows that Lucy is beginning to believe in her business, not to mention rebuilding her entire life after Martin's fatal crash. Now isn't the time to dampen Lucy's enthusiasm by burdening her with her own professional anxieties.

'You'll be turning clients away soon, or needing to employ staff. Or both! I'll see you later.'

Lucy's two o'clock appointment arrives punctually. She is a new client who made the appointment online, detailing her need to put on weight . . . and fast.

When Lucy welcomes Miss Jennifer Steed, she isn't what Lucy had been expecting. After taking in Jennifer's luscious long blonde hair, her overwhelming first impression is of a big, beautiful woman. Everything about her is ample, from her hair to her stomach, to her large brown eyes and jangling green and red beads.

Lucy immediately questions the accuracy of her memory. Perhaps she's thinking of another application? Certainly, this woman doesn't need help putting on weight.

'I hope I'm not late,' Jennifer says breathlessly. 'I didn't have the right change for pay-and-display, so I had to nip to Boots to buy something to get some change, and there was a queue, as you'd expect. It's always the way, isn't it, when you're running late? If I'd had tons of time, I would have had all the change I needed.'

'Don't worry, you're not late. Make yourself comfortable. I'm Lucy. Did you find us alright?'

'Yes, fine,' Jennifer says with an eager smile.

The office is in Shrewsbury, off the main high street on Byar Lane, which is a convenient and discreet location for clients. Shrewsbury is a great place to live and work, with the Shropshire hills close by. Unfortunately, there isn't any free parking, though there are plenty of car parks in town within walking distance, so clients aren't put off. Their rented premises is a single-storey building, which a passer-by might not notice if it weren't for the gold plate to the right of the front door stating Dr Glass's long line of qualifications.

One day, Lucy's name will be added to that shiny gold plate, but it's too soon for that.

'Thanks for completing the online form. Would you like a drink? Tea, coffee, water?'

'Water, thanks.' Jennifer knocks back a glass in one go, so Lucy refills it from the water jug. Lucy gives her a few moments to compose herself and to catch her breath. She notices how small and delicate Jennifer's feet are in gold pumps beneath the tent of her colourful maxi dress.

As Jennifer chugs the second glass of water, she takes a good look around Lucy's office. The walls are pale blue, with large, framed posters illustrating a healthy meal and a balanced diet with a lean and dressed chicken and curly leaves of Red Russian kale. Lucy has taken great care to balance useful information with feel-good measures displayed in bright fonts:

BE THE PERSON YOU WANT TO BE.
EAT TO BE WELL.
LOVE YOUR BODY.

'I like your posters.'

'Thanks.'

Lucy is both relieved and anxious as she skims Jennifer's application form. Her memory has indeed proven correct.

'Alright,' she says. 'So, I can see from the information provided you'd like to gain weight quickly. You are thirty-five and take infrequent exercise. What I like to do in the initial session is to get to know you a bit better and then devise a bespoke plan that's realistic for you to achieve your goal. Do you have an hour to chat?'

Jennifer nods. She arranges her long, patterned dress so that it billows out around her, freeing it from her large thighs. She reminds Lucy of a queen on a throne. Only a hint of her bountiful cleavage is on display, but her bosom jiggles with each slight movement she makes.

'Yes, that all sounds good to me,' she replies. 'I've been trying to gain more weight for about four months now, but I seem to have reached a plateau. I eat at least three thousand calories a day, more when I'm with Ross.'

'Ross?'

'My boyfriend. He's lush,' she says and tosses a tendril of hair behind her back, which curls around her waist like a Burmese python. 'We've been together six months.' She says it like they're married. 'He keeps a close eye on me.'

'Is Ross a doctor?'

Jennifer laughs. 'He's a baker. Well, more than that. A business owner, too. He has a bakery in Malpas—Pie in the Sky. It took him ages to decide on a name. Originally, it was a toss-up between *The Sweet Spot*, *The Muffin Man, and Sticky Buns.*'

'I think he made an excellent choice.'

'Me too. At one point, Ross told me it was going

to be called *Squashing Delights* and I about hit the roof. Squashings are what he likes me to do in the bedroom—you know, for me to sit on him and wriggle around a bit —and that's fine, but not on a shop sign. It might put some customers off their pastries!'

Lucy tries to keep a straight face as she switches the scales on. 'Go ahead and hop on so we can get a benchmark weight. Just remove your shoes, please.'

Jennifer has to use the arms of the chair to stand up and then climbs onto the scales without her ballet shoes.

'So, at the moment, your weight is ninety-eight kilograms.'

'Oh God, is it? I've lost two pounds,' she says miserably.

'Let's take a height measurement, if you'd like to stand here. Thanks. 168 centimetres. That's great. If you'd like to put your shoes back on and have a seat.'

'Ross took me out for a curry over the weekend, and it didn't agree with me. Prawn balti. I should have stuck with chicken biryani as I normally do, but he said to try something new—so me being me, I did.'

'Your body mass index, or BMI, for your age and height is thirty-two, which suggests you are obese. Your ideal weight for your build and age is between nine and eleven stone or fifty-seven to seventy kilograms, so you see, you are over what's thought to be a healthy weight.'

Jennifer waves an arm in the air, dismissing Lucy's information in one imperious gesture. Her bracelets jangle in discord.

'Being obese has several health risks, such as type 2 diabetes.'

'I'm not here to be healthy,' Jennifer says bluntly. 'I thought you said this first session was about getting to know me, so you know how to help?'

'I apologise. BMI is a useful starting point to go from. Over to you.'

'Right. In a nutshell, I want to put on another two stone,' Jennifer says matter-of-factly. 'There's nothing complicated about that, only my body has stopped gaining. I think three stone will make it difficult to get around and I need to work. Ross likes big women, you see, and I like Ross. Simple as that. He likes to watch me stuff myself. It turns him on. Should I tell you more about our sex life?'

This time Lucy puts her hand up and shifts uncomfortably in her seat. 'You already told me about the squashings. It isn't usually necessary to give a blow-by-blow account.'

'Well, Ross likes . . . certain things, and the bigger I am, the better. A few extra stone have made all the difference, but it's not enough.'

'Why is there an urgency to gain weight?' Lucy asks and begins to sense Jennifer's annoyance. 'Slow and steady is best where weight loss or gain is needed. The body maintains a healthy weight, which is gained or lost gradually. You will have heard of people going on crash diets with dramatic results, only to put all the weight back on—and more—once the diet ends.'

'Yeah, I know all that. And Ross and I know that big is beautiful.'

'I see. Does the overeating turn you on too?'

'I like food,' she says simply, 'and he loves a wobbly belly. It's his favourite bit of me.' She looks down at it with the expression an adoring mother wears when gazing at her child's head. 'And mine.' Lucy expects her to stroke the folds of flesh, but her hand caresses the slim arm of the chair instead.

'Eating ripe fruit in front of a partner can be very

erotic,' Lucy suggests. 'Pears, peaches, plums, strawberries, grapes. Take your pick, depending on the season. Oranges are good for your skin, hair, and nails too. A win-win.'

'I see where you're going with this, but Ross and I are incorrigible carnivores and sugar-junkies—and don't say fruit has sugar in it because it's just not the same, and you know it. Don't you enjoy the sweetmeat of happiness? Don't tell me; you only eat salad.'

Lucy laughs. 'I don't, of course. I love meat, but—'

'Health is so important. You said. Only, Ross is hungry for me, and I am hungry for him.' She bends and flicks her toes; the toenails are painted a fierce shade of pink. It reminds Lucy of summer cocktails. The absence of self-consciousness in her new client is refreshing, but concerns about Jennifer's requests buzz in her brain.

'I know what I want,' Jennifer states plainly.

Lucy looks back at the application form, feeling defeated. Her advice is falling on deaf ears. 'Are you troubled by the discomforts of over-fullness? I mean, does your body send you signs of physical distress because it can't handle the quantity? I have to ask these questions, as a nutritionist.'

'Look, thanks for your concern and all that, but I'm paying for this, and I want to put on two stone as quickly as possible. Yeah?'

'Let's move on. I see from your diet sheet that you eat a lot of fast food. It's high in fat, but it can make you lethargic. It's possible to gain weight from foods which are healthier. I can't condone eating fried and fatty foods to meet your goal.'

Jennifer shrugs.

'A diet high in good fats like avocado and nuts is an option, and smoothies high in protein, such as caramel apple shakes, as well as foods high in starch like rice and potatoes. Within a couple of days, I'll have a diet sheet for you, and I suggest you try it for a week and let me know how it goes. Return this time next week if you can, and I'll retake your weight. How does that sound?'

'Anything else I can eat? While I think of it, Ross and I are going away for a couple of days. He's treating me to a spa weekend, dinners included, and afternoon tea. It's that prominent place in Chester, by the racecourse.'

'I don't know Chester that well.'

'Anyways, I'll eat what he wants me to eat then, and more.'

'Why would you do that?'

'That's what we do. Ross usually chooses really well. And the most calorific, of course. He can eat what he likes and never gains a pound. Highly strung. Always on the go.'

'You could purchase a protein supplement if you wish, to add to cereals and drinks. To keep healthy, eat a variety of foods—fruit and veg—keep up the fluids—water—and take some gentle exercise, like using the stairs rather than the lift or an escalator. Yes?'

'Sex is exercise,' she says darkly, 'but he won't be wanting any if this doesn't work.'

Jennifer rises slowly from the chair and flicks her long hair over her shoulder. Lucy notices that her ankles and feet are swollen and, by the amount of water she's drunk, deduces there is quite a thirst to quench; an early warning sign of type 2 diabetes.

'I hope your little plan works. Ross is paying for your time.'

'Why don't you bring Ross with you next week? I have an offer on for couples at the moment.'

41

'I'll ask him, thanks, but I don't think so.'

'Or, if you refer a friend, you get one session free. Anyway, I hope you enjoy your weekend away. See you next week, Jennifer. Take care of yourself.'

Without responding, Jennifer leaves and lets the door slam a little too hard behind her.

Jennifer is not Lucy's first client looking to gain weight for sexual pleasure, but this one worries her. The previous client had enjoyed her fatness and overeating; it was a desire born out of self-love and gluttony. She isn't convinced this is the case with Jennifer, who appears to be doing it to sustain a sex-life with Ross. She hopes Jennifer will return. Lucy isn't exactly turning clients away just yet.

In her mind, Lucy has a duty of care to, at the very least, provide information about the risks associated with obesity and overeating. Binge-eating might be a topic of conversation that is off-limits with Emma-Jane, but Jennifer is a paying customer with eating habits on another level, let alone the risk of asphyxiation from squashing. If nothing else, meeting Ross would satisfy her curiosity about what he looks like and what Jennifer sees in him. Perhaps Ross will be more open to her advice? The thought alleviates some of the unease she feels in the pit of her stomach—but not all of it.

The office feels very still and quiet after Jennifer has gone. Lucy doesn't have another appointment until the following morning and, while she has admin and diet plans to work on, her mood isn't in the right place to settle and work. Pity she doesn't have someone to get out with for a quick drink, or a run along the river.

On the bright side, she does have a date the night after next. Perhaps he'll be the one.

In Carlisle, Lucy had had a few brief flings. One was

more sex than anything. The other fizzled out after a few months of dining out and dining in. So, since returning to Shrewsbury, she'd signed up with a dating agency. She figures if she keeps an open mind and expects nothing to come of it, she won't be disappointed. Meeting people is difficult, between working long hours and then using her free time for training or trips to Carlisle to see her parents. Her online profile specifies older men, those aged forty to fifty, because she thinks an older man is more likely to understand some of her foibles.

She stares at the wall, the messages in focus then blurring to a smudge.

BE THE PERSON YOU WANT TO BE.
EAT TO BE WELL.
LOVE YOUR BODY.

As Lucy stares at a poster on the office wall illustrating a colourful plate with pomegranate and avocado salad, part of her envies Jennifer and Ross's passionate relationship, even though their sexual habits aren't to her taste.

She can understand some of the pleasure of watching a person you love eat something delicious, but not a four-course meal! Perhaps once Jennifer gains just a few more pounds, Ross will be satisfied, and they will stop fixating on food. As it is, it seems like there isn't a cauldron big enough for her appetite for him, which makes Lucy's meals for one seem like gruel served up in minuscule wooden bowls, her kitchen a sterile shell of a place and her body a silent temple.

Someone will come along. At least, that's what her mother says. One day. Just when you are least expecting it. Just at the right time.

*Before I'm in my grave, I hope.*

# 6

Next door to Lucy's office, Emma-Jane makes her last client of the day as comfortable as she can.

It is 7:30 in the evening, a late appointment, which is Vanessa's choice. After losing her young daughter to an asthma attack, Vanessa is struggling with grief and severe depression. Avril had just turned ten and was Vanessa's world. The young woman brought her up as a single mum after Avril's dad made it clear he wasn't paternal material.

'I dreamt I grew dandelions in the earth, and they cast a spell,' Vanessa says. 'A gust of wind shakes just one dandelion, and I see Avril's face in it, in the white head of it. Then, it disintegrates into tiny pieces, and Avril is travelling in the air, floating.'

Vanessa raises one hand in the air as she describes the image.

'Then, I run to different windows—I don't know whose house I'm in—and I see her travelling by, carried on the air. I think I'm awake and I look at my alarm clock, then put the light on. On my pillow, there's all these white fluffy dandelion heads, all in little pieces.'

Vanessa smiles an innocent smile, almost childlike, her head on one side. She looks young and innocent.

'Maybe I'm coming to terms with Avril's death.'

Emma-Jane smiles, sensing that Vanessa desperately wants her to agree, but she does not want to read something into a dream which may or may not be there. There's progress evident in her appearance and the lucid description of her dream.

'You look well rested,' Emma-Jane says. 'It makes such a difference, doesn't it—to outlook, everything—when you feel refreshed? And of course, with time, the intense grief you feel will fade. In time.'

'Days like today I can believe that. Others, not so much.'

'That's normal. Are you ready to try hypnotherapy again today?'

Vanessa nods and climbs onto the couch.

'Make yourself comfortable and close your eyes. You're in a safe place. Take a long, deep breath and relax your back into the chair, relax your mind and your body, relax all those muscles and bones. Excellent.'

Soon Vanessa begins speaking through her hypnosis.

———

*I am in my bedroom changing the sheets when I hear Avril banging on the window.*

*'Stop that!' I yell. 'For heaven's sake! What has gotten into you?'*

*Avril is gasping for air as she stands by the window in the lounge. It looks like the pain is in her chest and the back of her throat and by the wideness of her eyes, the tightness quickly worsens. Avril looks scared. She is moving away from the window to the sofa. Her feet move like she's been dragged backwards, like she didn't choose to go that way.*

*Pedalling backwards, pedalling air.*

*More chest pain, like daggers now. Her chest rises with each tortured intake of air.*

*Eyelids flutter in an anguished face.*

*'Get . . . my . . . inhaler!' Avril bleats between coughs and*

*wheezes, a voice like her insides are blocked, like her windpipe is clogged. 'Quick . . . ly.'*

*I feel frightened. I know the signs. It's a severe attack.*

*Fuck! It's not in the kitchen drawer. I am an organised mum. Why isn't it in the drawer, where it should be? I am running, turning, twisting, looking high and low, and Avril is wheezing.*

*'M- mum!' she struggles.*

*I had seen the blue inhaler recently. I am sure of it. So how can this be happening? I look around the lounge and kitchen, looking but not seeing. Panic. Unable to take in what is happening and what will happen if I don't lay my hands on the inhaler any minute, any second, and time is ticking.*

*Make it stop. Stop the clock!*

*On the bureau there's a pile of old magazines, a few schoolbooks and one of Avril's soft baby blankets, which she refuses to part with. Perhaps it's under that pile. I look, rummage, toss it all to the floor. But no inhaler. I toss the cushions off the sofa and root under the seats and chair.*

*Be calm. You'll find it. Think, I keep telling myself, but it isn't working.*

*'Mum!' she begs. 'Hel–'*

*There's a look of terror on Avril's face as she falls to her knees, then onto all fours. An animal now. Primitive. Seeking survival. Her head hangs as if staring at the carpet, then rises with each attempt at breathing. Her breath is rattling now. There are no other sounds in the house, except the crumbling and sickness of Avril's lungs, like a hot wind trapped inside a small space, and my urgent footsteps running from one room to the next, from one cupboard to another, emptying drawers and ticking, ticking . . .*

*'Christ! Where is it?'*

*'Hel...'*

*I run to the bathroom to look for a spare inhaler in the cabinet. Relief comes when I see the blue and white box on the top shelf beside the Rennie, talc, and Head & Shoulders.*

*I grab it. 'Christ. It's empty.'*

*A flash of inspiration. My handbag. I upturn it on the lounge carpet. Nothing. I run back into her bedroom, where I keep another leather handbag for smart occasions, and I look in there, just in case. Nothing.*

*I am desperate now. Once or twice before, Avril has blown into a paper bag to regulate her breathing, so I rummage in the bin for the McDonald's bag I threw in there yesterday. The bag has got wet stains of grease on it, but it is good enough. Avril's eyes are bulging, and her chest is heaving.*

*'Take this! Blow! Blow. You can do this.'*

*Only she can't. She can't catch her breath. The panic owns her. I hold her head despite knowing it's futile. Avril can't blow into that bag any more than wipe her own nose. There's only the faintest recognition in Avril's eyes that I am there. The terror has gone. Now, it's nothing but still water. Stagnant.*

*'Don't die! Pleeeease!' I scream.*

*The crackling and rasping are poison in her system. Her body is shutting down. I know it, feel it.*

*'Oh God, Avril!'*

*I grab the phone and call 999. Her face is blue. They tell me to put my ear to her mouth. 'She's not breathing!' I listen for a heartbeat in her chest and feel for a pulse in her neck, her wrist. Nothing. Nothing. Nothing.*

*It's all my fault, because I couldn't find the inhaler. I wonder if I didn't dust properly yesterday, or whether the temperature is too hot or too cold in the apartment, whether it's the new carpet, the weather, whether someone at school has been horrible to her, whether . . .*

*I open her mouth and blow. Nothing happens. I try again and again.*

*'Oh my God. Oh my God. My baby!'*

*I lovingly stroke the fine hairs on her cheeks, still rocking her, just like I did when she was a baby.*

*I carry Avril into my bedroom and wrap her in my duvet, then I carry her downstairs to my car as though the warmth and movement and tenderness might resuscitate her. I put a seat belt on her. It's difficult to drive because of the tears and snot and it's hard to concentrate, but I pull up outside A&E and I don't know why I'm here, but it's all I can think of to do.*

*Inside there are too many people around, talking, watching, sitting, and there are too many bright fluorescent strip lights and lots of signs shouting one thing after another, which might as well be in a foreign language to me right now. My arms are heavy from carrying Avril. She's heavy and limp. I keep walking, not really sure where I am going or what I am doing. Everything is slow and weird, and people are whispering, until a nurse gently puts a hand on my shoulder and smiles kindly, with her head to one side. The nurse leads me to a chair and gently takes Avril out of my arms.*

*I realise I only have one shoe on. Then, I fall onto the floor and bang my head.*

⊱━━━━━━━━━━━━━⊰

By the time nine o'clock comes, Dr Emma-Jane Glass is exhausted and ready for home.

Vanessa left a while ago, but her recollection of Avril's death lingers in the four corners of the office. Some days are more emotionally draining than others. Both Vanessa and Dr Glass's other regular client, Drew Rogers, take a lot out of her because of their intense emotions of grief and loss and her need to maintain her distance. It's hard not to get emotionally involved with good people who are suffering.

Sometimes caring too much about clients like Vanessa is a bad thing, but seeing Celia will keep her involvement in check and help her to compartmentalize, to keep this professional obsession at bay...

At least, she hopes.

Emma-Jane finishes typing an email to Celia to arrange a supervised session. No matter how often she sees Celia to talk about her work, the job gets to her like an invisible splinter under the surface of the skin.

A festering splinter that no amount of squeezing and tweezering can remove.

# 7

The moon plays hide-and-seek as it slips in and out of the clouds. From behind the office window, the night is playful. There's an evening out there to be enjoyed. Late drinks, dinner, dancing. But Dr Glass has no energy or inclination for all of that, not when Vanessa's problems and distress are etched into the night's canvas.

'Are you planning to sleep on your couch?' Lucy asks with a fleeting grin.

Emma-Jane sweeps her black hair behind one ear, imagining herself wrapped in a soft, warm towel. 'I'm clearing my desk then heading home for a bath filled with Parisian oils. You?'

'Sainsbury's shop, then home to watch Lewis. Exciting times! See you tomorrow.'

'You might bump into Drew! He was on his way there. You'll probably find him at the deli counter. He's a foodie.'

'He just keeps getting better!' Lucy laughs, blushing. 'By the way, did you get that letter I left on your desk? It appeared under my door earlier.'

'I didn't. My desk is a mess.' Emma-Jane smiles, then lifts a box file and finds a beige envelope underneath.

There is no writing on the front. Just a stamp.

Her heart sinks.

She knows that envelope. Found one identical to it on her front porch earlier that morning.

'Thanks,' she says, as neutrally as she can muster to conceal her racing heart.

'You okay?' Lucy asks.

'Yeah, too much paperwork! See you tomorrow.'

Emma-Jane watches Lucy go, relieved to be left alone to open the letter in private. The envelope seems to shout at her to open it, so she decides to get on with it. The sound of tearing paper desecrates the clinical calmness of the office.

*First my home. Now my workplace.*

*Fuck.*

As she unfolds the letter, the words squirm before her like maggots until, blinking, they shift into focus:

*Dr Glass, the meddlesome, childless fool bent on advancing her own career at any cost. I expect you have been thinking about who and where I am. Think of me as an uncensored voice in the graveyard of your head. I am that feeling of hunger that keeps you awake at night. I am the umbilical cord, the noose, the tow-rope pulling you ever closer to the truth so you will see yourself as you really are.*

*I am watching as mothers give birth, or are given death. There's a cocktail of bliss, pain and love mothers feel when they give birth, but you wouldn't know about that. Nor how a small hand feels like the universe inside your own.*

*I send you this letter, which is nothing. Nothing. I am not sending you a child's school uniform, or their painting, or their favourite teddy. I am not sending you a photo of their firsts—first tooth, first curl, first shoes. I am not sending you a child's coffin. I am not able to amputate a limb to make you feel like I do. I wish, wish, wish I could, just as I wish you could smell an expectant mother's vomit and sour breast milk. I wish you could sleep in a room wallpapered with angels and clouds, and an empty cot beside your bed.*

*Who do you see in the mirror on the wall? Does that*

51

*face of yours fail to remind you of how fragile you are? How easily I can break you? How misshapen your thinking is in that bust of a head? You are misguided to think you are bulletproof when you are made of nothing more than distorted glass.*

*How pitiful it is that you are breathing when loved ones rot in the earth. I wish you could smell their stinking corpses and understand how enigmatic, brilliant, loving they were before the sun went down for good. The only comfort is it won't be too much longer till your test begins. For now, you are a glass woman living in a glass house. Just one stone aimed at your heavy heart will shatter you to pieces, I know.*

*I will expose you. Then, I will mutilate you with that broken glass.*

*Keep looking over your shoulder because I shan't handle you with care. Only the innocent children deserve that.*

*Wait for me.*

She stuffs the letter back into the envelope and inserts it between two files on her desk. It crouches there with the other letter she removed from her house. Both out of sight.

In her line of work, unstable minds are her bread and butter.

'It's nothing,' she whispers. 'Don't let it get under your skin.'

Like with the last letter, there's a stamp on the envelope but it's been hand-delivered. That's the bit which unnerves her—they have been to her home and now her office, in person.

What's next? Her white pillow for when she wakes up?

The power-game continues. Perhaps now's the time

to tell Celia or the police. She mustn't become paranoid. Then they will have won their game.

*I really need to get cameras installed.*

Outside the sky is murky, and the silence is dangerous. It isn't far to walk to her car, but it feels like she's speed-walked ten miles by the time she is inside her Volkswagen Golf with the doors locked. It's harder to trust the darkness. She immediately switches on the interior light and checks that no one is in the back seat before revving the engine and speeding home.

Headlights follow her all the way as a car drives too close to her bumper for comfort. At the traffic light at the last crossroads before turning right onto Boulter Road, the light turns red. She curses, locks the doors, and silently wills the light to change to green.

A horn sounds behind her.

'What?' she screams into the rear view mirror, suddenly blinded by the high beams. 'Idiot!'

The angry horn blares long and loud. As the light suddenly turns green, she punches the gas, speeds off, and manages to lose the other car.

Her face grey with fatigue, thoughts of her own death follow her home in another black, remorseless night.

*Wait for me.*

# 8

Jennifer's bloated, beaming face confirms to Lucy that her diet plan is working. She doesn't know how to feel—is it a success, or a failure? Now, Jennifer is back after two weeks and, with the practice being so busy, it has slipped her mind to speak to Emma-Jane about her concerns and the ethics of treating her.

'Good to see you. Take a seat.'

'Thank you,' Jennifer says breezily, giving Lucy a wide smile, which reaches her brown eyes. 'It's working!' She stands in front of Lucy with her arms outstretched. 'Five pounds—in one week! Ross is so happy. Me too! My boobs are bigger! Honestly, you should have seen his face when—'

'That's great!' Lucy interrupts, putting one hand up, quite unsure of where the conversation is going but not wanting to take the risk. 'I'm pleased you're happy; and Ross, too.'

'Ross is on his way. He should be here in a minute.'

'Excellent.'

'So, on to stage two. What's next?' Jennifer asks, collapsing into the chair. She dumps her handbag, an orange and black suede tote, to one side. She certainly knows how to make herself comfortable.

'Have you experienced any uncomfortable side effects from the diet plan?'

'Wind.' She laughs. 'And I've been weeing a lot. More than usual, I should say.'

Lucy leans forward in her chair. 'More than normal?'

'Don't look so worried! I feel fine!'

'I mentioned the risk of type 2 diabetes last time we met. Urinating often can be a symptom. Perhaps you'd like to be tested, just to be on the safe side?'

'Honestly, Ross keeps an eye on me, like I said last time I was here. I'm fine.'

'Any other side effects?' Lucy asks, using her notes to keep the consultation on track, which is harder with some clients than others. Jennifer leans forward towards Lucy and sticks her tongue out. 'Black tongue,' Lucy says.

'It wasn't like that before.'

'No?'

'No. It tastes a bit metallic. Have I got bad breath?'

'Have you tried scraping it with your toothbrush?'

'Not really.'

'If it's not a birthmark, it's most likely a disorder called "black hairy tongue." Excessive protein or poor diet could be the cause, or more oral hygiene is perhaps needed, which should help with bad breath.'

'I don't want dog breath for the weekend. Ross would hate that! What do I do?'

'Start with scraping the tongue with your toothbrush.'

'Blow me. I was feeling terrific about myself before you told me my breath stank!'

'I didn't say that.'

Jennifer is listening now. 'Ross has made me all these lovely meat pies with your protein supplement.'

'Health is so important. Perhaps your tongue is telling you to stop gaining weight.'

Jennifer rolls her eyes, like a child bored by her teacher's admonishing.

'I'll be adding more fruit and vegetables to your diet

plan this week—owing to that tongue of yours. As before, plenty of water. Less of the protein supplement, and choose red meat over white.'

'Alright then. Sorry for getting a bit arsy; only I love Ross, the sex, all that, you know.'

'No problem at all.'

'Do you have an appetite?' Jennifer asks suddenly, raising her eyebrows.

Lucy lets the question hang in the air between them for a moment. She could choose to ignore it, to maintain the professional distance between them. Or she could answer, and so halve it.

This big, beautiful woman is getting under her skin. Why? Jennifer defies the culture of size six and asks Lucy questions her own mother doesn't; nor Emma-Jane, for that matter. Jennifer is thriving on life, on sex, on food, and what does Lucy have?

'If you invited me for dinner, what would you cook?' Jennifer continues. 'Hang on. A wager! If I guess correctly, I get a free session and diet plan. Deal?'

Amused and slightly self-conscious, Lucy nods in agreement and begins to laugh.

'Let's see here,' Jennifer muses, eyeing Lucy closely. 'If you were letting your hair down, so to speak, surf and turf. Food after sex, um—I know I'm digressing—I'd say toad in the hole! A weekday meal, okay—lentils, lots of other pulses and mushrooms, seeds and stuff, bits that get stuck in your teeth. Spinach! A side salad with rocket. Maybe fish . . . Tuna. The sort of meal where you never feel full. How am I doing?'

'That certainly sounds like a healthy meal, a balanced plate.'

'Was I right?'

'Weekdays I eat a healthy diet, but weekends I'm not so strict, especially when I'm exercising. If I was cooking for you, I'd probably make us a chicken Caesar salad, with fruit salad and natural yoghurt to follow.'

'Yeah, I could get that down,' Jennifer says, smiling. 'But I'd still be hungry.'

Lucy hears footsteps, and then there's a knock at the door.

'That'll be Ross.'

Jennifer wriggles in her seat, preparing to stand up, but Lucy beats her to it and opens the door.

'Ross?' He nods. 'I'm Lucy. Come in.'

He ducks as he walks under the door frame; all six-foot-two of him, even though there are a few inches spare to clear his head. Lucy thinks he probably weighs less than sixty-three kilograms soaking wet.

'These are for you,' he says to Lucy, proffering a tray of sweets. 'Chocolate and orange cupcakes, white chocolate éclair, a raspberry jam doughnut, and a coconut slice. All freshly baked this morning. All very unhealthy and delicious.' He laughs.

'Oh, lovely! Don't tell anyone I'm a cake fiend. And so's my colleague next door, Dr Glass.' She puts the cakes on the table and Ross outstretches his hand. The handshake is soaking wet.

'Jennifer hasn't stopped talking about you since she came to see you. She's so happy about how much she's been able to put on.' He crosses his long limbs, his feet in distressed leather cowboy boots.

Lucy arranges her notes in her lap to give herself a moment to compose her thoughts . . .

They say opposites attract. Ross is as thin as a beanpole. Jennifer and Ross smile at each other, he takes her hand in his and holds it in his lap, as though it might fly away.

Jennifer hungrily eyes the cakes.

'I have tried recipes for healthier cakes for my customers at the bakery, with less sugar and butter, but the taste isn't good at all. We've had some success with healthier toppings, like yoghurt and apple. To be honest, I do so much baking at work that when I get home, I love cooking meat for Jennifer—fried, battered, roasted. We do it every which way, don't we?'

Jennifer grins.

Lucy tries to discreetly wipe her hand on her trousers. 'They look delicious, thank you. I'm just pleased Jennifer is happy with her progress, but I wanted to talk to you both about the risks of obesity. Some nasty side effects are showing.'

He turns to look at Jennifer quizzically. Jennifer sticks her tongue out, then sucks it back in again.

'Let me have another look,' Lucy says, leaning forwards. 'Obviously, I didn't see your tongue before you gained weight, but when a person puts on weight, the tongue can get fatter. The human tongue has a high percentage of fat. Does it feel bigger?'

Jennifer shrugs.

'Has your sleep been affected?'

'Not really.'

'Hop on the scales.'

The room feels hotter, smaller, as Lucy thinks about how to get Ross and Jennifer to listen to her, to stop playing their games with weight and squashings in bed.

'I think you have gained enough weight now and, in my professional opinion, you need to stop. It is my duty to repeat my concerns. It wouldn't be professional of me to help you gain any more weight. With your swollen black tongue and the other symptoms we discussed previously, my advice is to stabilise your weight. Or better still, gradually lose a few pounds.'

She looks for a reaction but doesn't get one from either of them.

'I think we should leave it here,' Lucy concludes.

Jennifer gives a moody shrug when it becomes evident that Lucy won't bend. 'I'll go somewhere else then, to someone who *will* help me. Money normally sorts out an overactive conscience.'

'Not to me, and not when it comes to the health of my patients.'

'That's crap,' Jennifer snaps. 'If you've got enough money, you can get whatever you want.' She crosses her massive legs, putting a barrier between them. It seems Jennifer is used to getting her own way.

Lucy doesn't want to argue the toss with a client who's getting increasingly agitated.

'I want to eat out tonight,' Jennifer says suddenly to Ross, sounding like a petulant child. 'Beef burger and lots of chips.'

'We can do that. As soon as I finish work, I'll take you. Where do you want to eat?'

Staring straight at Lucy, she says, 'Burger King.'

He kisses Jennifer's hand and keeps hold of it in his lap. Lucy thinks he'd probably lick her face right now if it made her happy. It's Ross who needs Lucy's help to gain weight, not to mention treatment for his dripping wet hands; she thinks he might be suffering from hyperhidrosis, which is not only unpleasant for him, but for anyone else he touches.

'Perhaps you'd like to see me on your own, Ross?

Here's my card,' she says, passing it to him while avoiding contact with his soggy hand.

'Not me. You know, life's too short to be miserable. See you.'

As soon as they leave, Lucy sighs. Then, she pushes a whole cupcake into her mouth. Cream and chocolate squirt onto her chin but she keeps biting and chewing, not enjoying it, but needing to simply fill the damned hole of being single when it seems almost everybody else is in a relationship, in love, in bed having great sex, or popping out children.

She doesn't feel in control of her professional decisions. Perhaps more experience really is needed before she opens her own practice. Her parents had said as much. It's not just the technical knowledge (which she has), but also the skills to get people to listen and to see sense.

To trust her judgement.

---

Lucy has to pay rent for her office on top of her flat, so she avoids spending lots of money at the delicatessen. But at the sight of Drew Rogers carrying a basket full of attractive-looking food hanging from one hand, and his charming tan brogues, she is instantly lured there.

Emma-Jane is the consummate professional who keeps details about her clients in confidence but, having an office directly opposite from her, Lucy does occasionally bump into Emma-Jane's clients. Some are less friendly than others. Drew is an exception. He is warm and handsome, not to mention well-dressed, and the owner of a farmhouse. More than once, she's imagined him sitting on an enormous sofa covered in throws and soft cushions in front of the fireplace, an open fire roaring in the hearth and his toes wiggling in the warmth.

'Fancy meeting you here,' she says, hoping the cliché will be read as that. She smiles, self-conscious under the bright, fluorescent strip lights.

Drew looks up, startled from his reverie; he was obviously immersed in the choice of delicious cheeses, meats, and salads. She watches his expression remoulding as he tries to figure out where he's met her before. She puts him out of his misery as a mother and a child squeeze past with a laden trolley.

'It's Lucy. I have an office in town, in the same building as Emma-Jane—Dr Glass.'

'Of course! You're the nutritionist,' he says, and she's surprised by the sudden light in his hazel eyes. 'How could I forget?' Drew takes her hand and kisses it. Lucy blushes and relaxes her shoulders, relieved he knows who she is. 'I'm shopping for dinner. One day at a time, you know. I'm rubbish at planning my meals ahead.' He turns back to look at the contents inside the deli counter. 'The olives here are excellent, and the salami.'

Lucy raises her basket to show him the contents for her own supper. 'I like the bargains close to their sell-by date.' Her basket holds broccoli, carrots, and asparagus.

'Are you vegetarian?' he asks, bending down a little to look. She takes a moment to check out his head of hair and the attractive silver threads in his sideburns.

'No, I eat meat and fish. "All things in moderation" is my motto.'

The memory of Ross and Jennifer flashes before her.

'Quite right too,' Drew says, though she can't tell whether or not he's sincere. He has three bottles of red plonk in his basket of goodies. 'Here's an idea. Let me cook for you—tonight, I mean, if you're free. There's more than enough for two here. We can see how the property developer fares against the nutritionist. Purely platonic, of course. What do you say?'

A little shocked, but flattered, she replies without delay. What was it Ross had said? *Life's too short to be miserable.*

'I say, why not?'

'Where are you from, Lucy?' he asks in an even, low voice. 'Does your hometown have a signature dish?'

'Good question. I'm from Carlisle, Cumbria. My parents still live there. It's a village near the Lake District. So, I suppose a signature dish would be Cumberland sausage and tattie pie.'

'What's in that?'

'Oh, it's delicious. Lamb, black pudding, and potatoes. Stodgy, hearty food; great after a long walk.'

'Sounds tasty for a winter dish. What's your number? I'll text you my address. See you there around seven?'

Moments later, Lucy has his phone number, his address, and the first date she's been truly excited for in a long time. Her heart thuds with excitement as she watches him walk away.

---

*What do I wear?*

Drew's farmhouse lifestyle builds in Lucy's mind as she applies a touch of eyeshadow and mascara: a farmhouse table and chairs, perhaps a Labrador who sleeps beside the stove, and a free-standing cream bathtub with lion's feet.

She imagines waking up in the morning to the birdsong behind linen curtains or Venetian blinds.

She adds a layer of lip balm.

*Get a grip. You're getting carried away.*

With a boyfriend, Lucy thinks, she could finally attend the weddings and christenings she's always invited to but regularly declines with half-arsed excuses. She could finally stop screaming into her pillow after disastrous dates, when the loneliness makes her feel uncomfortable in her own skin but the longing for male company lingers on, like a constant shadow.

She tries to look like she hasn't made too much of an effort, which is difficult to achieve when, in fact, she has.

As she drives to Drew's house, she tells herself, *It's just dinner. Don't expect too much. Don't expect a thunderbolt.* Perhaps she should call Emma-Jane to tell her where she's going for dinner, but what if she disapproves because he's a client? *She won't mind*, Lucy reassures herself, while resolving to tell Emma-Jane all about it tomorrow.

He isn't a client of Lucy's, after all.

Lucy parks beside a Range Rover and knocks on a chunky oak front door. When he opens it, she catches the scent of aftershave and sandalwood lotion. Not the zesty kind Martin used to wear. This is muskier, and not subtle. Before leaving her house, she sprayed perfume in the air and walked through it twice, only to feel it was too faint and immediately squirted her wrists and neck.

Now she's worrying it's too strong.

Drew's lips don't quite form a smile as he stands in the doorway, but almost. Enough to give the impression of one, and perhaps the promise of a real one later.

'I wondered if you were coming,' he says, and steps back to let Lucy into the house.

'Sorry, I got a bit lost. Your drive is quite hard to find in the dark. It's not a road I've driven before.'

'You're here now,' he says, giving her a chaste kiss on the cheek. It's a tepid welcome to the farmhouse she's so been looking forward to seeing after imagining it so vividly in her mind.

Lucy had predicted that it might be on the cooler side (unlike her little modern place, which is cheap to heat), so the brushed cotton top and trousers she'd chosen, with a suede jacket, feel like the right choice given the temperature inside. Drew is wearing a smart, open-neck shirt—no tie, unlike when she saw him in the supermarket.

'Come on in. We're eating in the kitchen; hope you don't mind. Let me get you a drink. Red wine?'

'Please. Just the one, and a small one at that. I'm driving.'

She follows him into the kitchen, trying not to stare at the house or at him too much. There's evidence of work going on with the dust sheet at one end of the hall and picture hooks left bare. In the kitchen there is an opened bottle of wine and vegetable peelings on the marble countertop.

'I hope you're hungry,' he says, pouring her a glass of wine, and topping up his. He gestures to a chair. 'Make yourself at home.'

Drew turns his attention to chopping onions like he's splitting the atom. Then, he becomes completely absorbed in cooking the steak. He adds butter, rosemary, and garlic to the skillet and, with a practised hand, tilts the pan from one side to the next to baste the steak. Lucy takes in the mismatch of old and new furnishings, the razor-sharp knives on the chopping board, and the photograph of a little boy positioned centrally on the window shelf, smiling behind the glass in a chunky wooden frame.

'Do you like cooking?' Drew asks with a razor-sharp knife in his hand.

'I probably should, given my job, but when it's just me to cook for, I tend to go for the quickest and easiest option.'

'Why should you? It sounds to me like you're too hard on yourself.' He looks her in the eye. 'Only do things you enjoy!' He hands her a spoon. 'Do you like the sauce?'

She swallows and nods her approval. He looks pleased.

She takes a sip of wine as he serves up the meal. 'This is a good wine,' she comments, and reads the label: Châteauneuf-du-Pape. 'Perfect with steak.'

'I think so. Plenty of body, but the key is to give it time to breathe.'

The quality of the silence changes. As she sits down, Lucy rummages in her mind for something to say. She sees the farmhouse kitchen table is simply laid. A large plate of meat and a dome of green in a salad bowl catches her eye.

'The food looks very professional,' she says and begins to eat.

'Presentation is important, don't you think?' he says, looking straight at Lucy and then back to his food that he quickly devours.

*He's ravenous*, she thinks to herself.

He swallows and clears his throat. 'Though good presentation can disguise a disgusting meal. I like presentation to be an authentic display of delicious food.'

She feels herself blush when her eyes linger over his coiled torso as he talks passionately, so she takes a sip of water to hide her face and to gather herself. 'I think it all depends on the dish and the occasion. At home, I eat a lot of salad with meat, with roughly chopped-up veg or fruit—depending on what needs eating—and it's delicious, but it always looks like a dog's dinner.'

'Dining for one. It's not always fun, is it?'

Lucy smiles as she tucks into the meal. 'It can feel a bit solitary if you're used to the company, that's true.'

'It's a pleasant change to share dinner with a woman who enjoys her food. My ex-wife, Evie, she would make all the right simpering noises when the food was being prepared but, as soon as she sat down to eat it, she'd play with it, move her fork around—it used to drive me mad. On rare occasions, she did well; she'd excuse herself before the end of the dessert to make herself sick.'

'Sick? Oh dear, was she bulimic?'

'I suppose so,' he says with a wave of his hand, as though dismissing the memory. 'Do you like crème caramel? It gives me an excuse to use my brûlée torch!'

'That sounds delicious, but I am getting full, thank you.'

She looks around the kitchen. The age of the place is evident in the thickness of the walls. She admires the stable door, the window ledge of chunky oak, and the red tiled floor. 'This is such a lovely house. As a property developer, have you done up a lot of houses?'

'Oh, yes. In the last ten years, I'd say more than ten. I buy smaller properties to do up and rent out, but I always have one large property to live in while it's being developed. I avoid capital gains tax that way.'

One wall is being replastered. 'Are you doing much work to the house?'

'It's all going to look different. A facelift of sorts. New carpets. It'll be decorated throughout.'

'Sounds more like reconstructive plastic surgery to

me, and it looks nice as it is . . . but I understand why you would want to change it.'

'Buyers at this end of the market have certain expectations. I'm not sentimental about it. It's a business, and it needs a facelift, anyway. Where do you live?'

'Renting a flat in Shrewsbury. Before I look to buy, I need to see how my business goes. It's very early days.'

'You should sound more confident than that. Believe in yourself. If you don't, customers won't. Think of yourself as your shop window. I mean, you look very trim and healthy, but it's more than that—you need a positive, can-do attitude.'

Lucy looks away to hide her jaded expression.

'Sorry, I'm lecturing you. I'm passionate about business.'

'My father tells me off when I'm negative about myself. He says there are plenty of enemies out there who will do that.'

'He's a wise man.'

'Ex-police.'

Once they have both finished the meal and while Drew puts the dirty plates in the dishwasher, she takes a closer look at the photograph which had caught her eye earlier. 'Is this your son?' she asks, gesturing to the image, hoping it will be a talking point to get Drew to open up a bit about his private life.

'James. It was taken last August on his third birthday. Evie, my ex-wife, is good with the camera.'

'I see that, and he's a sweet-looking boy. Curly blond hair.'

'He didn't get that from me as you can see, but he has my dark eyes.' Drew has his back to her so she can't read his expression. The silence feels thick.

'So, it's his birthday soon?' she asks as she looks at the wall calendar.

'Yes, the twelfth.'

'Have you and Evie been divorced long?'

'Long enough,' he says, then quickly changes the subject. 'How do you like your coffee?'

'White, one sugar. Thanks.'

He fills up the cafetière and carries it over to the table on a tray with cups and saucers. 'So, how well do you know Dr Glass?'

'Oh, I know Emma-Jane really well. I've known her a long time. Now it's great to be working alongside her.'

'Quite a history then?'

'You could say that,' she says. 'How about your history? You've been seeing Emma-Jane for a while now.'

'That's none of your business.'

She is taken aback by his sudden change in demeanour but forces a laugh to fill the silence. 'Emma-Jane and I are very different, but we get on so well.'

'Different in what way?' he asks, pouring the coffee and adding milk and sugar to hers.

'She's confident, self-assured, and terrifically studious. Her work is ... well, everything. If it wasn't for her support and encouragement, I wouldn't be working for myself, or in Shropshire. I'd be living with my parents in Carlisle, bumbling along.'

'It sounds like you respect her a lot.'

'Yes, I do.' Lucy takes a sip of coffee. 'Do you mind if I use your bathroom?'

'Ah, the downstairs loo is being updated. Up the stairs, take a left. The door has a brass handle.'

The stairs are wonderfully uneven, and the banister is old wood and beautifully imperfect, but the light bulb in the landing light has blown, so it's a semi-dark and slightly gloomy space.

Lucy doesn't allow herself to linger too long over the three framed photographs of James at different ages, positioned at even strategic intervals. The second-to-top stair creaks loudly, making her smile and remember stories of children sneaking out at night and being caught by the very same thing. When she opens the door to the bathroom, she gazes around for a few seconds with her mouth open at the contemporary bathroom suite and décor, the massive wall mirror and the wall-to-wall tiles. Even the floor is tiled in the same neutral shade of beige. The character of the place has been eradicated, replaced with bling.

On her way back down, Drew must hear the stair creak. 'In here!' he calls from a room off the hall, sounding slightly drunk.

Lucy follows the sound of his voice to the living room. 'Wow! I love an open fireplace. What a room to relax in.'

'Not furnished any longer, or lit, but perhaps another time we could eat in the dining room—if you have enjoyed my company this evening, that is. That has an open fire too.'

She sees his eyes are softer now, after the wine and the first course, and perhaps he is more at ease in her company. As much as she would like to stay and drink a second glass of wine, she has to drive home. Seeing a slight inebriation in his flushed cheeks makes her feel a little less vulnerable than she did when she arrived at the large, imposing farmhouse.

'It's been a lovely evening. Thank you.'

He kisses her goodbye, and she feels his flat hand linger against the small of her back. The pressure is just firm enough for her to want more.

She reaches for him, but he pulls away and closes the door in her face.

Leaving her alone in the cold.

# 9

Emma-Jane looks at her watch for the second time. Unusually for him, Drew Rogers is late.

If he doesn't arrive in the next five minutes, she will ring him on his mobile. Even though it's in her terms and conditions, which all her clients sign, billing a client for an hour they didn't actually attend feels most unsatisfying. The policy is there to protect her from potential clients who jib out at the last minute, or completely change their mind but fail to tell her.

Time is money. It is a business, even if it's the business of people's minds and health. Of all the people she's worked with recently, Drew knows time is money. It isn't like him at all to be late for an appointment.

It isn't good for her to worry about her clients needlessly, but she cares about them. Poor Drew, so depressed after his wife left him and took their child with her. She is about to bring up his details to ring him when the front door bangs and footsteps announce his arrival. A firm knock on the door confirms it.

'Come in!' Emma-Jane calls, keen to sound friendly and hide her annoyance at being kept waiting. There's bound to be a good reason.

Drew enters and makes himself comfortable in his usual chair, opposite Dr Glass.

'I called in at The White Lemon for my usual products, then the butchers for a ribeye steak and cured bacon and soon regretted that, I can tell you. The queue didn't move for ten minutes. People dither, have you noticed? I've made my mind up about what I want to buy before I go in, but others . . . Simpering, umming, and arhhing. Bloody annoying.' He sits stiffly with his arms on his lap, reminiscent of an army officer. 'I guess some people haven't got anything better to be doing.'

'Well, you are here now.' Emma-Jane sees he's wearing a new, expensive-looking watch and his chequered shirt complements his olive skin tone. 'How have you been since I last saw you?'

'Much the same. Sleeping better with a bit of help. Pills, a decent glass of whisky after a meal. Nothing too heavy, but it helps. I've been sorting through my wife's things. The farmhouse is . . .'

Dr Glass doesn't move or speak. She lets the silence do the work.

'Too big for me. It's a funny thing, I hadn't noticed it before, the size of it, even though it feels like . . . Evie is still there.' Unlike some of her clients, he's comfortable making eye contact with his chestnut, shrewd eyes except when his ex-wife, Evie, is mentioned. He takes a deep breath. 'I won't be developing the outbuildings. My plan was for us to live in the farmhouse, develop the rest and sell it off. Not anymore.'

'Good that you're sleeping better, and it's understandable to find the house bigger now that it's just you living there. Has sleeping better helped you cope with running your business and making those tough decisions?'

'It would seem so. I am decisive of late. I have a team of two who look after the maintenance and minor building projects. I trust them to get on with that side of things, so I manage my own time. Yesterday, there were a couple of houses of interest at auction at Birmingham Auction House but, when I got there, I changed my mind. I realised I don't want more houses, more tenants, more tax, so I spent the day in the Birmingham Art Gallery, something I've never done before.'

'That sounds good. A change. Why there?'

'Evie was a photographer and, at one time, we had dozens of her photographs on the walls in the farmhouse. I went there out of curiosity, really, to see what the appeal is. The pre-Raphaelite drawings and paintings held my interest, especially of Medea. Do you know about Medea?'

Emma-Jane shakes her head.

'She was a sorceress. When her husband deserted her for another woman, Medea poisoned her rival and the woman's two children.'

'Was the exhibition themed? I think in the past I've seen advertisements for themes or styles.'

'There were different exhibitions on different floors. It's a huge place. You should go. I was very taken with a sketch in chalk. So simple, in black and white, depicting a mother with her child feeding from her breast. It was called *Infant's Repast*. Exquisite.'

He glances up at and fixes her with his dark, unreadable eyes.

'Do you have children, Dr Glass?'

It isn't unusual for clients to ask her personal questions, so she isn't shocked by the impromptu probing. 'No, I don't.'

His face suddenly brightens, flashing a half-smile. 'I expect you have more female clients than male.'

'Why would you think that?'

'No reason.' He straightens an imaginary crease in his trousers. 'I'm thinking of dating again. Evie was vivacious, stunning. I shall do well to find someone as attractive. She had blonde hair. Your hair is very dark. Is it natural?'

A little surprised by the personal nature of the question and the rapid changes in subject matter, she doesn't respond immediately. Lucy recently told her about their meal together.

*Is he referring to their date?*

'Yes, it's natural. To think about dating again is positive,' she says, nodding encouragingly, happy to be on professional territory again.

'I've had the master bedroom and en suite redecorated to my taste, changed the mood. Previously, I never paid much attention to what went on inside the house; that was Evie's domain. She had everything she wanted. Jewellery, clothes, expensive engagement and wedding rings. My mother used to make the remains of a roast on a Sunday last the best part of a week and was buried wearing her wedding ring. You'd think Evie would wear her wedding ring like it meant something. Goodness knows where her rings are now!'

'It's good you're making it your own space, with your stamp on it. It's therapeutic to clear away things you don't need and to change the look and feel of a space.'

'Don't patronise me,' he suddenly snaps, then calms himself. 'Please don't.'

'I wasn't.' She pauses and waits for the sharpness in the air to dispel. 'I'm sorry if it came across that way.'

'I'm finding it increasingly difficult to come here and open up. It's an unnatural thing for me to do. Do you understand?'

'Yes, I do. That's why I suggested hypnotherapy previously, which you didn't like the sound of. How can our sessions be made easier for you?'

'You give nothing of yourself while I am expected to unstitch my insides and let them all fall out right here, on this carpet.' He gestures to the floor. It's a surprise to see his hands move from his lap. He looks down, as if blood and guts are there, glistening between them.

'It's your decision,' Dr Glass responds. 'You are in control of what we talk about, what you think about. I am only here to listen and to help you find a place in your mind where you are comfortable with past events. I want you to be comfortable in your skin.'

He places his hand back on his lap.

'Dr Glass, I know I'm good at what I do. I'm a successful property developer,' he says. 'I own five properties. Four are rented out at the moment and, when the fifth is ready, that'll get me a decent income. I pay more tax than I should. The money in my account and my assets confirm my success, but you? How do you know you're doing anyone any good?'

'That's a good question, and you're not the first client to ask it. Psychology is a science, but of course, human beings are complex. My aim, in simple terms, is to promote change in a mental or emotional state.'

'Change?' he asks, quizzically.

'In your case, that means alleviating some depressive symptoms to increase your sense of well-being and to help you deal with stress.'

'Then you're not helping me,' he says suddenly. 'It's not working.'

'I am confident in my diagnosis, Drew, and we are pinpointing the causes.' A sudden grin surprises her. 'You display depressive symptoms. A prolonged low mood, disrupted sleeping patterns, anger, irritability. Now is a good time to set a realistic goal for the future.'

'Claptrap.'

'Depression isn't something anyone can easily snap out of. Am I right in thinking you are angry with me because I ask you to talk about Evie? I understand it's painful for you.'

'Ah, her.' He looks up to the ceiling. 'You know she wore her camera like a placard. I should have looked at her photos more closely, and then I might have seen it coming. I could have done something or prepared myself at least. It was the shock. The devastating shock of her leaving. Visceral.' Drew's dark eyes look angry, but his expression is unchanged.

Dr Glass waits and lets the silence do the work.

'Have you ever had an electric shock, Dr Glass? Like voltage charging through your body. The pain and the lingering of pain through every vein and fibre in your body, which keeps on jarring because you're too stupefied to let go of the wire. There should be a law that punishes people for causing such pain to others.'

'Evie has caused you pain, and you are angry about that. The sense of loss is perhaps greater because you don't understand why she left you. Added to that, it came as a total surprise.'

'That's a succinct recap. Thank you. I see you are listening. Ten out of ten.' He smiles a sarcastic smile. 'I used to love watching the two of them in our house; a glass in my hand, or a mug of coffee, depending on the time of day. You know, when my son was born, it was like a miracle. I still haven't forgotten the first time I held him. Tiny hands. Small breaths, so integral to my own within seconds. And fingers, long and thin, curious about life and not afraid to touch. Evie said over and over how small they were. Helpless. That moment eclipsed everything in my life before.'

Drew turns his head and looks through the window, as if to turn his gaze away from the silence between them.

Sensing he doesn't want to say anything else, she responds, 'It is a lot to cope with when you were clearly in love with Evie and adored your son. You said they now live abroad with her new partner?'

'I used to think I saw tenderness in her eyes, or a subtle smile on her lips that was just for me. Love. Evie said she loved me all the time. Took photographs of the word "LOVE" made from sticks or stones, all kinds of things, which took time to arrange, to photograph and develop. It was a labour of love, I thought. Romantic. Silly, perhaps, but I thought there was truth in the clicks of her camera. But no woman would take herself and her child away if they knew and felt love like that.'

'You are hard on yourself. You weren't foolish to believe Evie loved you.'

'I was,' he retorts. 'It's arrogance. I had affairs and expected her to love me despite them. They meant nothing; just sex, entertainment, some ego-stroking because young, nubile women wanted me. I fancied them. Nothing more.'

Emma-Jane senses his mood swing, so remains silent. That face still looks relaxed, but the eyes and the tone of voice tell the truth.

'Go on.'

'That last time, I saw the panicked look she cast at the clock. An excuse about some appointment or other. She whipped James into her arms. A hasty chaste goodbye, like she couldn't get away fast enough. She'd been crying. I kissed her goodbye, and her mouth had shrunken to a bee sting. I said goodbye, and that was it. I thought they were coming back. If I'd known that would be the last time I—'

'What would you have done?'

'Begged her to stay.'

'Drew, have you given any thought to the suggestion I made last time we met?'

'What was that? My memory isn't what it was.'

'I'm not here to tell you what to do, of course, only you are a man of means, and perhaps you have already explored this route. A team of professionals could help you find your wife and son and legally secure access arrangements for you.'

His jaw tightens. 'It's out of the question.' He stops talking, perhaps unable to speak for a moment. His brown eyes shine with emotion, hurt cleaving through him. 'James was busy playing with his toy tractor when she walked out of the house, carrying him in her arms. I didn't even kiss him goodbye. It's too painful to talk about James anymore. He is my only son. My boy,' he says with emotion. 'I'm done talking. You seem to be done listening.'

'Hypnotherapy might help you focus and then relax. It's something I can offer you. Do reconsider. It's quite a common treatment for depression or long-term conditions like breaking bad habits and treating PTSD.'

Drew sighs profoundly, and his eyes darken further.

'No.' The sternness in his tone catches her by surprise.

'Would talking about your affairs in more detail be helpful?'

'What more is there to say about them? Kat was the last, and I have no interest in her now. The woman had delusions of grandeur, and she meant nothing to me. Not then, not now. I'm a virile man of means. Women like me.'

'Do you regret your affairs?'

'Why should I?'

'How did Evie feel about them?'

'She knew about them, if that's what you mean.' Drew clears his throat. 'That's all for today, Doctor.'

'We have fifteen minutes left.'

Drew rises suddenly from his chair. He looks at the two uneaten cakes on the coffee table. 'Pity you haven't eaten those. They might sweeten you up.'

'See you next time, Drew.'

As soon as the door is closed, Emma-Jane flops onto her sofa.

After the first three sessions, in which Drew was tearful and restless, she noticed his hands rarely moved from his lap. He's a model of self-composure and control, a mirror image to her in many respects, as she has learned to keep still to encourage the client to speak.

She sighs and shoves the first cake into her mouth, then immediately eats the second one. Feeling full and thirsty, fat and out of control, she closes her eyes.

If anyone is in control right now, it's him.

# 10

'Candles! They look lovely in here with the red walls—oh! And your antique furniture! I love that large chest with gold handles.' Lucy blushes with pleasure as she catches Drew's eye and walks around the dining room of his farmhouse.

The lit candles are a romantic touch she appreciates, on top of the enticing aromas coming from the kitchen. Drew looks so handsome in a navy striped shirt and tan chinos. It's such a treat to have dinner cooked for her by this handsome, successful man.

Ever since their last date, Lucy has felt lighter. Hopeful. *But why did he slam the door on her?*

Above them, the central light directly over the dining table is a rustic iron chandelier with six candelabra bulbs. It casts an additional warm, honey light. Drew toasts her glass before they sit at the table. Then, he leans forward and kisses her softly on the mouth. The kiss is long and gentle. She closes her eyes and luxuriates in the dark sensuality of it. Everything else moves out of her consciousness; there's just him and his lips.

'Wine and kissing go so well, perfect in fact; like smoked salmon and scrambled eggs,' Drew says.

'Or tuna and pasta! Carbs and protein!'

'So true.' She notices him looking at her again, and each time her tummy does a forward roll. 'Candlelight is flattering, isn't it, and atmospheric, especially in an old place like this. I'm not as young as you. I need all the flattery I can get.' He chuckles.

Lucy is surprised by his self-deprecating comment. 'Don't be daft! You're what? Forty? I'm not far behind.' She can't read his expression to see if his modesty is genuine or if his ego is being sufficiently stroked, so Lucy decides to change the subject to a neutral topic of conversation. 'How's your week been with the sale?' she asks. 'You mentioned this place is going on the market.'

'Yes, it is. A private buyer has approached me about this place and, provided we reach a mutual agreement, I will save myself about six thousand pounds in estate agent fees. God only knows how they justify their rates. I upset the director of Morris Estate Agents, a man named William, who I said as much to. I've bought and sold properties through them for years and had them manage the recruitment of tenants.'

'That is a lot of money, just for selling a house. Most get found and sold on Rightmove, anyway.'

'Precisely. How about your week at work?'

'I took your advice. I've taken the bull by the horns and spent double my usual budget on advertising, and I've sent tweets at the same time each day, around eleven, like you said, when people are thinking about a coffee break and gearing up for lunchtime.'

'Has it had the desired effect yet?'

'I took two bookings this week from the advertisement, and I've got around twenty new followers. Plus, several new enquiries. I'm definitely going to keep it up.'

'Excellent. You will come out of the shadow of Dr Glass's business then, and you'll be flying with new clients and confidence in yourself.'

'Oh, I don't see it like that at all. We complement and support one another, but I recognise I need to do more of my own business generation. With the summer coming up, people will think about getting in shape for bikinis and shorts.'

'That's a good point. See, having a confident mindset works wonders.'

Lucy raises her glass. 'To confidence.'

As tempting as it is to glug back the wine, Lucy takes a modest sip, thinking of the drive home and of work tomorrow. She can hardly lecture her clients about sticking to less than fourteen units of alcohol a week if she's knocking it back.

'If the business keeps growing, I may look to buy my own property early next year. Rent is dead money, after all,' she says with a smile. 'Perhaps you've got some tips for me on where to look? What are your rental properties like?'

'For rental properties, I follow a few simple rules. Terraced or semi-detached houses. The newer the better, I'd say, unless you've got DIY skills or know good people. I'm lucky: I have two labourers, AJ and Pete, who take care of the maintenance and building side of the business. Anything old and you could face a nasty surprise like rising damp, or worse, subsidence, which can be expensive to put right and, for someone needing to purchase with a mortgage, almost impossible to buy in the first place—and more difficult to sell.'

'Are those all your rules?'

'I buy close to decent shops, like a Spar or Co-op. In this area, it tends to be Co-op. Many of my tenants don't own a car and so they need to be able to walk to a local shop for their groceries. It's a selling point.'

'So which areas of Shrewsbury do you buy in?'

'My rule of thumb is generally only a three-mile

radius from the town centre, and the closer to the centre, the more rent I can charge. My strategy has been to hang on to the properties for as long as I can afford to, or until they are on the cusp of needing work. Some of my tenants have been there for over ten years and think of the house as their own. I have two properties which are empty at the moment. A previous tenant ransacked one of them. I can't tell you what a mess they made of the place.'

'That's rough. What did they do, exactly?'

'About five grand's worth of damage, that's what. It's not habitable as it is.'

'That's awful! Do you know why the tenants made such a mess of it?'

'Why do some people do what most animals don't? I have no idea, nor do I have time to dwell on people who are a waste of space, as far as I'm concerned. If they've got issues, or something to say, then speak, seek help, communicate, but to wilfully destroy the interior of a house . . . That I cannot grasp or respect an iota.'

'No. It's unbelievable.'

He shakes his head. 'If I didn't have a business head, it would feel almost personal.'

'Apart from my parents' house, I can't say I have any attachment to a building because I've moved around so much. I lived in halls while I studied at university, which was fine, but not exactly home-away-from-home. Mum and Dad's place is the closest to a home so far. I think that while you're renting, you're always half on the move, even when you're not aware of it. I suppose once you've got your own place you buy more and more stuff. It becomes a big thing to move, whereas for me it's a few bags, a suitcase, a duvet. Not much more.'

'It's a healthy thing to live like that rather than being

burdened with possessions and expense. I've realised that since I've had to confine myself to a couple rooms here at the farmhouse while it's having a facelift. It surprises me how little I really need here. The kitchen, a bed, a sofa. At one time, we lived in all the rooms.'

'Well, it's a lovely place. Did your wife take these photographs?' Lucy asks, getting up from the table and peering at the framed shots on one wall of the dining room.

He nods.

'They're excellent. Not that I'm an expert, but I'd like one of an atmospheric landscape on my wall. Like this one. Where was it taken?'

The focus of the shot is an old sycamore tree, set in a dip in the landscape, like the land has bowed down to worship the beautiful tree situated in a barren spot. There is light and dark between the branches and beneath the tree's canopy is a dainty cross.

'Local. Must be. We've always lived in Shropshire. It'll be Nesscliffe. I've kept those shots because my son, James, loves trees. This one especially. He says it was Robin Hood's Tree. He has a terrific imagination.'

Now that she looks at it closely, it's almost certainly Sycamore Gap, near Hadrian's Wall, at Hexham. Lucy looks askance at Drew's handsome face. She doesn't know him well enough to read his impassive expression, so she's unable to judge whether she should correct him or not about the location of the sycamore tree. Drew is a private man and might not want to talk about it for reasons she can only guess at.

Sycamore Gap, or the Robin Hood Tree—as she called it as a child, like James does—is a popular spot for photographers, but in Evie's version the wooden cross at the base of the trunk is distinctive. It's a little creepy seeing the cross there, knowing that James loves the tree. The monochrome shot makes it look sad, haunted even.

A strange choice, given James's fondness of it.

Drew tops up a large crystal wine glass with red wine. She hears the glugging sound as her mind works over something: the familiarity of the photograph scratches at something in her mind, like she's seen the composition of tree and cross before. But where? Unless Evie's photography was published in newspapers or magazines, it's unlikely Lucy would have come across it.

'Has the photo been printed or displayed anywhere else?' she asks. 'It looks familiar.'

Drew laughs a hollow laugh. 'Evie was an amateur back then. A good one, but I very much doubt you've seen her work before.' He tilts his head back and takes a swig of wine.

Lucy dismisses the uneasy thought and tries to think about the evening meal she is about to enjoy. How can she have seen the photograph before? She knows how the mind can play tricks. As she looks more closely at the photographs on each side of the Sycamore Gap, she sees Evie had taken close-up shots of the foliage from underneath the canopy.

The tree must have been special to them both.

'It just reminds me of something—maybe something I saw in the newspaper.'

'I'll bring the main course in. Won't be long.' His sudden change of the subject catches her off guard.

'Alright. Shout if I can help.'

She moves to the other side of the large dining room, where there's a dark wooden chest. Its surface is bare, except for a bowl ladened with a rainbow of fruit.

It catches her eye, the fleshy plums and dark cherries especially. But on closer inspection, she sees that the fruit is spoiling. Fur clings to the flesh of the plums and one has imploded to reveal its guts.

'I hope you like salmon and prawns. It's tagliatelle.'

Lucy backs away from the bowl and joins him at the table, hiding her distaste with a fake smile. 'Looks delicious. You're an excellent cook. Martin, my ex-boyfriend, was a whizz with the BBQ, but not so keen on using the oven.'

'You broke it off because of a terrible dish,' Drew laughs. 'Didn't you?'

'No. He was killed in a car accident.' Drew immediately falls silent, and Lucy decides to kill the awkward silence. 'We'd just got to the stage, after three happy years together when, well, we were ready for a more serious commitment, I lost him. It was a while ago now, but he was very special to me.'

'I'm sorry.'

'Better to have loved and lost than never to have loved at all. Isn't that what they say?'

'You think so?' he asks, doubtfully.

'Ask Emma-Jane. She's the expert.' Lucy smiles.

'Oh, is she in a happy relationship?'

Lucy laughs. 'With her job, yes.'

'Does she know you're here this evening?'

Surprised by the question, Lucy shrugs. 'Of course.'

'What do you miss the most, now that you live alone?'

She is taken aback by the shifting questions, the personal nature of his queries.

'The sound of someone disappearing from your life forever is ear-splitting. I have the radio, TV, the lights ... Even the stupid fan in the kitchen, just for background noise to substitute the noises Martin used to make.' Surprised by the sudden personal admission, Lucy thinks before she speaks, but Drew continues before she has a chance to.

'I find the sounds of cooking replace some old sounds: her shoes on the tiled floor, for example. But nothing can replace the joy of a child's laughter or their running along the landing. James walked nowhere. Always ran.'

'It got easier. After losing Martin, I mean. At first, it seemed like there should be a hole in the pillow beside me. I had long periods when I didn't think about Martin. Since moving back to Shrewsbury, that's not been so easy.'

'Love is sadistic,' Drew says suddenly. 'It unskins. Vampires, bloodsuckers, the horror on TV—all that slashing, hacking, sucking—it's nothing compared to lost love.'

Lucy isn't sure whether he's joking. He looks thoughtful—or is he acting?

'I think a lot about the shape and feel of loss,' he continues. 'I even visit art galleries in pursuit of seeing it artistically presented, but I haven't had any success so far. I read sometimes, of course, but I'd still like to see something visually interpreted. Of course, you can see loss everywhere, as Dr Glass has shown me, if you let the greyness of loss colour your perception. That's not what I mean. In my darkest of moods, I did, yes—not so much now, I'm pleased to say, ever since I started planning my future.'

Lucy adores the way he speaks, the way his eyes glaze off into the distance. To a place she'd like to accompany him.

'She's very good at her job.'

'Yes,' he says, refocusing his eyes on Lucy. 'And you are her number one fan!'

'Can I see the rest of the farmhouse after we eat?' she

asks and her stomach grumbles. The aromas from the kitchen smell delicious and, because she has normally eaten by this time, every minute feels like two. Her hunger is like a third person at the table.

He puts his glass down.

'Unfortunately, that isn't possible.' He pauses for a moment and half-smiles, perhaps recognising he was blunt. 'There's still a lot of work going on in many of the rooms. Perhaps another time. I hope you will not rush off now.' He leans forward and his shadow falls over her and the table.

There is no mistaking the signal. This time, no door is slammed in her face.

The kiss is gentle and searching, almost as satisfying as a full stomach until he bites her lip and makes it bleed.

It frightens her, but still she wants more.

# 11

Emma-Jane doesn't need to ask Lucy how her most recent date with Drew went. She can tell by the serene expression on her face and the quick way she giggles at the smallest things.

It's lovely to see her friend happy, but it worries her that the romance seems to be moving very quickly, with them seeing each other every other night. Not that it's any of Emma-Jane's business, but it seems like Lucy is well and truly head over heels for someone she barely knows.

In her office, she watches Lucy flick through pages on her iPad while she sips a mug of tea, humming all the while. Emma-Jane puts her head to one side as she tries to isolate her feelings of concern. It isn't jealously at seeing her friend happy, is it? Is it protectiveness? She isn't sure. Although Drew has his issues, she can understand what Lucy sees in him.

He is a client; perhaps that's what it is.

She leans over to take a closer look at Lucy's screen and sees images of a sycamore tree, one after the other: sometimes in colour, sometimes in monochrome.

'Are you planning a hike somewhere? Looks remote, wherever it is.'

Lucy doesn't look up. She scrolls to another image, more of the same. 'No, just surfing.'

'What are you looking for?'

'Nothing much.' She suddenly gets up from the chair

and stretches. 'I'm going home. Do you want me to lock up?'

'No, I've got a late one with Vanessa.' They are always tough sessions, and Lucy knows it.

'See you tomorrow then. Night.' Lucy gives her a supportive smile before leaving the office.

In their last session, she had suggested Vanessa keep a dream diary to bring with her but, when she arrives an hour later, she is empty-handed.

'Make yourself comfortable, Vanessa,' Emma-Jane says, after the usual preamble to the start of a session. 'Have you been out anywhere since I saw you last?' she asks, disappointed to see the colour that was in her cheeks paled to an alabaster hue.

'Only the cemetery; to the shop for food but I bought nothing in the end; to put the bin out . . .' Vanessa wrings her hands. 'I started walking to her primary school at three o'clock, because that's what I used to do, to collect her. I forgot she—' Her voice breaks. The crack is as loud as crockery smashing on the floor.

'Three o'clock must be a difficult hour. Your mind has gotten used to a particular routine at that time. We get trained, conditioned, to do things at a certain time. Is there a new routine which could occupy that time? A new habit to replace the old, perhaps?'

Vanessa shakes her head. She looks thinner and tired, growing more waif-like with every visit. That glow in her aura following the dandelion dream has long gone. This Vanessa is a ghost of that self.

'I had another empty apology from a neighbour. More empty words. Sounds. They might mean something to them, but not to me. Meaningless. I wish they wouldn't say anything to me. What do they know about emptiness?

Why are they sorry? How dare they speak Avril's name to me?'

'Go on.'

'I felt angry, and so I dropped some litter over the hedge when they'd gone. Silly, but I felt better for a while.'

Emma-Jane stays still, waiting for Vanessa to continue.

'Someone else, last week, told me to keep my chin up. Not a friend; someone with a nice face I used to chat with now and then. He said, "funny how life goes."' Her eyes widen. 'Funny?'

'You felt angry, and that's a normal, healthy reaction to grief. Dropping litter was a small liberation. When you experience loss, you will go through stages: denial, anger, bargaining, depression, acceptance. Some days you will feel all of them at once—'

'You've told me that before, Dr Glass. I know you want me to move on with my life, but I want to hang on to the old, good times. The special ones. I can't do anything else. Why would I replace my love for Avril with something else? I wouldn't be me then. Because she is no longer with us, it is right I am incomplete.' She sighs loudly. 'It's only right.'

'You are brave. There was no warning to prepare you for Avril's sudden death. You were happy and well. Then suddenly, everything changed. Your life looks and feels completely different now. No one expects you to keep going like everything is as it was before. Be gentle with yourself, and maybe allow yourself some pleasure. A meal out, a trip somewhere in the fresh air, perhaps?'

'I don't want to. It's pointless. Might as well play a video game. How does buying a hot sausage roll from a café or a gastropub or an expensive hair product make it any better?' Suddenly she looks up at the ceiling, like she's heard a gunshot and a bird is about to drop into her lap. 'I don't think you understand me, Dr Glass.'

It's hard to hear. 'Then help me to,' she says calmly. 'Talk to me.'

Vanessa looks at her like she's shouted swear words. Her pale, heart-shaped face bobs above her tiny shoulders like a balloon. 'My friend, Edith, said I should have another child. I laughed when she said it. Imagined myself walking down the high street, with my purse in my handbag, nipping into a few shops to browse the babies. Hold them in my arms like I'm trying one for size. Edith's never had kids. Just dogs. She thinks it's like getting a new dog when the old one dies. I hadn't realised how much I don't like her till then.'

A lorry thunders by outside. *Speeding*, Emma-Jane thinks, and she suddenly remembers the rain. The car on her tail. The letters.

*Could Vanessa have written them?*

Emma-Jane shows she is listening by sitting forward a little.

'Vanessa, I am not here to tell you to move on, or to put it behind you, to go on holiday, or buy a dog, or take up gardening or cooking, for that matter. Your friend, Edith, means well by encouraging you to get pregnant again, thinking that if you have another child you might feel like your old self. You may never feel like your old self again. Space and time, quiet, is perhaps what you need most, to allow you to know your loss and your grief.'

'When will I cry my last tears?' She looks down at herself, her narrow legs, the bony hands in her lap twisting a cotton handkerchief. It looks like it was her father's handkerchief, or a man's, at least. The amount of cotton on that little lap catches Emma-Jane's eye. A dainty hanky wouldn't absorb the river of tears. She needs a man-sized one. A giant one, for an elf of a person.

'There's nothing left of me except grief for her. To come here, to get out of bed and start a new day, it takes all my energy, like my heart doesn't work properly.'

'Are you eating well?' She already knows the answer. Vanessa's faded jeans look baggy. The thinness of those legs makes her tan, leather boots look like they belong to someone much taller. 'Even just a bit is a good start. Things you fancy. Do you like soup? It's easy to eat and digest, and fresh soup can be very nutritious.'

'I was going to eat before I came here, but then the post came. Something for Avril. I opened it. One Christmas, she wanted to adopt a donkey. They sent her a photograph and a thank-you note for the donation. I can't bring myself to cancel the subscription, to tell them she's dead. Her post is piled neatly at one end of the kitchen table.'

'Could you set yourself one goal? Perhaps to put the post in a drawer, or somewhere less prominent? It would be a step forward, when you're ready, to coming to terms with your loss.'

Vanessa shakes her head. 'I dreamt about Avril last night but, as soon as I woke up, I couldn't remember a single detail. I laid there with my eyes closed, hoping some recollection might come. It's like she is robbed from me all over again. Missing. When will I accept I won't find her again? When will I stop looking?'

'Is there a way you can say a goodbye to Avril? A goodbye isn't stopping you from loving her. You can give yourself permission to say goodbye and still love her. Love yourself, too. Be kind to yourself.'

'I love myself. I do. I want to set myself free.' She sobs.

Emma-Jane hides her disquiet as Vanessa cries.

'Do you think I'll know when I'll give up waiting for that light at the end of the tunnel?' She sighs. 'I'm sick of looking down the tunnel. It's dark, so dark, and long.'

'No one is expecting you to do anything except to be and to feel. If you want to cry, then cry. Take each day at a time. Can you picture Avril smiling, laughing?'

'I picture her a lot. I picture her on the other end of an imaginary phone, like you told me to. I wish she could answer.'

'Did you give writing your feelings any more thought?'

'Yes, I've made a start.'

'That's excellent. A new purpose can be a good thing. Well done! Perhaps bring a piece in if you'd like to. I would love to read it.'

'I'm rewriting some of Avril's favourite movies. Cinderella, Snow White. Avril loved those stories, but they all end happy. I am rewriting them, just for adults, with a realistic ending,' she says, wiping her eyes.

'You are right. Life isn't a fairy tale.'

---

Emma-Jane feels hollow after the hour with Vanessa.

She emails Celia, her clinical supervisor, for an appointment to talk about her cases to offload and evaluate how she is handling Vanessa and Drew. It seems like there is no garment to fit Vanessa's grief. Drew is grieving too, in a different way. She finds the quietness of Vanessa's sad smile moving, and she respects the way she wears her pain like glass: transparent, fragile. So brave, to not wear a brave face; to wear a real, feeling one.

Not like Drew.

She glances at the time on her laptop to find it is almost nine o'clock. Lucy left two hours ago. It would be sensible to lock the front door at this hour, but she doesn't plan to stay in the office for long. No wonder her head is pounding, because she can't remember when she last had a drink of water or something to eat. Breakfast, she thinks, apart from biscuits and cake. The pain starts on one side of her head, then works its way around the circumference of her skull.

While the session is clear in her mind, she writes her notes detailing what she and Vanessa covered, whether her diagnosis still stands, and any signs of progress or concern. She also monitors her own response to her client, in terms of transference. It's usual for her to type quickly and to push the keys firmly so it drowns any other sounds out.

The sharp and sudden beep of an alarm makes her jump.

She glances behind her at the window and glimpses flashing red from a nearby building, a solicitor's. The alarm has gone off, as it has once before, and that had been a false alarm. She struggles to keep her focus.

Emma-Jane reads the notes she has made, pushing through the tiredness and headache to get the job done so she can get home, take a bath, and finally relax.

*Relevant issues: Vanessa is rewriting fairy tales. Revisiting Avril's childhood and changing the ending of the tales to 'realistic.' Lack of hope. Battling depression and lack of empathy with friend, Edith. Does she want to move on? Suicidal thoughts. Looks thinner. Talked about not looking for a light at the end of the tunnel. Not sure she wants to live in the present.*

The door handle to her office turns. She frowns, watching the metal handle move forty-five degrees. It's probably Vanessa. *Not more to deal with.* The day gets longer, and the handle keeps turning.

'Vanessa?'

Alarmed by the lack of response, Emma-Jane stands from her desk, bile rising in her throat. With her eyes screwed up, she peers through the gap into the darkness.

'Is that you?'

She pushes the office chair behind her, surprised by the sound of fear in her voice and the tightness growing in her chest like a tumour. A scent, not entirely unfamiliar, catches her nose, tickling her memory. The wheels turn and slide as the chair skids behind her.

Then, there is an agonising silence. The door is ajar.

'Hello?'

Her eyes narrow to focus on the darkness spilling into her office like black blood. Someone is there, waiting, standing behind the door. Watching. Playing.

Her hand lunges for the key in the lock just as the door flies open and she freezes like a deer. Her stomach twists in fright, but she recognises the tall figure standing motionless in the doorway. The man associated with that scent.

'Drew?' Relief washes over her.

She is about to speak to him, ask him if he needs something. But before she can do anything else, Drew suddenly grabs her roughly round the neck, as if she were a stray, vicious dog. She thrashes in his firm grip, one that is resolute and cruel. Panicking, her legs kick out at the door and the desk, in desperation to be free.

'No!' Her tone is indignant, shocked. 'No!' she screams. Has her client suddenly lost his mind?

*Is this happening to me, right now, by him?*
'Get off!'

Strands of hair catch in her mouth and, with her arms held tightly behind her back, they remain on her tongue until the chloroformed rag is placed firmly over her open mouth. The vile odour brings on another wave of thrashing, sending a pile of papers flying off the desk and onto the floor.

The most recent hate letter tumbles to the carpet, landing face up.

*It was him.*

Then limpness, a loss of focus, like the office is moving away from her. His arms and fingers still tight, the gag fat inside her mouth. *Is he going to rape me?* Her eyelids flutter like trapped butterflies. She can't scream. She's powerless.

A final stab of fear jitters up her spine and then numbness pulls her down, as if under the sea, as the drug takes full effect. Moaning and growing limp in his grip, she stops trying to fight back and lets her rag doll arms fall to her sides.

———————◆———————

He lays her down on the carpet, a shape of entwined limbs and hair, and rearranges her so she is lying neatly, face up. He kicks her leather chair out of the way to make more room for her legs, which splay out. Drew switches the light off in the office and a ghostly glow from the computer is an echo in the room.

It is good that she fought. He wouldn't want a pushover to convert to his way of thinking. A feisty, intelligent woman. Looking at her now, she is attractive, in a dark-haired way—not his usual type.

It's her learned mind which interests him. The pliable nature of it. The synapses and the neural pathways have been corrupted. He needs to change that. Make Dr Glass see clearly.

The alarm continues to sound down the street and the light flashes on and off through the blinds, lighting the room in a scarlet hue, like the red-light district. There is no alarm to sound in this office building, except the internal wail and siren of Emma-Jane's frightened heartbeat. Drew smiles with triumph when her head lolls to one side, like she's been lobotomised. The red light flashes on and off over her face and body, across the desk, up the walls. *It's almost erotic*, he thinks, and lets the moment linger, savouring it, before the next stage.

This is the last time he will see this office. Not that he'll miss it, especially that chair. There's another chair waiting for Dr Glass to sit in at his property. Not a comfortable one—the chair isn't about relaxation; it's about surrendering and listening. Concentrating.

Months ago, Dr Glass had spoken confidently on local radio about that woman, Angela Lamb, who killed herself and her son, Teddy. She defended the monster. Sympathised with her. The thought puts a bitter taste in his mouth.

He spits on her. The glob of saliva lands on her neck.

Knowing she won't be unconscious for long, he focuses on what he needs to do to eliminate her records of him: his address, phone number. Drew wriggles the mouse to her computer, bringing it back to life. He puts his name in the search box, wanting to delete his contact details. Time is precious; he has to get her into the car and to the house before she comes round. Abruptly, he yanks the filing cabinet drawers open and rifles through the papers, but he finds nothing with his name on it.

'Fuck.' He scratches his head. Then, an idea comes to him. He clicks on her email and sends a brief message to Lucy. He smiles, knowing that trusting, gullible Lucy will believe it. All of it. The woman has her uses.

*Late night yet again. Taking a few days off from work. Need a holiday.*

Would she sign it 'love'? Probably. Lucy is her number one fan, after all.

*Love, Emma-Jane x*

The floor is covered in papers that have toppled from her desk, which he collects into a neat pile. He returns the upturned pot of pens and pencils knocked over by the tussle to its proper position. Lastly, he puts the two hate letters he sent her into his back pocket. Looking down at the slack features on her face, her arms and legs akimbo, he thinks, *Dr Glass isn't so respectable now.* A grin spreads across his face. He's got a few things he wants to teach her.

His letters were a tasty little starter before the main meal, which she will enjoy from a location of his choosing. The letters took time, care, and there was an element of risk with hand-delivering them, especially to her house. All that glass—how perfect that Dr Glass should live in a glass box. You'd think she'd have a clearer perspective on life, but no.

It's taken several months of planning to get this far, and several pointless hours with her, in this very room, talking, talking, talking. Did she listen? Soon, she will spend hour after hour on a chair. One she will be tied to, and cuffed to for good measure, to be sure he has her full attention. He deserves nothing less.

He bends down and strokes her thick, black hair like she's a pet cat. Drew notices her nails are painted a dark purple hue and the thumb nail is chipped. A small imperfection. Did the fall do that? This time next week, they will look different again.

'Ready for your little holiday, are we?'

Not taking any chances, he handcuffs her wrist to the heavy wooden desk before he moves his Range Rover. Mud has conveniently smeared the number plates. Ten minutes later, he pulls up as close to the office building as possible. The streets are quiet now, and the stuttering streetlight lends him a helping hand to move in the shadows.

He dresses Emma-Jane in his dark overcoat and pulls a cap over her head. If someone were to see him heave her into the Range Rover, they might be forgiven for thinking the person is worse for wear, and Drew is doing a good turn in helping them get home. A smart car, and smart dress. It helps.

'There we go,' he says loudly over the sound of the alarm, in case anyone is watching. 'Soon we'll get you home to bed. No more whiskies for you!'

In the leather passenger seat, he fixes her seat belt before turning on the radio to Classic FM. The empty house is only a few miles away, bur far enough to enjoy Beethoven's *Symphony No. 5*, followed by Vivaldi's *Four Seasons*.

He turns up the volume of the radio. His mood is buoyant as he pulls away, the red light and alarm still flashing, still sounding—but no one cares enough to stop and stare.

# 12

The worry of his mobile phone ringing at the late hour reshapes AJ's body into an exclamation mark. Erect from his bed, he travels to the small landing where his phone is resting like a toad in the dark.

'Who the hell is that?' Hannah asks from the bedroom.

'Drew,' he says, sounding more alert than he feels. He answers. 'Hey, Drew. No worries. I was awake anyway.'

'Bullshit,' Hannah mumbles and sighs, pulling the duvet up to her chin. Drew talks for several minutes. She thinks, *No doubt giving orders, listing instructions. Why doesn't he call Pete? It's always bloody AJ. He's too soft, that's his problem. Too decent.*

'Downstairs?' AJ asks. 'Yeah, we'll get on to that tomorrow. Where are you staying then? . . . No worries . . . Not a problem. Bye.'

Hannah switches on the sidelight to see AJ's boxers are bunched up under his balls. He scratches them, looking perplexed.

'What did he want?' she asks, as he climbs back into bed after readjusting himself.

'I think he's a bit drunk. Didn't realise the time. He wants me and Pete to get the rest of the farmhouse sorted, now that he's moved out proper like. Honestly, Hannah, he was slurring, and at one point he hiccupped. I 'bout laughed.'

'Where's he living now, then?'

'He didn't say. He's only just moved his stuff out. One

of his other properties, I expect. There's four or five of them. To be honest with you, I'll be glad to be away from the bloody farmhouse. It gives me the creeps, all those empty rooms and outbuildings.'

'It's not like you to be creeped out by something like that. What's with you, AJ?'

'I just don't much like the old farmhouse, to be honest. I prefer to work outside, and Kat—that redhead I told you about—she keeps pestering me and Pete about where Drew is living, his new phone number . . . She's sniffing around the place asking questions, like a bloody sniffer dog in heat.'

'Tell her to get lost!'

'Drew's my boss. His personal life is his own business, and he's pretty stressed out at the minute anyway, but his shit stinks as far as I'm concerned, and I'm getting caught in it.' AJ drops his head on the pillow like it weighs a ton.

'Have you told Drew about her pestering you?' she says with an accusing gaze. 'He needs to know if she's coming round all the time. Honestly, AJ, I think Drew would want to know.'

'No, I haven't said, because the bloke isn't my best friend or anything. If she doesn't take the hint soon I might, in case it gets out of hand. He's obviously dumped her, and she doesn't like it. Pete thinks she comes around at night, because the barriers were moved, but I don't know about that.'

'Really? She could go to prison for stalking Drew. I read about that in my weekly mag. For her to be calling round after what's happened sounds wrong to me. Insensitive, at the very least. I mean . . . After. Anyway, this bloke—'

'Are you hungry?' he interrupts. 'Fancy toast or

something? I'll make it.'

'It's one o'clock in the morning. I've got work tomorrow. So do you, for that matter.'

'Piss off. I fancy jam and toast.' He flings back the duvet and pulls on one of his old T-shirts, a pint of Guinness printed on the front. 'Do you want some or not?'

Hannah puts her arms above her head on the pillow and grins. Her boobs peek and bounce above the duvet.

'I'll take that as a yes.'

One bulb in the kitchen has gone, so it's a dim, gloomy light, but enough to switch the grill and the kettle on and butter four pieces of white bread. It's one of Nigella Lawson's tips for delicious toast—the double buttering, with a touch of salt. As soon as the toast is done, he butters it a second time and races upstairs with a tray.

'You'd better be awake!' AJ calls as he climbs the stairs, the aroma of warm toast making him salivate.

'There's not much chance of getting some kip around here while you're banging around down there! Are you sure you haven't invited Drew over?'

He feeds her a slice of toast. 'You know me better than that!'

She likes to be fed, like a tamed wolf. 'Mmm,' she says, and licks her lips, conjuring images of the moon. 'Delicious.'

A rivulet of butter runs down her chin, which she wipes off with a finger. She licks and nuzzles like a wolf. AJ feels the blood returning to his penis, an ache. He feeds her a second slice, still warm and buttery, the colour and heat of sunshine. 'You do something to me, Hannah.'

Hannah passes him a mug of tea from the tray and takes one herself, which she slurps loudly. The surge of blood in his penis drops like a cold temperature, but the static of her is loud in his brain. He puts his mug and plate on the carpet and reaches for the sidelight to switch it off, wanting to be close to her, to listen to her heartbeat. Hannah puts her mug down too and snuggles up to AJ with her head on his chest.

'I love you, Hannah,' he says. 'I'm going to make you proud one day. I am.'

'Silly,' she says, stroking his chest. 'I already am, and I love you. I couldn't do what you do. You're good with your hands. Not many men can say that, and especially not the men I work with all day long, in suits and ties and manicured nails, who are so fussy about everything.'

'Fussy about what?'

'Parking in the same spot, for instance. Or having their coffee break at the same time every day. Eating the same bloody type of biscuit, even! I just find them a bit prissy. Not real men like you, who needs a bath at the end of the working day and has muscles from hard graft, not a stupid weight machine in the back bedroom.'

AJ laughs and cuddles her. 'Do you remember that episode of *Only Fools and Horses*? The last one, when they became millionaires by chance. God, that would be amazing. You know, to have your luck turn like that after years of scraping and grafting.'

'I love Rodney.'

He laughs, remembering a short story he'd read in one of her weekly magazines. The theme was basically that we are all lovable rogues and insecure monsters, hoping someone will find our quirky or monstrous side lovable. Even people like Rodney find love and fortune, becoming a Drew Rogers of this world.

'Listen, we gotta keep saving and then buy a place to do up. We would have to put up with the dust and mess, but it'll be worth it when we sell it and buy the next one. I can do brickwork, carpentry, some basic plumbing. You'd do a grand job of the interior design stuff.'

'I'd love that! Curtains, soft furnishings. Betsy at work buys loads from TK Maxx; you know, designer stuff, but on the cheap. Her house is amazing!'

'What's your dream home?'

Hannah sighs, and he is more aware of her warm breath and body than he wants to be now when he needs to get up early. Suddenly, she laughs. 'You know, nothing too fancy. I like cosy. A cottage would be nice for just the two of us. I like beams and fireplaces and uneven floorboards.'

'Sounds like a builder's nightmare!' he says, relieved she didn't say a mansion or a castle. Laughing, he hopes she won't give up on him and run off with some rich, clever bloke. Would she keep loving a version of him without edges or weaknesses? Sometimes he hates himself for being so average, so sometimes he cuts with a razor in the morning to make himself as imperfect as he knows he is inside. 'I can live with that, as long as you're happy.'

'But we're going to go on holiday, aren't we? Somewhere hot. I'd like Greece. The beaches in Corfu look amazing. Just a week of sunshine is enough.'

The corners of AJ's mouth tighten. With it being the middle of the night and feeling uncertain about where future pay cheques will come from, all the summers ahead appear as a desert, with him labouring his way up one sand dune of a thousand feet after another, his workman's boots sinking into the sand with every stride he takes. The image is so vivid he can hear the wind and feel the sweat drying on his back.

The room settles in readiness for slumber as the aromas of toast and butter and pipe dreams fade into the four corners of their rented house. Hannah's breathing becomes slow and deep, but sleep is a mirage for AJ, who turns on his side and holds his pillow to his head in the vain hope it will stop whirring. In the morning he will dress, eat a cooked breakfast, mop up the egg with a slice of bread, get into his grimy white van and put in a hard day's work lining Drew Rogers' pockets by improving one of his many properties. Then he will come home, knackered and hungry, and watch the television until he finds the energy to make a meal for them both; something quick and cheap, like spaghetti and meatballs.

He rolls onto his other side, away from Hannah, and stares at the red digits on the alarm clock. The feeling in his stomach can't be hunger, not after the evening meal and then the toast they've just eaten. What is it? He sees their regular Thursday night meal—the pale noodle flesh of spaghetti on a plate beside minced meat, smeared in blood-red tomato sauce. What is it that will make him feel better?

But he knows. He thinks about it every day.

AJ's belly will not feel full until he's got enough money to not worry about getting sick or losing his job, not earning a month's pay and being sunk under that red line that gets harder and harder to cross every month. He feels like a lad in an egg and spoon race who keeps tripping over his feet and dropping his egg.

Failure. Sometimes he thinks he can smell it on himself.

It's in the corner of his eyelids some nights, when he is too tired to blink, let alone speak to Hannah. There's a weight on his eyelids now, an antique coin which belongs to a billionaire, pushing his lids down. Tiredness. It's there all the time. Even when he wakes up. He's not even thirty yet. What will it be like when he's fifty, sixty, seventy?

Primary school. He's been thinking about it lately. The reports his teachers sent home. If he'd tried harder, would it be different now? All that ink, that paper, those classroom walls and a strange person standing there at the front, like an omen. Are his van, his toolbox and his muscles, his strong, toughened hands, the sum of him?

He strokes his bicep; it's firm and bulging from labouring, not hours in a gym. Earnt. Not glistening under LED lights in a fancy mirror-clad place, sitting beside babes in Lycra with hair in pigtails bouncing like a rabbit's tail left and right.

Graft. Hard graft. Muscles that could do damage to a person.

If he so chose.

# 13

Spurred on by Ross's incoherent murmurs, Jennifer wriggles and gyrates some more on his face, pushing his head deeper into the anti-allergy pillows on their bed.

'Mmmmm . . .'

'I can't hear you!' Jennifer exclaims over the rustling of cotton from his limbs swimming on the sheet.

'Mmmmmmm . . .'

A slap on her enormous bare bottom prizes open her mouth like a fish plucked from the sea but the stinging pain quickly fades until he slaps once more, followed by a flurry of them, battering against her skin in an unreadable morse code.

'That hurts!' she says, pushing down some more, imagining the angry handprint left behind on her bottom while now partially enjoying the tingling sensation.

'Fffffff . . .'

Ross's moans and his kicking legs returns a smile to her lipstick and jam-smeared face. She arches her back wearing a rueful grin, and her long hair spills like water between his naked limbs.

*I'm the queen of squashing.*

'Ahhhhhhh . . .'

He moans some more from the depth of his lungs, as though from the bottom of the sea. She imagines the pleasure he feels and wriggles some more until his moans are thinner. Weaker.

'Ahh . . .'

'What?' she says, suddenly stopping the wriggling and the cessation releases a pocket of air against hot pink flesh like a popped bubble.

His limbs fall slack on the King size bed, copied in the mirror at the dressing table where Jennifer's jewellery is the most colourful thing in an otherwise white room. One foot of his is partially caught in the net of white sheets.

Now conscious of the heat, the sweat on her skin, and Ross's silent stillness, she sits and listens. There's a 'not thereness' about him at odds with the sensation of his stubble beneath her.

'Ross?' Her voice rises uncontrollably. 'Ross!'

Unable to lift one leg, she rolls over to one side, but rolls back, frenzied and fearful she will land on the lavender carpet in a puddle of flesh.

'Are you saying the safe word?'

She tries to climb off him again, but she can't rightly shift under her own weight, especially with the handcuffs.

'Oh my god! Oh, my fucking god!'

With wild eyes, she reaches for the sheet, the mattress, something to get a handle on. But her hands are sweaty and greasy. 'Ross! Help me, oh God,' she wails, sick with terror, her voice hoarse and primitive. 'No-oh-ooh-ooh!'

Jennifer wraps her hands around the wooden headboard and once content she has a firm hold, hoists her behind from the throne of his face, and looks down at a dead man.

# 14

On her way to work, Lucy distracts herself by checking her emails on her phone. It surprises her to receive Emma-Jane's email telling her she is taking an impromptu holiday, but she has been working some long hours lately.

*Good for her.*

That's not the most pressing thing on her mind, however, having listened to the local news on Shropshire Radio in the car. Lucy fights the tears pricking at her eyes as she strides from the car park to the office and the tragic news begins to sink in. She puts a hand over her mouth to keep the pain inside as she jogs along the pavement and, as soon as she steps inside her office and closes the door, breaks down into floods of tears.

Ross is dead.

Ross, attentive and doting beside Jennifer. She can see them sitting side by side now, holding hands, in these very chairs. She thinks of Jennifer in her chunky red and green beaded necklace. A mere pendant would not have been any kind of statement, not even a full stop. She can hear her bangles jangling and the swaying of her hoop earrings. That, and the bounce of her ample bosom, jostling with the banter of her clothes, the clashing colours, fabrics, patterns, buttons.

Is Jennifer dressed in monochrome now? She'd once said she likes to play her accessories loudly, like trumpets. Is the bugle playing 'Taps' now? Is she wearing her signature plum lipstick like a bruise? They were so in love.

*Poor, poor Ross, and Jennifer.*

Lucy doesn't know whether to sit, or to stand, or go for a walk, or do nothing. Hide. Run. Is she to blame, somehow? If only Emma-Jane was here to talk to. It's futile, but she checks to see if Emma-Jane's office is empty, just to be sure. Seeing that it is, next she dials Jennifer's number, and it immediately clicks to voicemail. The first time she hangs up, then she rings again to leave a message of condolence. It's something. What else can she do?

'Jennifer, it's Lucy. I'm so sorry. I've just heard about Ross. It's terrible. I don't know what to say. Please, ring me if you can. Take care. Bye.'

Moments later the mobile rings, showing a number Lucy doesn't recognise, but she answers it on the second ring. Her heart thuds. If it is Jennifer, what can she say? Will Jennifer be angry with her?

'Hello? Lucy speaking.'

'It's Jennifer.' The tone is emotionless, entirely out of character. If she hadn't given her name Lucy would not have recognised the small voice on the other end of the phone. It's almost childlike, like she has magically shrunk.

'Jennifer! Oh God, thank you for ringing me back. I'm so sorry about Ross. I've only just heard. It's—'

'The police interviewed me. They questioned me. The officer spoke to me like I was a fucking cannibal or something. Like it was my fault! I loved Ross!' She sobs and Lucy waits, one hand over her mouth. 'I won't be charged. They know it was an accident, but they made me feel responsible!'

Lucy doesn't know what to say next and is ashamed, in part, by feeling relieved Jennifer isn't angry or blaming her. 'I'm so sorry. Wh—'

'It's my fault,' she wails. 'I suffocated him. One minute we were hugging, and then ... squashing ... crushed under my ... I wish I was dead.' And she hangs up.

Lucy immediately tries to ring her back, but there's no answer. Has squashing killed Ross? Did her weight block his windpipe? Did the air in his lungs run out while she was sat right on top of his face? She puts her head in her hands, hating the image, and hating the anxiety caused by knowing about their sexual preferences and playing a part in them by making Jennifer heavier.

*Does that make me culpable?*

'Oh my God.' She dials Emma-Jane's phone, desperate to talk to her friend. What should she do? The phone clicks to voicemail so she leaves a message begging her to ring back and hangs up.

Ashamed by the selfish thought that she might be culpable, she thinks of Ross and remembers a quotation she'd read, something about eating being touch carried to the bitter end. *How true that turns out to be,* she thinks sadly. Lucy paces the office. *What do I do now? My reputation. My fragile confidence.*

*Ross is dead.*

Perhaps she isn't cut out for this work. She should return to Carlisle, live with her parents for a time, while she sorts her head out. Lucy looks again at the chairs Ross and Jennifer had so recently sat in, held hands in, talked excitedly about their future in. Soon he will be in a casket, motionless, in the dark, buried. His heart still intact, but frozen. His hands, cold.

Unable to spend another minute in her office, she throws a few things into her handbag and heads home to pack a bag for a few days away. The further away from Shrewsbury, the better. Half an hour later she points her car north, toward Carlisle and her parents' house.

*Running, yes, I'm running. But who wouldn't?*

On the way, she phones her clients and postpones her appointments. It isn't the professional thing to do but she is in no fit state to work. Goodness knows what advice she'd dish out. After Jennifer and Ross, she doubts she will have the confidence to open her door again. *No wonder Emma-Jane needs a break*, she thinks, dealing with death and grief day after day, hour after hour.

The journey to Carlisle is one she knows like the back of her hand. Usually, she phones her mum just as she leaves the A69 because the route from that point to their house is less than thirty minutes. She usually says she is less than an hour away, preferring to arrive in good time so her mum doesn't fret. Since she turned eighty-six, she's become a worrier.

Lucy occupies her whirring mind by imagining herself sitting at the kitchen table with them, tucking into Mum's home-made Victoria sponge cake. Dad slurps his tea, holding forth on some subject or other and then Mum plans the Sunday roast, even though it's only Thursday. The image is comforting. Hopefully, Jennifer will have a family to comfort her in her hour of need.

An hour later, Lucy has a change of heart about immediately going to her parents' house. She decides against ringing them to tell them about her imminent arrival. It can wait for a few hours. She turns right towards Hexham instead, and parks in a familiar lay-by with easy access to the footpath which runs alongside Hadrian's Wall. The sun is shining, and it is a quiet and beautiful place to get some exercise and de-stress.

She changes into walking gear in the lay-by and packs a rucksack with a few supplies and extra layers. Her phone is on the passenger seat. It's been on silent for the journey, and it's been a refreshing change not to be a slave to messages, but she takes it with her, just in case.

The terrain is largely flat at first, and wonderfully serene after the booming in her brain. The events of the day begin to lose their jaggedness after an hour and a half of brisk walking. A buzzard's lonely cry from above announces its orbit before it lands on the wall ahead and remains motionless.

*Its necklace of feathers is beautiful*, she thinks. *Perhaps it's looking for its mate for life. Like me.*

*Like Jennifer will.*

Lucy likes the freedom of rambling without a fixed route, just to walk one way and then back the same. Keep it simple. Not that she has an OS map with her, anyway. She knows the area fairly well, having walked here with family and friends. During the peak of summer, they tended to avoid popular sections of Hadrian's Wall—like Segedunum, the most Eastern fort on the Wall—because tourists would flock there, changing the atmosphere of the place. Over the years, Lucy has found the least popular sections to walk, where it is possible to not see another soul for miles on end.

Bliss.

It's the rugged, remote landscape she likes, and the simple beauty of fields grazed by sheep rolling for miles. Large chunks of the walk are edged by Hadrian's Wall: made from hand-carved stone, weathered by storms and wrapped in moss. Almost two thousand years old. She walks for several hours in the company of the remains of forts, the skulls of sheep who didn't last the winter, and distant farms. The solitude and isolation among the crags and stiles, beside the heritage of the Roman wall, is a perfect antidote to a chaotic, stressed mind. It's quieter, but not quiet.

*Ross. I can't believe he's dead.*

With each footstep, though, Lucy puts distance between herself and poor Ross, and the professional conflict she'd felt all along in treating Jennifer. Now Ross is dead, and there is nothing she can do about that. As Emma-Jane says, there are people who go through Lucy's door who should go through hers instead, but you can't force them. Perhaps she and Emma-Jane need to intervene, to work together, but it's easier said than done. Lucy decides to text Emma-Jane to let her know where she is but, as soon as she reaches for her phone, she sees the battery is dead.

She'd forgotten to put on airplane mode to save the battery, and the roaming satellites have sucked it dry.

'Shit.'

Annoyed with herself, she stuffs the useless phone in her rucksack and keeps walking, even more briskly than before. Gradually, the temperature falls, which tells her she must soon turn back the way she came, but not just yet. The sun is going down, throwing her shadow in front of her for company. Lucy strides towards a lonely tree, suddenly feeling alone herself now that the light is fading and the landscape is losing its colour.

Even the grey stones of the Roman wall take on an austere, barren face, while the heathers and mosses pale into the semi-dark. The tree looks both beautiful and forlorn in the fading light; its branches extend like arms and the twigs of fingers point to the sky and to the earth, to heaven and hell.

The darkness is coming.

If Lucy hadn't been enjoying her walk so much, she

wouldn't have walked so far in one direction. Five miles, or more. That'll be ten by the time she's back at the car.

'Oh God.'

Panic doesn't set in just yet. The sound of birds hiding out of sight, the dots of sheep on the skyline. It's all so wild and beautiful. Nearby, there is a bothy, a stone cottage now dilapidated; shelter for animals, at one time. She moves closer to see it better and feels like she has gone back in time to a gentler way of life.

Then she sees it on the horizon:

The Robin Hood Tree, not a nebulous shape but unmistakably Sycamore Gap. Given that she's walked so far, it would be silly not to see it close up. It rises from the contours of the landscape like a giant, taking her back to the framed photograph in Drew's farmhouse. The one Evie had taken.

*Local.* That's what Drew had said. *Nesscliffe.*

*James loves trees.*

Even before she reaches Sycamore Gap, Lucy suddenly remembers where she'd seen Evie's photograph before that day with Drew. It was in the newspaper, and above it was the tragic article about a mother who took her own life and that of her son.

The Robin Hood Tree.

The woman's name had been *Evelyn.* That much Lucy remembered. Evelyn.

Evie.

Lucy puts her hand to her mouth to stifle a sudden sob.

*Drew's wife. And his son.*

They had died here, at this very spot. A rope, a modern-day hanging. Their throats and lungs had given in. Evie Rogers had hired a 4x4 to drive them as close to Sycamore Gap as possible so that it wasn't far to walk with James and the step ladders. The poor walkers who discovered the dangling corpses found toys at the base of the tree. Dropped teddies, probably fallen from a height, from James's hand, and ...

The cross. Lucy remembers the wooden cross from the photograph.

*James loves trees.* Drew told her that, but not the rest. *Dead, not divorced, not abroad. Dead and buried.*

Here.

She shivers now. The tree branches seem to bow down as if in mourning, weighed by terrible sadness and understanding. The little cross Lucy saw in the photograph is gone, but sadness is fixed in place by the roots of the tree.

'Why didn't you say something to me, Drew?' She shakes her head, struggling to process the tragedy. She puts her head in her hands; the horror of understanding, the darkness and the isolation exacerbated by not having a useable phone.

'Oh God,' she says, tearful now.

The starry sky is all twinkling silver glass eyes watching from afar, waiting to see what she will do next.

'I'm such an idiot.'

The wind through the branches sighs as images of Drew, Ross, and Jennifer click through her mind. The low, sad sound of the wind sends her eyes up to the dark network of branches and light-green leaves. Feeling self-pity and desperation, Lucy closes her eyes. Her skin tingles.

The blonde, beautiful wife to a successful businessperson. That was the gist of what she remembers reading. A young mother, and a blond little boy. Found hanging from Sycamore Gap. Her stomach churns. Maternal filicide. Lucy even knows the correct term, from Emma-Jane's published article on the subject in that scientific journal.

*Poor Drew.*

Why a mother would deliberately kill her own child makes no sense to Lucy. The bleating sheep on the nearby grassland seem to mourn the human tragedy and echo the sound of sadness in stereo.

She sheds a tear for Drew's loss, for the dead mother and child, and for herself, for almost falling for someone who isn't who she thought he was. A widower, someone who didn't let her see all of the rooms in the farmhouse. Was it because, behind closed doors, the memory of what was once loved inside is painful?

Drew, a man who kept his past a secret. *But why?*

Why pretend Evie and James were still alive, knowing all along they were dead and buried? The thought unsettles her. She hopes Emma-Jane has helped him deal with the tragedy. All that loss . . . Not one, but two members of the family. At once. How terrible. To wake up one day and your life will never be the same again. Lucy knows grief after losing Martin. If only Drew had opened up about it, they might have helped each other.

She sits down beneath the tree's canopy to pull out an extra top and a beanie hat from her rucksack and adds them to her layers. She is shivering from shock, and the temperature has dropped again, more so under the shade of the sycamore. Her nose drips from the cold and from crying. It's a disgusting thing to do but, without a tissue or company, she uses her tongue to wipe the snot away; as much of it as she can.

Lucy is sitting where Evie and James sat in their final

moments. She rests her back against the sturdy trunk, wishing it were a friend, a warm human to lean against, with smooth skin and a sense of safety that comes from companionship. She misses human company as much as the sun in that moment. If only Emma-Jane was here. Even the white phosphorescent face of the moon is blocked by the leafy canopy and network of branches, some as thin as the bones of a skeleton.

She shuffles forward from under the lone tree. The remnants of clouds are barely perceptible in the sky above. They could almost be a vapour trail from a plane jetting off on holiday, perhaps to a warmer climate.

*Getting away from it all. Are you flying off somewhere nice, Emma-Jane? I wish I was with you.*

The branches stir, this time vigorously, and a symphony of sighs and moans begins, broken by the sudden sound of a child's voice in her head. Did James plead with his mummy to remove the rope? To take him home to Daddy? Did he beg and wail, *Mummy! Mummy! I don't want to play anymore.*

James's name is luminous in her overactive mind: it could be written on the wall, on the trunk and in the sky in sparkling white lights. The tree hasn't moved an inch, but it feels as though the branches have wrapped themselves around her wrists and ankles like handcuffs. If only her imagination would stop working, stop painting a grizzly picture of a child's corpse dangling from this branch like some Gothic Christmas decoration.

The sheep bleat and the sudden forlorn sound in the dark makes her head jerk. Lucy is suddenly sick, bends over, and releases until there's only bile and retching. The stench of Ribena, coffee, and the remains of muesli churn her stomach.

Exhausted from the long drive and even longer walk, then the puking, and with a body starved of food and water, Lucy forces herself to take several cautious sips from her water bottle. She then wipes her eyes and nose to try to get a grip of herself. The problem is, Lucy is completely drained.

Sapped.

Shivering, she rubs her arms and pulls her coat over her hands. Once she feels better, she'll walk back. It'll take time, but she's fit; she can do it. Five more miles. It's a distance she's walked before.

Her eyelids feel heavy. She gets up again because she has to keep going, no matter how much her body is screaming to the contrary. Her boot collides with a stone jutting from the ground and she is propelled forward, landing face first. Winded, she stays prostrate on the ground, moaning with pain to her forehead, hands, and knees. She waits to catch her breath.

For a split second, she closes her eyes. Then, she falls into a deep sleep.

When Lucy wakes, two hours later, her hands and face hurt with the cold from a hard frost. Although her stomach is rumbling from hunger, she can barely breathe, let alone eat. The full moon and frost cast the landscape in an auroral light, duping her into thinking it is morning at first. But then she sees the twinkling grass and brittle white blades. Even Hadrian's Wall has a ghostly glow. Low-hanging cobwebs are intricate lace patterns festooned between branches, some as tenuous as kitten's whiskers. Fallen leaves sparkle with frost in a parody of Christmas festivities.

She puts her hands inside her coat to warm them up and blinks to wake herself up properly. The temperature is so low that her breath hangs in the air like smoke. Stars pepper the vast sky above.

Lucy has never felt smaller or more alone.

'Hello!' she shouts. 'Is anyone out there? I need help!'

A sheep bleats. In that moment, she wishes she could push her face into its wool and wrap her arms around its well-fed, padded body to ground herself, to be sure of the world she is living in, so she doesn't disappear into the horizon.

'Come on, Lucy,' she says, her breath hanging in the air. 'Get up, get walking, get back to the car.'

Slowly, she stands, her legs stiff from sitting in such an awkward position for so long. The remote rural landscape feels hostile now; she longs to see rooftops, traffic lights, and flashing neon signs for pubs and takeaway. Anything to punctuate, tame, and colour the planet. If only she could smell fish and chips, with salt and vinegar and a squirt of ketchup!

Then, Emma-Jane's voice and face pop into her head. They were at the office, when Emma-Jane had said that Drew was divorced. Drew had said 'ex-wife' when they had dinner. Not 'dead wife'.

Lucy stares at the tree. But that's not what happened. He's not divorced.

*He's a liar.*

Emma-Jane probably doesn't know the truth either. The unease spreads up from Lucy's stomach and into her throat. Maybe Drew hasn't told his therapist. Her stomach clenches again.

Lucy runs for half an hour under the stars—loaded with history, a past which is following her every step—and then slows to a jog until her legs and lungs are too tired to keep moving at speed. To cover the miles as quickly as she can, she walks, then jogs, walks, then jogs, at intervals. The moon is still eerily bright in the sky, lighting the way back to the car. She has no idea how long it will take or what will happen to her next, but she will not stop moving until she knows where Emma-Jane is.

By the time Lucy returns to her car, she is crying with exhaustion and worry. The smallest thing is too much to bear. First, she can't find a phone charger, and then she can't get the seat belt on, but she has her car keys and a bottle of water.

*Think positive. Get back to Shrewsbury. Don't cry.*

That's as far as she can think right now, so she points the car south and drives, hanging on to one thread of good fortune—her parents haven't called the police to commence a missing person's enquiry.

But where is Emma-Jane?

# 15

When Emma-Jane comes to, it's as if she's watching a film made with a handheld camera.

The hand that clasps it is shaking too much. Gradually, the film jerks, and then, when she realises it isn't a video, the wind is knocked out of her. She notices the Anaglypta wallpaper in an unhomely lounge stripped of furniture.

Cuffed and tied to a chair, this is her cell.

Worryingly, the wallpaper is splattered with dried blood, like the scattering of scarlet stars across a pearly cosmos. Her blood? Looking down at herself, she doesn't appear to be bleeding, but those splashes of blood are a portentous constellation she cannot navigate by.

Above her head, the naked light bulb does nothing to alleviate the gloom of the room, which is heightened by the sound of rainfall outside a curtained window—that, and the proximity of her captor in her peripheral vision, asleep on a mattress in one corner of this bare room.

Drew Rogers. A client. A successful man. But a troubled man.

Before she speaks, Emma-Jane tries to process what has happened to her, the chain of events leading to this abduction. The smell of the room she finds herself in is something new. Besides her own personal body odour and the reek of urine from having peed herself at some point, there is a distinct smell of washing powder from Drew's clothes. Rose, or jasmine, or something. She imagines pink packaging. Her hands shake, wrists bound by handcuffs.

She can recognise the positive potential of having a captor with scrupulous self-maintenance. It hints of self-respect, self-regard, so he might be open to discussion about the consequences of abducting her. Perhaps?

*Or perhaps not.*

Not so long ago, there had been the sound of a washing machine, and perhaps a dryer, which had connected her with reality and domesticity. A house, a flat, a home. *He is clean. He is clean.* It gives her a whiff of hope that Drew hasn't lost his mind entirely and might see sense. There's a cat flap somewhere. It rattles. To see someone's well-fed cat right now would be comforting.

*Drew sent me those hate letters. But why? If he lost his mind, why has he brought me here?*

The ceiling is stained grey, presumably from age or cigarette smoke. That might explain why the cover of the smoke alarm has been removed and the wires wriggle naked from the ceiling. The two kitchen chairs in the room are wooden, splattered with flecks of white paint. Her abduction has been planned. This empty property, his packed bag, the sessions they shared leading up to her abduction. Did he court Lucy for information about her habits?

Lucy. A surge of warmth and hope passes through her veins at the thought of her friend, somewhere out there.

Meanwhile, with every passing minute, Emma-Jane stinks. Sweat first, then urine, then shit. *Why degrade me this way? Have I wounded him?*

As thoughts fire into her brain, she sweats. The combined increase in body heat, her own waste, and the stifling heat in the room make for a most potent stench. He must enjoy being in control of her habits: when she is clean and when she is filthy. Like now.

Not wanting to alert her captor that she is awake, she swivels her eyeballs as far right as they will travel. His shoes are tan and clean. Expensive. Definitely leather. The socks are navy, with some kind of logo on the side. This well-dressed man had penned those hateful letters and drugged her.

How deceptive appearances can be.

The last thing she remembers is being in her office late at night. Was there an alarm? Bit by bit, she remembers talking to Vanessa and feeling concerned about the deepness of her depression and unwavering grief. Then Emma-Jane remembers typing up her notes on the computer.

Drew came to her office. Must have waited for her to be alone. She sees herself sitting at her desk, typing, looking at the computer. Then she looks at the door handle. It was turning. She sees herself standing up. The door opens. How long ago was it that she had been in her own office?

Drew wakes, sits up on the mattress, and rubs his hands over his face. That familiar face, and yet, a stranger's.

'Hello, Dr Glass.'

'Drew,' she says. 'Why? Why am I here?'

He rises slowly from the mattress, straightening out his trousers as he approaches, then settles in a chair directly opposite the one she is strapped to.

'You cut to the chase,' he says with a wolfish stare. 'Welcome to your new abode. Shall I call you Dr Glass, or something else?'

'That depends on why I'm here.' She waits for an answer, which doesn't arrive. 'Something makes me think it's not for free therapy, so you may as well call me Emma-Jane.' She studies his face, surprised at how handsome he is, even after a rough night's sleep on a mattress on the floor. A monster of a man would befit the situation and make it easier to accept. 'Are you going to tell me what the hell I am doing here?' She tries to lean forward, only to find her torso is strapped tightly to the chair. There's no wriggle room. The tar of anxiety suddenly clogs her veins.

'How does it feel to be in the chair, to be the one required to trust, to be open and honest about your deepest and darkest secrets? Here I am, listening; an interesting twist on our usual situation, wouldn't you say?'

'Is that it? Role reversal? I didn't know drama was your thing.'

He raises an eyebrow.

'Am I to be punished for something I have done, or not done? I have only tried to be a good therapist and help you, Drew.' She stares at the curtains, frustrated she doesn't know what time of day it is, or even what day it is. 'Am I here because I failed you in some way? Or simply because I am a therapist?'

'There's no rush for you to know. You will see.'

'Is this about control?' she asks, rattling her cuffs. 'I want to know, Drew!'

He slaps her hard, and her vision swims.

'This is not like your sessions, spent with half an eye on the clock. We have way more than an hour of each other's time, so stop asking questions. I will tell you when I'm good and ready.'

She strains to listen to sounds beyond the living room. She yearns to hear a car, a voice, footsteps, something to tether her to a place in space and time instead of floating in a white, blood-flecked void. Are there people nearby? Someone will notice she is not where she should be. It's only a matter of time before she's discovered.

Lucy. Lucy will know something is amiss.

'Where are we?'

'This is one of my many properties. Empty, obviously. Between tenants. I put my team on hold just for you. I can see you're happy about that. Once we're done, they'll come in, make the place as good as new for the next owners. I'll sell it. I'm done with my lettings business.'

'Is that part of the plan you spoke about?'

'Yes, as a matter of fact, it is. So, you do listen. Bravo,' he says, clapping. 'And you remember. I'm impressed. It was fun to talk to you, really. You're very patient, and you are better than some, I'm sure. My wife saw therapists, lots of them. They never made the slightest bit of difference. A complete waste of her time and my money. I told her as much.'

The sound of a heavy-goods vehicle in the near distance gives her hope she isn't far from civilisation. Drew notices her twitch of hope.

'Don't get too excited about being discovered any time soon. I took the liberty of using your computer to email Lucy. Told her you're enjoying a holiday, after a lot of stress at work. You've been working late a lot recently.'

So, he has been watching her. A creeping chill works its way up to her neck. She fights the urge to sigh heavily, not wanting to give him the satisfaction of knowing he successfully read her thoughts. While moving is out of the question, her mind is performing, and that is all she has to hold on to right now. Her throat is dry from lack of water, her head throbbing from dehydration. The room is hot, airless.

'Can I have a glass of water?' she asks. The last thing she needs is to feel dizzy or faint, and have her faculties fizzle out.

He opens a small bottle of water, sips it, and then pours it straight into her gaping mouth. She can't swallow quickly enough. She chokes and splutters, the water trickling down her neck and onto her blouse. When the bottle is half empty, he stops pouring and sits down again, watching her cough and gasp.

'You needed that, didn't you?' he says, smiling.

'Thank you.' She licks her lips to savour every drop of water. 'Why am I here, Drew? Come on.'

His eyes are so dark and unblinking they could be holes. Just like in her office, he doesn't just make eye contact. He holds it.

She flinches when he bends down behind the chair and removes the weights so he can swivel the chair and her around to face the kitchen. Then he drags the chair closer, so she can see the kitchen surfaces, the oven and even the back door. This is a whole new horizon for her.

'Like the view?' he asks.

'It's a change.'

'I enjoy baking for relaxation. You can watch how it's done.'

Judging by the vein throbbing of his temple, blood is hammering in his system. He cracks an egg on one side of the glass mixing bowl and expertly separates the yolk. After adding the rest of the ingredients, he beats the mixture into submission and dips a finger in to taste.

'A little boy has twice as many taste buds as an adult,' he says. 'But there are still several thousand to send signals to the brain. Salty, sugary, spicy, savoury, sour. A tongue is as unique as a fingerprint.'

Seeing his controlled rage in the rough unscrewing of jars and the deft use of the knife through the butter, she doesn't let her fear show. The surreal nature of the experience is so terrible it is almost laughable. Each movement he makes is sure, precise.

'I made James a cake for Halloween. He loved it! Orange and chocolate cake, decorated with ghosts made from white chocolate.'

Cocoa powder, caster sugar, and icing sugar are in view. 'What kind of cake are you making now?'

'Blood-Red Velvet Cake. Three layers, cream cheese frosting, and blood-red ganache. I use oil-based food colouring for the blood so it stays separate from the white chocolate the cake is smothered in. Of course, the finishing touch is a blood-splattered knife protruding from the middle of the cake, but we'll come to that later.'

Her stomach churns at his mention of a bloody knife, almost like a secret ingredient to the recipe in his mind. Is he going to poison me, or kill me with a kitchen knife? For now, at least, it seems the muscle of his tongue will get a workout with eating and swallowing the cake. Perhaps that will satisfy him for a time.

The lid on his emotions is screwed on tight between jars he has not shared with her. Yet.

'I love the smell of a cake baking in the oven. It's the smell of families,' Drew says. 'Don't you agree?'

He slams the cake mixture into the oven. Then, he unzips a leather holdall perched on top of the washing machine. At the sight of a small, sharp cutting knife, Emma-Jane sharply inhales and leans backwards in her chair. The chair lifts on two legs, but something behind her knocks the chair back onto the grotty grey carpet.

Drew rolls up the sleeve of his shirt. She stares at his bare arm in complete shock.

Jagged lacerations are etched into his forearm. An unmistakable sign of self-harm. As his therapist she should have known, but he'd kept the dark habit a secret.

The scars and fresh marks send another jolt of fear through her: her diagnosis had been depression, but this habit points to an inability to verbalise emotional pain, sometimes self-loathing and other issues, to seek release from self and feelings of hurt, anger.

A sudden desire to help this poor, suffering man grips her as tightly as he had gripped her neck the night she was abducted.

*Am I here because Drew needs me?*

He looks longingly at the blade and then at her. 'Some people have tattoos. I prefer scars. While the cake is baking, there's work to do.'

He rolls the sleeve up a couple more inches and the old scars, like welts sucked by leeches, stand at attention on his forearm. He stares straight ahead, as if he is stuck at the traffic lights, waiting for it to change from red, to amber, to green. Emma-Jane knows what he's going to do and can do nothing to stop it, but she has to try.

'It's much easier for me to be open with you here,' he says, then removes his shirt and trousers and she gasps. 'Don't worry. I'm not going to touch you.' She gasps again at the ugly patchwork of yet more extensive scars. Cut after cut has been made across his stomach, thighs, torso. Some still fresh, bleeding a little, open like a dribbling mouth from the gauze beneath his clothes. Most are scar tissue; a sad shade of pink that will never disappear.

'Some scars have names like "Christmas," "Halloween," or "Birthday" and "Bramble" and "Talon," for those that are just plain horrible. This new scar will be named after the cake, to mark our first day together.'

'Be kind to yourself, Drew. You're distressed.'

Drew doesn't appear to hear her. She senses his

tingling, pulsing skin. She yanks at the restraint around her middle as he makes a deep incision in his thigh with the knife. He looks at her angrily, as if she's to blame for his distress. The silence is almost as terrifying as noise because of the anarchy living inside his head.

'Your pain, Drew, doesn't have to make you do this.'

'It's James's birthday soon. I've been counting down to it with these marks, you see. I like to look at the scars, the grooves of different length and depth, depending on how much pain I'm in. Scars are perfect for someone like me. You see these,' he says, holding up his arm. 'These can't be erased, nor can the damage that's been done. I cannot undo the reason for them. James, my flesh and blood.'

Her heart thumps in her chest and sweat trickles down her back. This poor man. She has failed him as his therapist. There's so much pain and distress here, she had no idea. He fingers the blade, and a poppy-red bead of blood sits on the end of his finger. She can almost taste the foul stench of their sweat, caused by the stifling heat in the room.

'Please! Don't, this—'

'Shut up. Watch. Don't speak.'

*It's like bloodletting,* she thinks, as he reaches for a plastic container to catch the dripping blood. When will it end? She has treated clients who self-harm, mainly females and children or adolescents, but never has she witnessed it in proximity like this. For men, there is often a cultural taboo. Perhaps that's why he didn't tell her about the grim habit.

It is impossible not to feel pity for him, knowing that self-harm can be a predicator of death by suicide, and an expression of a deeply troubled mind. It isn't what she expected. Her diagnosis that he was depressed because his wife had left him was wrong, and that, almost as much as the loss of her own freedom and dignity, troubles her. Perhaps Drew isn't the man she thought he was.

He's not only unstable, he's also an impersonator.

Her own safety and survival take over her thoughts as his face twists and contorts in pain. What if he bleeds to death? Then she might slowly starve to death in this very room. The window provides a possible means of escape, if she can break free from the chair and throw herself, or something, through it. She doesn't have the luxury of knowing where the key to the front door is, or the general layout of the house yet.

Drew makes a second incision, even deeper than the first one. He gasps, but looks pleased when the blood dribbles into the container. 'Whenever James drew or painted me, I had a fat stripy tie on.' He grimaces. 'You know, his outfit was all wrong the last time I saw him, in his mother's arms. It must have been new clothes she bought especially. A going-away outfit for the occasion. Navy blue. Such a grown-up colour. Against his fair hair, it made him look pale.'

A look of dark relief washes over his face as the blade cuts his skin once more and the blood rolls. The expression is of a pleading, begging man, but the pity she had felt is replaced with fear for him and her. His dark glassy eyes frighten her the most, now he is really hurting. Will it be her turn soon? Spots of blood land on the kitchen floor, a cream and brown patterned linoleum which has seen better days. He inserts the knife into the plastic container, then lathers the blade in his blood. She shuts her eyes to the horror and hears him open the oven. The aroma of the delicious cake confuses her senses.

'Open! Open your eyes. Now! I am in charge. You will

only learn if you do what I say! Understand?'

Startled, she nods compliantly. Her eyes jerk open and she stifles a sob in the back of her throat.

'A perfect cake, risen to perfection!' Drew clears away the mess while the cake cools. 'Now, for the decoration.'

The red ganache on top of the white icing is horribly realistic. Knowing the knife wedged into the centre of the three layers of dark sponge is smothered in real blood, she wonders if he added other ingredients to the mix without her noticing. Poison?

Her training conflicts with his demands to remain quiet and only watch, to be a passive observer of such human pain. It goes against all that she believes and has shaped her career around.

'James loved apple crumble and custard. He'd eat it for breakfast, lunch, and dinner, given the chance.' He looks up, rambling, perhaps delirious now. The cake is like a third person in the room. Malignant. She isn't sure if it's the pain and loss of blood or if he's been drinking. Perhaps both.

'Love. I held him in my arms. I felt love; he must have felt it, too.' He holds his hand in the air as if to catch the faint beam of light peeking through the blind, then returns to decorating the cake.

'Drew, please. Stop. Talk to me. I can't sit here and watch or say or do nothing when you are in such pain. Tell me. Help me understand. I am here, listening.'

'Yes,' he says, sniggering. 'You are.'

The hideous cake takes shape. *His hand has well and truly come off the tiller,* she thinks. She closes her eyes for a second, and when she opens them, the cake is presented on a white plate on her lap. He remains standing right beside her: the knife in his right hand, and his arm is still leaking blood.

'You are going to eat some home-made cake, aren't you?'

It's not really a question. She knows it, and despite the blood and the fear and the conflict she feels, her stomach grumbles loudly. Soon she'll start to feel weak. Her mind won't be as sharp, and that frightens her. Her brain is her ally. Staying on the right side of him and remaining alert are her priorities.

*Block out the rest,* she tells herself.

'Yes, of course I am.'

Drew smiles, pleased with her response, and gets down on his knees. He cuts a slice and feeds it to her, piece by piece. She keeps her eyes closed, pretending she is ignorant to what is entering her mouth, and forces herself to think about the view from Corbet Hill, across the Shropshire and Welsh hills.

'James. Forgive me, James.'

She opens her eyes to see Drew's head bowed in prayer. The words of contrition loop in her head, stirring feelings not of fear now, but sadness. The cake drags down her throat. The bloody icing, too.

The dark patches under his eyes make him look twice his age. This pitiful, troubled man. He looks so utterly vulnerable now, after appearing handsome only so recently.

'I want to help. I do,' she says after a large gulp of cake. 'You loved James. Dearly. Let me help you.' The clink of her cuffs is hateful as she attempts to stroke his dark hair, his tear-stained face. He rests his head in her lap, passively, and closes his eyes. His blood leaks onto her shoe. A red pupil staring right back at her.

The space behind the locked front door is another country; she needs a passport to access its vistas. A picture of a beach, a calm, blue sea comes to mind. All those foreign trips she's thought about and never taken. Will she get the chance now?

An image appears, of a mermaid washed up on the shore, drying out, marooned. Doomed, and changing into some other thing. She hates the chair and its anchored position. It skewers her to the spot, like a lump of meat. Her shadow stretches out in front of her, over his head.

Drew is asleep, snoring on her lap, his head placed just where the bloody cake had been.

Finally, she allows her walls to come down, and begins to sob.

# 16

AJ takes no pleasure in removing the nameplate from what was once James's bedroom door.

He remembers having a hand-scribbled KEEP OUT sign on his bedroom door as a child. Not like this wooden, hand-painted sign, which probably cost a packet. James's is written in black slanted letters, like a signature, and in one corner there is a little boy running with a cat.

Will Drew want to keep it?

Unsure of what to do with the sign, he tucks it under his arm and ventures down a set of concrete steps.

In Evie's darkroom, there is a black box with a lid. Inside, there's mainly photographs of Drew's son, James, and weird-looking landscapes. Before switching on the bulb in the darkroom, he is struck by the luminous finger marks on the walls——a child's hands, finger-painted in fluorescent green and pink, starting at the floor and working their way up the walls and to the ceiling.

*Evie and James must have had fun doing that,* he thinks, then switches on the light and places the sign in the bottom of the box.

Back in James's bedroom, on the inside door of the wardrobe, his ever-increasing height had been marked with dates and ages. The marks are in pencil; fine stripes one after the other, marking the passage of time and the rapid growth of a little boy.

AJ had never spoken to the lad, so he doesn't know why it's upsetting him to feel his absence and relics of his short stay here. He turns the radio up and gets on with pulling the multi-coloured bunting down from above the curtain rail, then makes a start on painting the wall. James is perhaps too young to paint or scribble on his bedroom walls like AJ had done as a kid. The four walls look pretty clean and fresh to AJ, but he'll do what the boss says, to keep him happy.

He finds photographs, still in their frames, in the top drawer of the boy's chest of drawers. The sunshine yellow of James's hair is as bright as an egg yolk. He is sitting on a green stretch of grass. He guesses Evie was behind the camera, taking the picture.

In another framed photograph, James is sitting on a ride-on tractor with green wheels and a yellow seat. He straddles it like he's riding the king's horse. The plastic wheels catch on the grit and gravel, so he looks to be pushing hard to get to where he has to go. The wheels are rolling, and Evie is watching James push himself along like it's the most amazing thing she has ever seen. Drew was there for that occasion, it seems, behind the lens.

AJ thinks about his own childhood: he had shared a room with his older brother, Jake, who liked to regularly remind him of what a stupid kid he was and what an amazing, clever guy his big bro was. Annoyingly, Jake had been right about being clever, as he's made a mint in banking and works for himself, when he can be bothered, as a broker.

The familiar sound of tires grinding on gravel sends him outside to the front of the farmhouse. He knows who is driving the battered red sports car. Kat Jones shimmies between the barriers like she's in a nightclub and heads straight to AJ.

'Back again!' he says. 'You'd think you live here.'

'Wish I did! Is he here?' Kat asks, to which he shakes his head, keeping his response to a minimum. He thinks he can feel Pete staring at them from inside the house. She pouts her reddened lips to show her disappointment. Anyone would think a camera was on her, the way she throws her long, red hair over her shoulder. 'When did you see him last?'

'About a week. He's busy,' AJ says with a frown, stopping himself from moving away when she approaches with a confident stride.

'Give him this, will you?' she says, passing him a white envelope addressed to Drew in black, scrawling handwriting.

'I can't promise when I'll see him to give it to him,' he says, but takes the letter anyway and stuffs it into his back pocket. He hitches up his loose jeans.

'Yeah, you will,' she says, with a knowing smile. When he doesn't respond, she shrugs and walks away to her car, tossing her hair over her shoulder in one deft movement. For a young woman, Kat Jones has bigger balls than most blokes he knows. The car door closes with a slam, and she revs the engine louder than she needs to. A pathetic kind of fanfare.

Pete appears from the doorway. 'How come you two are all matey?'

'Drew was seeing her, that's how.'

'So?'

'She lives in one of Drew's terraces, on that estate near town.'

'Which one?'

'Hartlepool Estate. I did some work there and got to know her a bit. Needed a new shower fitting.'

'You never mentioned that when she's been here

before.'

'No, well, it was a few months back since I saw her last, that's all, Pete. That was before . . . before all this.'

'Well, are you going to read the letter? I'd like to if you won't.'

AJ hesitates.

'You look guilty as hell,' Pete says. 'You and her haven't—'

'No! I wouldn't do that to Hannah, or to Drew. Jesus! Give me some credit.'

'Come on then. Let's take a peek. I'm guessing it's a crawling, gushy kind of letter, wanting him back. Worth a laugh, eh?' Pete makes a fake lunge for AJ's back pocket.

'Piss off. It's Drew's business, alright? Let's get back to friggin' work,' he snaps. 'The envelope is sealed, anyhow. Drew would know.'

Pete holds his hands in the air in mock surrender and pads off up the stairs. AJ pats his back pocket. The envelope is burning inside, heating his lower body and up his spine, to his neck and ears. He scratches his head and decides to forget about it for the time being and get on with earning a living, while he's got an employer and a pay cheque.

'Bloody hell!' Pete exclaims suddenly as he opens a bedroom window, shouting down to AJ. A car arrives. 'It's like Piccadilly Circus around here!'

Pete comes back outside to stand beside AJ. An unfamiliar figure, a scruffy-looking woman, slowly climbs out of her car with heavy legs, like she's been in hospital for a time and is convalescing. It looks like such a huge effort to walk.

'I'll go,' Pete says, and AJ shrugs his answer. Pete tries not to stare too hard at the white-faced woman. 'You alright?' he asks. 'Can I help?'

'Is Drew here? I need to see him,' she says, swaying a little.

'He's not here. This place is being sold. Are you a friend of his?' Pete thinks she is going to break down in tears by the way her face screws up.

'Yes. My name is Lucy. Where can I find him? It's urgent.'

'He owns a lot of property in the area. He'll be staying at one of those. That would be my guess, anyroad. Me and AJ are just labourers for him.'

She nods her understanding, as if talking takes too much effort.

He takes pity on her and a thought pops into his head. 'He owns a place on Hartlepool Estate. He always buys places to rent out near Co-ops. You could try there first.'

'Thanks.'

'Mind how you go now.'

---

Hannah glances at the flickering fluorescent light in the entrance to the bar. People are going in the opposite direction to them, which isn't a good sign. The indie band has been on stage for less than ten minutes.

Hannah's silver make-up and tight trousers are like honey to bees. AJ likes to see her dressed up and attracting a few looks. There are plenty of blokes in there with more money and better looking than he is. He pushes his chest out, happy she's with him.

'Watch it!' Hannah spits when a pissed-up bloke in a

rugby shirt stumbles in her path. She strides confidently, with AJ in tow, staring at her tight ass.

Inside, he scans the room for a table and, finding none, makes a beeline for the bar, where there are free bar stools. There's too much security in the form of burley bouncers to feel at ease, but it's nice to come into the warmth after the damp and drizzly walk there and sink a few pints on a Friday night after a long week at work.

'What are you drinking?' the bartender asks. 'It's happy hour on pints.'

AJ catches a whiff of sweat, Strongbow, and Monster. 'Carling, and a snakebite and black, please, mate.' He slides onto the stool beside Hannah and removes his leather jacket. 'As it's happy hour, we might as well have two of each then, hey.' He stifles a burp, but Hannah catches the smell of luncheon meat and spring onion pasty and pulls a face.

His phone suddenly rings and the shape of his face changes like plasticine. He stares at the screen a while before answering it. Hannah knocks back her pint as soon as she knows it's Drew because that usually means it's going to be a long conversation. The man calls at all hours and keeps AJ waiting for him on jobsites because he forgets to turn up. Lately, he's vanished.

She waits for AJ to hang up before unloading her gaze. 'Now what?'

'He's got a private buyer for the farmhouse and another terraced place he owns.' He runs a hand through his hair. 'He's selling up, Hannah. Wants to cash in all his property, or as much of it as he can at the moment. It's confirmed. I'm gonna be out of a job.'

'That man. He's a fucking tool!' she says, twisting the pendant on the end of her necklace. 'What's his game?

One minute it's flat out with refurbs, the next you're bloody out of work.' Hannah frowns as someone barges past.

'I think he's got major personal problems. I can't be out drinking when I'm about to be out of work.' He drinks his pint down in one go and takes a sip of the second one. 'Can we go?'

She lifts the half-drunk glass in the air. 'I've not finished. We've only just got here, and I got showered and dressed specially to go out. We hardly go out these days, although the band's not up to much, I admit.' She takes a long drink. 'How much notice has he given you?'

'He didn't say precisely. It's vague, like. Could be a couple of months, or a couple of weeks.'

'The man has to give you at least a month's notice. That's basically the law.'

'He pays me cash in hand. Drew can do what he likes as I'm just a casual labourer. Moneyed blokes like him don't give a toss about people like me anyway.' AJ knocks back more of his drink and wipes his mouth on the back of his hand. Despite the brew, he doesn't look refreshed. He gazes at the bar optics, like there might be an answer to his work worries there.

'Why are you so down? You'll get another job.'

AJ looks away and stares into his empty pint. 'I wish I was born with a silver spoon in my gob; then I wouldn't be working my bollocks off for a few quid.'

'We're doing alright, and we've got each other. I wouldn't want to be Drew right now. Not for all the money in the world.'

AJ raises one eyebrow and takes a sip of his second drink.

'Bloody Drew!' Hannah continues. 'Just lately he

keeps messing up our evenings.'

'Well, he won't for much longer, that's for sure, because he won't want anything to do with me.'

'So, our plans go up in smoke, just like that?'

'I'm going to speak to Pete about working for him, or working for ourselves, but as a team. We work well together. He's good on the plumbing side of things, but I can do the carpentry and brick work. He's better at painting and decorating and the admin side. We can get some fliers out in the local paper to drum up some business.'

'When will you speak to Pete?'

'Soon. I promise. We need to get money together so we can buy a place to renovate—two or three bedrooms, walking distance from a shop. That's what Drew's done.'

'The best ideas are often the simplest,' she says, and peers at her glass. 'Maybe one day you and I will be millionaires, living in our own palace.'

AJ stares bleakly at the woman he loves, fearful that one day he will lose her to a rich, lucky tosser like Drew.

# 17

Drew had once told Kat where the spare key to the front door of the farmhouse was kept: in the single-storey outbuilding, under a terracotta planter on the far right.

The key is small and cold in her hand as she strides towards the oak door to unlock it. Any day now, she will be booted out of the house and moving to the other side of the country to stay with her cousin. One final stop at the farmhouse is all she wants.

There's no sign of AJ or his co-worker, so she seizes the opportunity to look around. It's a place Kat had fantasised about living in happily with Drew. That fantasy had died the same day as Evie and James.

*Welcome home, me! As if.*

The kitchen is as she remembers, except the Belfast sink is empty and it smells musty, not like the brisk scent of washing-up liquid. Without the hot water running, the window isn't obscured with steam, as it was on the day she was last here.

For all the character and status of the farmhouse, she thinks it has a relatively modest kitchen, with a beige Aga cooker, now sleeping and out of date, and an incongruous-looking fridge—an American one, with double doors.

This room had been Evie's domain. Drew had told Kat that Evie was the sort of mother who was so organised, cramming her handbag full of stuff to meet almost any eventuality, so it was terribly heavy to carry around. There were countless lists stuck on the fridge door, as Kat recalls:

shopping and such like, reminders and messages—'Call school', and 'James dentist at 2 PM.'

The rest of the kitchen has recently been stripped, with only the dark beams left to give it a homely feel. Kat investigates the space, imagining where the kitchen table and four chairs would go if it were her house. Perhaps she would have a plant, a dresser, and a proper oven and microwave instead of an ancient Aga.

Her hands are on her hips and her lips are slightly pouting when the cat flap opens to a ghost of a cat. She lets out a nervous laugh at being frightened by the wind and nothing more. The moment lengthens. She looks down at the red tiles to see a dead mouse on the floor, in the exact spot she had told Evie that Drew was leaving her and James for a new life with her.

*You say Drew is leaving me and James to be with you?* Incredulous Evie had said it more than once. Perhaps three times. *You say Drew is abandoning us?*

The way she'd said 'abandoning us' had bothered Kat, even then, and it still does. Posh. Indignant. Shocked. A lullaby pops into her head.

> *Rock-a-bye, baby,*
> *In the treetop.*
> *When the wind blows,*
> *The cradle will rock.*
> *When the bough breaks,*
> *The cradle will fall,*
> *And down will come baby,*
> *Cradle and all.*

'Not my fault,' she says to the dead mouse. 'That's dead and buried, and so are they.' Kat kicks the mouse to the far-right corner.

It's the other rooms she wants to see to satisfy her curiosity before she leaves Shropshire for good. The rooms she's not visited before.

*It's now or never.*

In the living room, Kat imagines herself and Drew in wingback chairs on either side of the fireplace, and James playing with a few toys on a rug in front of a lit fire. The hearth has a distinct presence in the room. In the evening, Drew might drink a tumbler of whisky; Kat perhaps a glass of wine, or a gin and tonic with a slice of lemon in a crystal glass. She imagines expensive engagement and wedding rings on her left hand. She sees Drew stretching his legs out, his arms behind his head in a pose between smugness and arrogance, relaxing after the heavy strain of the working day and basking in his success.

She had loved him, wanted him all to herself, and had imagined herself here, in his bed, dining at the kitchen table. Silly her for thinking he planned to leave all this to be with her. For thinking he loved her back.

The French windows at the rear of the lounge, a recent addition not entirely in character with the farmhouse, let very little light into the living room because of the small panes. It chops the natural light into little pieces. The fragmented light is depressing, like prison bars. A soft sound, like a cushion falling off a chair, stops her thoughts in their tracks.

*The room needs heating, good airing, that's all*, she concedes, before moving down the hall.

The dining room has been stripped of furniture, presumably in readiness for its new owner, except for a few pieces. There is a dark wood chest—a large piece, perhaps antique, with a lid and two drawers with gold, delicate handles. Perhaps the chest was too heavy to move, or the purchaser took a fancy to it, as well as the grandfather clock which has stopped working, and the enormous gilt mirror above the hearth.

She lifts the lid off the chest and peers inside, as if it were a coffin.

The day she arrived at the farmhouse to speak to Evie had been a Wednesday. It was the day after AJ had fired her up and led her to believe her dream was about to come true. She remembers because her first thought that day had been to put the rubbish out for the binmen before it was too late (again). She'd rushed outside in her dressing gown and slippers, only just in time for the dustcart, and got to talking with one of the refuse collectors. He'd taken a shine to her and made some comment about how someone like her should live in a castle, or a listed building. By the time the dustcart had finished emptying the bins on her road, she'd made up her mind to speak to Evie.

Red hair. Perhaps that's why she's impulsive and temperamental. She looks at her reflection in the mirror and takes a strand of her long, red hair in her hand. Even if she cut it all off, it wouldn't change her character. Not like Samson in the Bible. Kat stares in the mirror for so long she senses an intense gaze on the back of her head. She turns, expecting someone to be in the room, but there is no one.

Just her conscience. Guilt.

Looking back into the mirror, Kat pushes her hair away from her face, closes her eyes and shakes her head, enjoying the feeling of her hair waterfalling down her back, touching her spine, her bottom. Drew had liked her long hair and would entwine his hands in it.

She shudders. Her conscience is getting the better of her, because there is only her in the room, besides the dark wooden furniture and the mirror. The carpet. The four walls, wallpapered, and the characterful fireplace. Kat takes a deep breath.

She hears a sudden click. The centre light switches on with a harsh glow from the naked bulb. Another click, and the sidelights to the left and right of the hearth illuminate.

Kat swallows down the bitter taste in her mouth. Why have the lights come on? It must be old wiring in a place like this.

The grandfather clock suddenly moves its rigid hands to twelve o'clock. The logs that had been left to the side of the grate tumble onto the carpet, leaving splinters of wood, bark, and an odour of smoke behind. Or is that her imagination? A solid log rolls further than the others, to within touching distance of her feet.

'For fuck's sake.'

Kat closes the dining room door behind her to explore the rest of the ground floor. Further down the corridor, she opens a door to a small room furnished with a desk. A box sits on it invitingly. The rest of the room is bare. Kat removes the lid from the box and peers inside, fingering each photograph in turn, one after the other. James, Evie, James with Drew, then one miserable black and white landscape after another. No wonder Drew had wanted a bit of life and colour with Kat.

*Who could blame him?* she muses, tossing her hair over one shoulder.

The sound of a door latch lifting tilts her head around the dark room. Upstairs is where the sound is coming from, she thinks. At the bottom of the staircase, Kat imagines making a grand entrance at one of their house parties, dressed to kill. In her mind, she hears the sound of high heels above her head, striding along the catwalk of the landing, then down the stairs, click, click, click like a camera. And slowly, so slowly, Drew's head turns to stare as he grins at Kat, his new wife.

A silly fantasy.

The cold, musky smell of the empty farmhouse brings Kat back to reality. She has seen enough. There's no Drew, no marriage, no happily ever after.

Not here, anyway.

# 18

Lucy has been to Emma-Jane's house, the office, and Drew's farmhouse, but there's no sign of Dr Glass.

If only she'd answer her phone, then Lucy's mind could rest. Drew doesn't answer his phone or return her calls either. It doesn't feel right.

Clients of Emma-Jane's have left messages on her office landline and pushed notes under the door. Vanessa, a fragile looking woman, looked desperate when Lucy told her Emma-Jane wasn't available today. Lucy doesn't know whether to contact the other clients or not, to make up a plausible excuse for Emma-Jane's disappearance. But one thing Lucy does know is that something bad has happened, because Emma-Jane wouldn't leave her vulnerable clients in the lurch.

*No way.*

Lucy might as well be standing on a rooftop and watching life go on below. Out there are those who look like everybody else, who blend in confidently with each season, while the storm inside them is building, building, taking ugly shape and form, until their traumatised self is reborn into a vengeful, malicious version of the original. These traumatised people sleep deeply, eat well, and each day are a step closer to finding out what they are capable of, the cloaked people they can be. These are the people Emma-Jane tries to help, tries to make happier.

*Someone has taken her*, Lucy thinks. *Someone who appears to be someone they're not.*

Lucy knows the Hartlepool Estate and is parked outside 12 Erin Row within the hour. Now that she's here, she feels less sure of herself, of what to say, of how to explain her uninvited appearance.

There is a red sports car on the drive to number twelve, next to a SOLD sign. The car has seen better days. The vehicle is a siren on an otherwise quiet street with mainly modest, small cars parked neatly on the front drive or white vans on the kerb. This house is neat. She can see why an astute entrepreneur like Drew would buy the property for his rental business and wonders why he is selling it now.

After taking a deep breath she walks up to the house. The bell doesn't work, so she knocks on the central, frosted glass pane in the door.

A young woman, perhaps nineteen or twenty, with fiery red hair and wearing leather gloves, answers the door. The volume of the television in the background is horribly loud. It sounds like a game show, with lots of clapping between talking.

'Sorry,' Lucy says, seeing the woman isn't pleased to have an unexpected visitor. She takes an involuntary step back. 'I'm Lucy. I was actually looking for Drew Rogers.'

The young woman frowns. 'He was my . . . is my landlord. Well, he is until I get kicked out when the new owners move in.' She aggressively gestures to the SOLD sign. 'This isn't a great time, actually.' She holds her gloved hands up in a way of explanation. There is blood on them; some fresh, some dried. 'I was just feeding my pet between packing up.'

Lucy doesn't know what kind of pet needs to be fed something bloody and presumably alive, but it isn't at the top of her priorities to ask. The woman's voice is captivating: low and husky. She tries not to stare. 'Does Drew live here?'

'Drew Rogers doesn't live here, no.' She laughs. 'Have you been to the farmhouse?'

Lucy nods.

'I know he's got two houses just out of town.' She looks up as she tries to recall where they are. 'Not far from the Co-op.'

'Which Co-op?'

'I dunno. Who are you, anyway?' A defensive hand slides onto one hip, which looks faintly amusing because of the glove. Conversation doesn't seem to be her strong suit. 'Did someone send you? I've got another week before I'm meant to be out.'

Lucy gives her the warmest smile she can muster under the strained circumstances. 'I need to speak to him about a friend of ours. I haven't heard from them in a while, and I'd like to get in contact. I won't bore you with the details.'

'A woman friend?' she asks sharply, with narrowed eyes.

Lucy lies. It's a decision made in a split second, purely on intuition. 'No. Eric Stash. So, you say you're a tenant of his?'

The woman nods, clearly not forthcoming. There's a smell of something unpleasantly tangy emanating from the house.

'Do you have his phone number, by any chance?' Lucy asks, hoping it will be a different one to the number he gave her.

The woman disappears inside and returns with a corner ripped from a notebook. 'Here. Can't say if it's still in use. He's not exactly communicative of late.'

Lucy folds it in half and carefully puts it into her pocket. 'Thanks. What did you say your name was?'

'I didn't.'

With that, she slams the front door. The letter box rattles, a tinny sound. Through the frosted glass, she sees the woman's figure move into the back of the house. Lucy is relieved to get away from that front doorstep, from the clasp of elephant grass which has spread uncontrollably in the small patch of front lawn ... and those bloody gloves.

She drives a short way down the road to pull in at a garage with a Costa Coffee, tittering at the name she'd invented, Eric Stash. Parked up, she tries the phone number the woman had given her, her heart thumping in her chest. She has no idea what she's going to say, but if she thinks about it too long, there's a chance she will jib out.

The phone rings and then immediately clicks to voicemail. The recording is automated, giving her no reassurance it is Drew's phone. Has she been fobbed off by the woman in gloves? She takes a deep breath and rings the number again, but the same thing happens.

'Bollocks.'

Now what? There's about ten Co-ops in town, and more on the outskirts. Lucy sighs. Neither Emma-Jane nor Drew return her calls, and the unease she feels continues to grow. If she has to drive round all of the local Co-ops and talk to all the shop assistants, she will. If that's what it takes.

The more she learns about Drew, the more worried she feels for her friend.

Lucy parks up beside the Co-op on Angel Street, on the outskirts of town near the River Severn. She gets out for a walk with no plan of what to do next, only feeling full of nostalgia and memories of her and Emma-Jane spending time here. There are hundreds of buttercups and crossworts turning the fringes of the roadside into golden bobbing heads, but still, the sky hangs lower and lower above her head.

*It will probably rain*, Lucy thinks, seeing grey clouds above. She has to keep looking. But where? Who should she speak to? She admonishes herself for not bringing a photograph of Emma-Jane with her. Then she scrolls through the photographs on her phone and finds one. Should she randomly stop people and show them the photo?

The river seems to look back at her in desperation, while willow trees twist their branches like they are wringing out their wetness. There is no order to the undergrowth or the landing places of sticks and branches. The unplanned architecture of nature is all around her, abundantly lacking in symmetry. Unsure of what else to do, Lucy keeps walking.

*Please let Emma-Jane be alright.*

*Where are you?*

On a trip to the Lake District some years before they graduated, Emma-Jane had explained the water cycle to her, detailing several processes, including evaporation and condensation. Lucy glances up at the clouds leaking droplets, perhaps originally from this very river. If water can change state, be carried to a new place, perhaps Emma-Jane can too.

*But where?*

Years ago, they'd loved cycling this way, out into 'the green,' as Emma-Jane called it, though Lucy loved the water more than the green space. They'd ride in single file, taking it in turns to lead the way down the paths. Lucy liked to be at the front best, which suited Emma-Jane just fine, as she rode at a slower pace. Exercise had never been her thing. Even so, as mature students, they'd often walked along the river.

Emma-Jane had been such a conscientious student, and always a thoughtful, loyal friend. Without her friendship during university and then after the death of Martin, Lucy wouldn't have managed to keep going.

*I can't fail her now.*

# 19

It is eleven o'clock in the evening and AJ has talked Hannah into snooping around the farmhouse for a bit of a laugh. Hannah stuffs her hands in the pockets of her bomber jacket to keep warm, as it is cold and stale in the house.

'Any furniture or stuff that's left is up for grabs,' he tells her.

'Serious?'

'Fuck him. Drew's given me notice. I don't owe him nothing. The place is sold.'

'I hope the new owners don't show up!'

'They won't.'

The interior doors to each room have been closed. As they open the door from the kitchen into the hall, it emits an unwelcome creak. Hannah looks up at the beams in the ceiling; the wood is old and weathered. She stands on tiptoes to touch it, but she isn't tall enough.

'It smells a bit musty, doesn't it? I suppose old houses soon get a bit damp when they're not occupied. Colder than our house, and we don't have the heating on.'

AJ doesn't respond. He's used to working in all temperatures. 'I reckon Drew doesn't know what day it is. Anything that's left in the farmhouse is here because he doesn't want it, or he can't get it shifted and stored. Come on. What he doesn't know won't harm him. The bloke's loaded, so I don't know why you're worrying about a few sticks of furniture.'

'If you say so.' Satisfied, Hannah relaxes and kisses him. She tastes of chocolate and old coffee grounds. He watches her move around the dining room with soft rabbit's eyes, like she's browsing in a department store, making everything feel lighter. 'Have you spoken to Pete yet about working together?'

'Not yet,' he says flatly. There is a dark chest against one wall, too big for most modern houses. 'This is nice.'

She admires the fireplace hearth and the mirror above it. 'That mirror's lovely.'

AJ immediately tilts it forwards to take a look at the fixing on the wall and see if it can be removed. 'You'll have to help me take it off the wall. It's awkward, for one.' She moves to get into position to help. 'Not now. Let's have a look round the whole place before we load the van up.'

Hannah giggles with excitement while he looks at himself in the mirror and rapidly frowns. His reflection is impaired by finger marks where his eyes should be, and a child's smudged handprint right in the centre of his face.

A small remembrance of James, one that Drew insists not to wipe clean.

AJ can't help but feel somewhat sorry for his loss. A perfect circle of breath forms where his mouth is.

'Gosh! It's perfect for a medieval banquet in here. What's that drink they used to have?' She touches her top lip. 'Mead! That sweet wine stuff. With a big, long, dark wood table and, in the centre, between the candles, an apple stuffed into the mouth of a pig's head! You'd sit at one end and me at the other!' She leans over the table.

'What are you doing?'

'Lighting the imaginary candles. Hey! You could have a fab game of real-life Cluedo in here. Was the murder weapon a candlestick or a poker?'

'You've been watching too many films and reading rubbish magazines, if you ask me.' He can tell she's enjoying herself, though, and loves her sideways smile. 'Did I tell you I spoke to Kat the other day? Drew's bit on the side.'

'What's she got to say for herself?'

'She looked rough.'

Hannah looks pleased.

'I think she's a bunny boiler. I feel a bit sorry for her, to be honest.'

Hannah looks at him with longing. 'That's 'cos you're a good guy, but not everyone is like you.'

AJ moves to the window and looks out into the darkness. 'There's no light pollution here at all. No traffic noise, nothing. If we had a place like this, we could do it up proper, from top to bottom. Not rush through, like Drew has. A place like this needs time and attention to detail—'

A sudden movement in his peripheral vision shuts him up. He doesn't move or speak. All his senses are acute and on red alert.

Hannah is gazing at the photographs on the wall. 'These are nice. Odd that Drew didn't take them with him. Wasn't Evie a photographer?'

AJ nods.

'Shall we take 'em? They might have some value.'

'Na, they look a bit creepy to me,' he says dismissively. 'If we keep saving up for a deposit, we could buy a tumble-down place and do it up while we live in it. There isn't much I can't do myself. Pete's been doing that on and off for years, living in his van at first, and now he lives on his own in a decent semi with three bedrooms and a conservatory. We gotta get our feet on that first rung of the ladder. I'm sick of renting a shitty little house. It's dead money, month after month.'

'We will get there, 'course we will,' she says and then kisses him. 'I'm sure of it. You and I are going to make our dreams come true. You're really hard-working and soon I'll have passed my first accountancy qualification.'

Hannah lifts up a frame and removes the photograph from the picture hook. 'I like this photo of the tree.'

Then, she screams.

Where the picture was, there is one word scrawled on the wall in what can only be blood:

**BITCH!**

Hannah drops the frame. The glass smashes.

'Jesus!' Hannah cries from between her fingers, both hands clamped to her face. She crouches down to look more closely at the photograph and notices the little cross beneath the massive sycamore.

Something AJ once told her about Drew clicks into place.

*His wife. His son.*

The jerking movement of AJ's head to the window finally wrenches Hannah's watery gaze away from the glass and photograph on the carpet.

'Shit!' AJ suddenly lurches for Hannah's hand and yanks her up, then tows her out of the dining room. 'There's car lights! I think it's Drew. We've got to get out of here!'

'But it's them. His wife. His kid.'

'Let's go, for fuck's sake!'

He pulls her out through the front door into the sobering fresh air. And like two cursed witnesses silenced by fright, they disappear into the cloak of night.

# 20

Emma-Jane's bones feel like rusty hinges as she climbs the stairs to the bathroom.

Once inside, she stretches her arms and back, trying to loosen the tightness in her muscles and tendons. It's like corrosion; the sitting, the sedentary hours and days. A tin can left out in the rain. Left for too long she will rust shut, and then she will break.

*Snap.*

There isn't a lock on the bathroom door, but Emma-Jane doubts Drew would come in unannounced. He doesn't threaten her in that way. She runs a bath rather than take a shower in order to make the most of the privacy and the opportunity to cleanse.

After four days, she is allowed a bath. His acts of cruelty and kindness are as irrational as he is.

While the bath fills, she goes to the toilet, then brushes her teeth with toothpaste and a finger.

*Ah, bliss.*

To be allowed to spend time in the bathroom is a rare luxury. She makes the most of it by stretching her arms, muscles, and neck, and then she strips. It isn't normal to feel so grateful for basic hygiene, but she does. How quickly simple things she once took for granted become special again, like cleanliness, privacy, the sound of running water, and the faint aroma of scented soap.

Before climbing into the bath, she looks down at her body, the soft rise of her tummy and the dip of her belly button. Her thighs are still generous, she thinks. If she were at home, she would shave the crop of dark hair under her armpits and on her legs, which has grown a lot in such a short space of time.

In the bath, she scrubs her skin, hopeful of removing the dead flakes, the dirt, and the stains of the last four days. *How long the days are*, she thinks, as she washes her armpits. He's told her it's Monday and she hopes that means Drew will leave the house for appointments. Living so intensely side-by-side is a curious strain, especially when she is used to living and working alone.

Now that she is alone, she can think of her captivity as an experiment. During her degree, she'd read about plenty of psychology experiments and critiqued them. Here she is: the subject. The conditions so far haven't been too bad: loss of freedom, restricted movement and food and water, observing self-harm, the degradation of her own filth to erode her . . . what? Femininity?

He enjoys control, for sure.

The question of the experiment is, *will he let me go?* If he does let her go, it will be for a reason she can't grasp. When she's reformed? Broken, like him?

That twitch in his eye is getting worse. He now drinks wine during the day and in the evening. Perhaps her death here is inevitable, after all.

She submerges her head in the water. Her hair fans out and she is serene, for a short time. Here, she feels like herself, and the pressure of her captivity idles away. In the warm water, the buzzing numbness and humming stiff joints uncoil and relax, after hours sat in the same position as a statue in a deserted museum while buses, trains, and bicycles faintly rumble outside. Perhaps there are posters shouting MISSING above her photograph on lamp posts, shop windows, and bus stops. She hopes Lucy will start to question things now that it's been four days. Emma-Jane is rarely out of communication for so long, be it 'on holiday' or not. She likes to keep in touch with Lucy.

*Lucy will know. She must . . . or else I'm dead.*

With her head above the water, she makes herself comfortable and moans with pleasure, only to fixate on a cobweb in one corner of the bathroom. A fly is trapped inside its silvery thread.

She knows how it feels.

'Clothes are outside the door!' Drew calls from beyond the door.

She flinches and covers her breasts with her arm. 'Okay, thanks.' She hears him descend the stairs and relaxes again. Appalled by the colour of the bath water and the soapy scum around the rim, she pulls the plug and rubs herself down with a towel. Embarrassed by her own dirt, she swills the bath clean.

There is only one towel. Drew uses the same one for his showers. The strange intimacy of the situation unsettles her; to be captive and intimate all at once.

Why doesn't she hate him yet?

She finds grey tracksuit bottoms, a black hoody, and a pair of red socks behind the bathroom door. Her breasts move inside the hoody, and her pubic hair brushes against the soft fabric of the tracksuit bottoms. Despite being dressed in baggy clothes, she feels vulnerable and self-conscious about her womanly shape. Thank goodness she isn't on her period.

Emma-Jane takes one last look through the bathroom window. The pane of glass is frosted for privacy and there isn't anything to indicate where she is. There is a faint sound of traffic, but no vehicles that she can see. People watching sunsets belong on another planet, which she can only wave to, like a star in the vast sky. To think the oceans are out there, where people walk their dogs along the beach, and children poke at dead jellyfishes, awed by their transparency. If only she could run into the sand dunes and wait for help to come.

The soap she used was pine-scented; the closest she will get to walking beneath pine trees and breathing in their aroma. People out there have washed their sheets and pillowcases and they smell of lavender and jasmine detergent as they flap and wave on washing lines in the fresh, fresh air.

*Where am I?*

'Are you finished in there?' he shouts, and then his phone rings.

*Be strong,* she tells herself. *Be strong and you'll get through this. He needs me as much as I need him.*

She sits on the side of the bath, listening to Drew on the phone. It sounds work-related. Her heartbeat spikes when she thinks he will be called away to work any minute. It's a mixed blessing: there is a fear he won't return and she will die of starvation, or it will grant her a window of opportunity to escape or be rescued.

The phone call is finishing up, so she makes her way downstairs, feeling self-conscious about her body. If only she had a clean bra and pants.

The washing machine is switched on. Drew is standing in the way of the front door, which has a cat flap at the bottom. It sways tantalisingly.

'Bye,' he says, then hangs up and puts the phone in his pocket. He looks her up and down, like he is seeing her through a new lens while remaining firmly in front of her exit to freedom.

She misses her home, the bright kitchen especially. Even the empty red biscuit tin on the table and the ugly salt and pepper pots by the cooker. The stainless-steel toaster and the scratched chopping board, years of rusty bread knife scars slicing over its wooden face. The annoying kitchen clock. The dozen tins of Baxters soup she likes stored in cupboards she rarely opens. The sharp kitchen scissors dangling from a hook.

'Thanks for the clean clothes,' Emma-Jane says. She slides into the lounge, surprised to see several bags and a suitcase in one corner and the mattress made tidy with a sleeping bag.

*Don't get depressed*, she thinks. *What a stark, nasty room it is.* An image of her light-filled house provokes longing for her home, her routine.

To look at him now, dressed in a clean shirt, pressed trousers, and polished brogues, he looks like a respectable, rational citizen. Handsome, with dark, curious eyes. She knows he's wearing bandages under his clothes, only after gently cleaning his self-inflicted wounds and applying antiseptic cream.

A secret shared.

She too is clean, no longer a mess of stinking piss and faeces and sweat. When he moves closer to replace the handcuffs, she sees comb marks in his hair, which are strangely touching. In those steady eyes of his, she sees something which scares her.

What is it?

*He isn't bad.*

As she looks at his benign expression, the stories of his son return as clear images: each one a sharp thorn, a splinter embedding itself deeper into her skin.

*He was a good father.*

If she were to be trapped here for a year or more, what vestiges of her old self would be left? Of that respectable psychologist who wrote the article 'Altruistic Violence in Maternal Filicide.' Of the hard-working student, the loyal friend to Lucy, the neighbour who keeps herself to herself. Just four days and the situation isn't black and white, but various shades of grey. Faces and places are blurred, as though they are travelling in opposite directions. Why doesn't she do something to make them stop?

'Do I have to be tied to the chair? I won't run. I promise,' she says softly.

He nods his head, but his gaze lingers on her. 'I have to go out for a short while.'

She wishes she could cross her arms to conceal her loose breasts, but now she is back in the chair and handcuffed, so she crosses her feet instead and focuses on one corner of the room she hasn't seen before.

'You're nervous,' he states. 'I'm not going to hurt you.'

She doesn't know if she believes him.

# 21

It's seven o'clock in the evening and the sound of traffic and conversation outside has filtered to a thin residue of noise.

Lucy finds the door to Emma-Jane's office slightly ajar when she returns. Sniffing the air for clues, she wonders if there is a smell of perfume. Coffee? Has she been and gone?

Her heart quickens as she runs inside to meet a tidy desk, an empty chair, the laptop switched off, and someone sitting on the couch.

'Oh! Can I help you? Is it Vanessa?'

Vanessa nods and sits up a little. Her eyes are watery and far away.

Lucy pulls up a chair beside her and softens the tone of her voice. 'I'm Lucy,' she says. 'My office is just opposite. Dr Glass is away at the moment.'

'No, she can't be,' she says, like she is answering someone else's question, and then she closes her eyes.

Lucy stares, unsure of what to do.

'I want her to read my stories.' Vanessa rummages in her handbag and removes a notebook. There is an open bottle of pills in there and a glass bottle. Vanessa clears her throat, and Lucy catches a whiff of something sour. The woman's tussled hair partly obscures one eye, but she doesn't seem to notice that, or Lucy.

'I will build a new country,' Vanessa proclaims, 'and make mirrors which heal fragmented reflections in a rainbow spectrum of light, each expression a prism and of perfect wavelength. I will slip through gravity into character.'

The phone rings and clicks to voicemail. Still, Vanessa doesn't seem to hear anything except her own rambling thoughts on the page. Lucy sits forward on the seat, unsure of whether or not to move.

'I'll throw a tapestry over the sun to protect Avril's skin. I will stitch her name into the stars and inscribe her initials in the sand, on the rocks, the barks of trees. I'll make her a necklace of red berries and holly, and a dress in the deep pink and red hues of a sunset. The hem will catch the clouds and be pulled along in the direction of the wind.

'The pebbles in the river sing; the blossom and the robin, too. They call me now to be with her. I hear beating wings like ravenous clapping, mastering the sky, turning heads, flying close to the sun like Icarus.'

Vanessa wipes her tears and puts the book down.

'I wanted Dr Glass to read them, but she isn't here.'

'It was very moving,' Lucy says, tears glistening in her eyes. 'I will tell Dr Glass about your writings and, when she's back, you could read them to her.'

Vanessa shakes her head, sending a tear down one cheek and into the side of her mouth.

'I don't think I'll be coming back.'

# 22

Emma-Jane jerks awake, and for a moment, she is confused.

She can't hear the idiosyncratic sound of the heating coming on in her own home, or the water in the pipes. She hears a man's voice talking on the phone. Footsteps. And then, she remembers where she is and who she's with.

She imagines it's a Saturday morning and she is walking to the dry cleaners to drop off her weekly work attire. The post office is next door, and then there is a newsagent, where she used to stop for a Diet Coke and a magazine. It's an ordinary street, with a boarded-up record store, a wine bar, and a florist with a yellow door. There's no graffiti, and she likes that other locals are well dressed and walk briskly with a coffee in one hand and a phone or a lead for a small dog in the other. This is where she lives. A professional, a single woman happy to live alone, successful. A simple life suits her. It's work-biased, a life watched through glass, perhaps, but she is doing something good with her time to help others.

Is her disappearance in the local news? Does anyone notice she isn't there? She imagines that street a little differently now: with fewer people, the shops shut. It unsettles her otherwise to think life is carrying on as normal there while she is marooned here, this respected woman of the community known by shop owners.

Isn't she?

Drew looks at her with intense eyes, like he wants

something from her. A cure for his pain? Part of her wants those secrets he keeps.

'Why me, Drew? It isn't a random act or a random choice for me to be here, to spend so much time in a chair, here, with you. Is it a power trip? A role-reversal thing? Revenge?' She swallows. 'And if so, revenge for what?'

He takes his time to answer. That's his way. They've had so much time in each other's company that she senses when he is thinking. It seems she can hear it. Then he reaches for her hand, and his touch is warm.

'I can make you a better therapist,' he says evasively.

'How so?'

He strokes her fingers, one by one, then places his hand against her palm. Her skin is finally soft. 'By spending time in this chair, as a patient and not as the therapist who is in full control, you'll understand the pain, the shame, the anxiety, and the humiliation. To willingly put yourself in a chair like that takes great courage by the patient. Did you know that?'

'Yes. I see my supervisor regularly,' she quips.

'That's different. Two professionals. The dynamics of power are very different between a patient and a therapist; and a therapist and her supervisor.'

'I never minimised how hard it is to take that step. It isn't my job to judge.'

'You do a lot of listening in your job, and little talking. You listen for inconsistencies in the patient's story, don't you? You assess constantly.'

'It's my job to identify psychological conflicts, the origins of pathology, anything clinical to best help them. Yes. Is that about control? Making me sit here, stinking and wet from my urine in this fucking chair?'

'I haven't heard you swear before. It suits you.'

'No, it doesn't.'

'A sign that you aren't in control. It isn't pleasant, is it? You know, it's hard to really know what is real to the patient, and what is real to everyone else. It seems to me that you and I are very alike. We share something. We both like to be in control.'

Emma-Jane averts her gaze to the grubby carpet. 'Therapists and patients must ethically maintain boundaries.' She pulls her hand away and closes her eyes, seeing tiny stars behind her eyelids.

He laughs. 'Is that a quote from a textbook?'

'I still don't understand. Why me? Therapists choose which patients they work with. If I feel I can't help someone, I refer them on.'

'What goes on in this room is confidential.'

'Doctor-patient confidentiality protects the patient except in safeguarding issues, but who is the doctor here? I thought I was the patient?' She smirks.

He folds his arms and crosses his ankles. The room is tense and stiflingly hot. If only she could open a window, flood the room with air and sounds of the outside world. A crack in the curtain allows a slice of light to fall on the carpet, showing the perfect circle of a cigarette burn.

'My wife took her own life, Dr Glass,' he says suddenly. 'And my son's.'

'What? You told me she—' She stops herself and keeps perfectly still for a few moments.

At last, Drew Rogers is telling the truth.

'I'm sorry, Drew. That's a terrible thing to deal with.'

'Why would you be sorry? You defender of murderous mothers! Compassion? What compassion have you shown to the fathers who are left behind? How can you understand my feelings?'

'Help me understand,' she says. 'Tell me. Why did Evie take her life? James's life?'

'To punish me! Punishment,' he yells. 'But I suppose in your next article, you will just use some more big words to justify her actions. 'Altruism? Is that what you'll say? It was a fucking punishment. I had affairs, several, and a business to run.'

'My article,' she groans. 'So that's why I'm here.'

Drew continues, deaf to her reaction. 'As a baby, James didn't sleep well. Then Evie had a miscarriage. I suppose she was unhappy; she wanted more from me. Bulimia, depression, smashing things, but I never thought for one minute she would do what she did. Be so spiteful, so vengeful. I had no idea she hated me that much. All those years, I thought she loved me. I just can't see how she could hate me that much to kill her own son. I can't see how anyone could do that to a little boy, a beautiful little boy who had all his life ahead of him.'

She shakes her head, feeling his pain. 'I'm so sorry.'

While Drew is vulnerable, when he is grey skies and heavy white clouds, she could almost reach for him. It's an impulse she's felt more than once, and it scares her that she might be experiencing Stockholm syndrome rather than genuine empathy, or even something more. Love? If not love, then what? Attachment?

It isn't loathing. It would be simpler if it were.

'I don't pretend for a minute I was a perfect father or husband. I wasn't, but I loved Evie. I would never have left her, not with James so young. It's difficult to know now, after what she did. I heard you on Shropshire Radio, you know, and I read your article, and everything seemed to fit into place then. I needed to meet you, to try and see how a doctor, a learned person, a female, could write those things. I kept meeting you, I kept paying, and I kept hating you because you were real. Human. And yet, what you wrote was so cold and callous. So . . . wrong!'

'I don't know what to say.'

He looks up at the ceiling, thinking. 'What was that line you said on the radio?' He touches his chin. '*Murder can be motivated by altruism.*' Drew laughs a cold, sardonic laugh. 'A doctor, a learned woman—and yet, so horribly ignorant and misguided.'

'I—'

'I'm talking. You fucking women. What do you know about how men feel, about our hearts, how we love our families? You know nothing.' He clears his throat. 'So, you are here, Dr Glass. It's part of your education and training. CPD,' he says. 'Think of it as being a student again, extending your knowledge of the mind. Of course, this time you have no option but to stay in that chair, to watch and listen. I think if I gave you an alternative, you wouldn't learn by your own free will. You wouldn't understand, but now you will see. You will see what it's like to be a victim of maternal filicide. To use your words, you will see inside my heart and mind. Now, you see this knife?'

'Yes.'

'Soon you'll understand.'

'Please. I've seen enough, Drew. I've even eaten your blood. I've sat in my own stink. Please let me go. I have always expressed sympathy for the victims. The police don't know about your hate letters.'

'I decide when you can leave,' he growls. 'When you can move a muscle, in fact.'

'Let me go and they don't need to know about this. I will be your spokesperson. I will write and publish an article; I will tell your side of the story this time. If you want that, you have to let me go. Please.'

'When you come home after a long day's work to find your wife and child have left you,' he says, 'and that your life will never be the same again, you expect some kind of debris, something that manifests the car crash in your existence. A snapped heel. A stray toy. An unmade bed. I came home to a clean, neat house. Everything was horribly in its place. Except for a note on the door of the fridge.'

'Tell me. What did it say?'

'"This dish is best served cold."'

'What made her do it, though?' Emma-Jane asks. 'She knew you had affairs and was okay with it. Something must have happened. A trigger.'

'Whatever it was, I'll never know. We'll never know.'

Drew gets up and pads upstairs. She hears him rummaging around up there and then he spends ten minutes in the kitchen, filling up the sink. There's a smell of bleach. Bile comes up into her mouth.

*Oh God. He's going to poison me. I'm going to drink bleach. Burn my insides.*

*A slow and painful death.*

He returns, holding a plate of food. A sausage roll and a cupcake. Then, he removes the cuffs. Famished, Emma-Jane does not care whether there are drugs or poison in the food. She wolfs it down. He passes her a bottle of water and watches her drink it in one go.

He produces a comb and a pair of scissors from his rucksack and starts combing her long, black hair. At first, she tenses her shoulders, but after a while she relaxes and succumbs to the intimacy of the gesture. Her hair's usual gloss is lost under grease and dirt. He combs as gently as possible, but her neck is occasionally jerked back and side to side.

Easy enough to snap.

'There were more people I didn't know than people I did know at the funeral of my own wife and son. Imagine that. Every chair *was* filled, and they kept looking at me as if to say I was to blame. As if I was the one who murdered James.'

He sighs.

'I had Evie wear her mother's pearl earrings because she liked to wear them for only the best occasions. I felt she deserved an open casket after putting on such a show of her unhappiness. I insisted they dress her in red; a colour she loathed. The dress was hers, but I can't remember her ever wearing it. She said it drained her of natural colour and clashed with her blonde hair. It gave me some comfort to think of her in an outfit she hated for all eternity.'

'What are you doing to my hair?' Her voice sounds funny to her, like it's a long way away. She realises she's drowsy. Soon, she'll pass out.

So, the food was doped.

Sometimes it's a relief to not be conscious. Not that she has any choice in the matter.

'It surprised me how good a job they did of concealing the ligature marks and the bulging of her eyes from the asphyxiation. That's what they do, I suppose, day in, day out. Conceal the horrible reality of death on a face. James deserved the dignity of a closed coffin, with the finest peach silk interior. The coffins were so dark they were almost black. His was such a small one, too.'

'Please stop,' she groans as he combs harder. But he keeps combing and roughly jerking her head with the knots.

'My wife was blonde. I used to like blondes. It's a good thing Lucy doesn't dye her hair blonde.'

'Lucy? Don't you dare—'

'Obviously at first, I saw her just to learn more about you. But actually, to my surprise, she is pleasant company. God knows my wife spent enough on her hair over the years. She used to say her hairdresser was a friend, a counsellor, and a hairdresser all in one. I guess they have to listen to a paying customer drone on about themselves so they can justify their charges and take twice as long as they need to.'

'Wh—'

'Evie used to buy glossy magazines: the new trends sort, the fashions. She had bright plastic fingernails up to the day she left me. She scraped, rather than touched, me. I should have noticed. They were shining, often red and perfect, but the day she left to hang herself and James, she wasn't wearing them. I suppose they would have gotten in the way with the noose and the knots . . . I see you have short nails. Practical.'

'You couldn't have known, Drew.'

'I miss stroking James's hair, and his cheek. It was as smooth as a stone from the river.'

'Ouch!' she shrieks. He yanks through a final knot and begins cutting her hair.

'One day, I will start a new family. Someone young, fertile. Have a boy, of course. He'll hear stories about magic trees and forests, Hansel and Gretel, Little Red Riding Hood. No rope swings, of course. James. We'll call him James.'

'Sha—' she slurs, and then her head drops like a stone down a well.

'Sweet dreams.'

Satisfied that the shorter length is like his wife's hairstyle, Drew releases Emma-Jane from the chair and drags her into the kitchen, where he's placed a second kitchen chair by the sink.

He pulls on the gloves.

When Emma-Jane comes to, she sees several inches of her hair on the floor. The smell of bleach is stronger than before, and she knows what he's done. In her peripheral view, the straw-like colour catches her eye.

Her glossy black hair had been her best feature.

A tear rolls down her cheek and into her mouth. She tastes the salt, happy for a drop of water and a human reaction in private. Her teardrops reassure her she is still Emma-Jane—still human, female—no matter how damp her armpits and groin, no matter the microbes festering and stinking.

To be bleached blonde couldn't be further from her natural colouring. She knows why he's done it. If she looks like Evie, whom he loathes, it will be easier for him to harm her, kill her, even. What's next, she's less sure about.

Ordinarily, a hair disaster like this might make her tearful. But not now. It's only hair. She's just glad it's still growing. Perhaps he's dyed her hair to move her to some new place, so people won't recognise her.

*Is anyone looking for me?*

Is she even a red dot on someone's map? Perhaps her supervisor, Celia, her neighbours, have noticed her absence. Are there messages on her landline and mobile delivered in urgent, agitated tones?

As the days go by, perhaps someone will act on the

vacancy of her home, her office. Maybe Derek at the dry cleaners, or Maureen at the Post Office. Maybe one of her clients has acted on a suspicion that something isn't right because she is a reliable, punctual professional. Vanessa might call the police and they'll come looking for her, like the prince with a glass slipper.

Might Vanessa sound the alarm, or is Emma-Jane just a forgotten acquaintance?

# 23

It dumbfounds AJ when Drew picks up his phone. It's the first time in a week he's answered his phone calls; AJ usually leaves a message and waits for a call back. Even Hannah looks surprised to hear Drew's voice on the van's speakerphone.

'Glad you called. I could do with your keys to the farmhouse. I need you to hand them over.'

Surprised by the upbeat tone of Drew's voice, AJ raises his eyebrows at Hannah. 'I could drop them off at the farmhouse. We're not far from there now, as it happens.'

'Perfect.'

Drew hangs up before AJ can clarify whether Drew is at the farmhouse or not, but he figures he can always leave them in the hiding place and text him.

Hannah looks nervously at AJ. 'Do you think he knows?'

'What?' he says with a shrug, keen to hide the tension building across his shoulders and neck at the sound of his ex-boss's voice. He'll be glad to cut all ties and start afresh.

'About us sneaking in the other night.'

'We didn't take anything, anyway. The mirror would have been all wrong in our place. If he knows, I'll say we were checking up on something. Don't worry; if he was angry, I'd know.'

'I'm not going inside the house. I don't mind standing in the yard with you, but that's it.'

'Suits me. Drew would have to drag me in there.'

Hannah giggles nervously.

'We'll only be there for a few minutes. I promise.' He touches her hand and she laces their fingers together.

Ten minutes later, they pull up in front of the farmhouse. 'Is that Drew's motor?' Hannah asks, wide-eyed. AJ nods, hating that Hannah is impressed by the Range Rover, by money and by swank, by the soft leather seats in a vehicle that lifts the passengers to a height where they cannot help but look down their nose at people in regular vehicles. Pete reckons a high-spec vehicle like that would have cost around seventy thousand pounds.

*Him too*, he concedes.

Drew is inside the Ranger Rover, talking on the phone.

AJ looks at the farmhouse, inconspicuous and unchanged. Doors and windows closed and locked on secrets. The house looks respectable enough, though; money can hide dark secrets, which poverty cannot.

Opposite the farmhouse, there's an old shippon built for lambing at one time. At one end of the yard, there is an old barn, once home to cattle when this was a working farm. The open sheds are now home to nests of starlings in the spring, and to a family of doves, who come and go and coo. If anything, it's those outbuildings that reflect the true identity and history of the place and the previous owners. A lost way of living. A kind of history remembered. AJ almost pities the new owners who have bought the sad farmhouse.

*Will Evie and James haunt them?*

All the buildings are neglected and uninhabitable in his mind; even the charming facade of an old farmhouse which pretends to be welcoming, warm, a family home. Once, it had been.

If Drew hadn't changed his plans, AJ could have been working for twelve months, possibly two years on those outbuildings, earning a decent wage to get himself and Hannah on the property ladder. At twenty-eight, he isn't even on the bottom rung.

As he closes the door of the van with a slam, he's reminded of the antique chest in the dining room. The jealous streak in him wants Drew to be dead inside and for the chest to open and close, like the lid on a coffin at an open-casket service. He glances up at the house briefly—it's watching his every move. He half expects the door to suddenly open and smoke to rise from its chimney, only it's Drew who opens and closes his car door with an expensive click.

'AJ!' he says cheerfully.

Hannah hops out of the van to join them, looking a little sheepish.

As always, Drew is smartly dressed in a shirt, navy slacks, and brogues. It's his usual look: countrified, but businesslike. AJ looks Drew up and down, just like Drew looks at Hannah, while she smiles benignly at him.

'You must be the lovely Hannah,' Drew says, reaching for her hand, which he lightly kisses. He is the epitome of charm and agreeableness. A true snake charmer. 'Good of you to drop by. I'm here to say farewell to the place. The new owners move in next week.' He steps back with his hands in his pockets, looking at the property. 'Mixed emotions to see it go, which I didn't think I'd have.'

Hannah shuffles her feet and is about to say something when Drew continues.

'I expect the new owners will develop the outbuildings, carve it up into two dwellings. That was my original plan until . . . things changed.'

AJ passes him his keys to the farmhouse and says ingratiatingly, 'Are you happy with everything Pete and I have done to the inside? That's why I was calling you.'

'The place is sold. I haven't been inside, AJ. I've no intention of entering, either,' Drew says, smiling. 'I can trust you, can't I, without having to check your work with a red pen?'

'Sure. Only you normally like to. I left a box in the darkroom. Mainly photographs, and a few bits I wasn't sure whether or not to skip.'

Drew's phone buzzes in his pocket. 'Well, nothing important then. Thanks for dropping the keys off.'

A sound causes them to turn and look back in the farmhouse's direction: a light tapping, like a fingernail on a window. *Tap-tap-tap.* AJ and Hannah exchange a knowing glance while Drew looks at each window and then takes a step back.

'Must be a bird trapped inside. Rooks used to get stuck in the chimney. Damn pests. Well, thanks for the keys. Lovely to meet you, Hannah,' he says with a half wave and moves towards his vehicle, seemingly in a hurry to get away.

AJ doesn't take the hint. 'Hold up!' He likes to see strain on the man's face, to delay Drew; make him wait, like he has made AJ wait time after time on jobs he forgets to show up for. Once, you can forgive someone, but when it's a regular occurrence, that's just plain disrespect. 'I haven't seen you in a while,' AJ says. 'Did you get my messages? Kat's been here a few times.'

'Sorry, yes, busy, busy. Anything urgent I need to know about?'

'I dunno. Kat left a letter for you. I have it, but it's at home.'

'Next time I see you. It can wait. I guess you'll be glued to the TV tonight with Liverpool playing Manchester City?'

Hannah rolls her eyes. 'You bet he will.'

'I won't take up any more of your time.' Drew turns to leave again, then stops in his tracks when AJ speaks again.

'Pete and I are setting up our own business.'

'Excellent. You will make a talented team. I can put you in touch with a few contacts if you'd like. Developers who need regular trades on hand. The chap who bought this place might be interested. Worth a try.'

'Yeah, I'd appreciate that, though I expect if he is a developer, he'll have his own labourers.'

'Quite possibly. People's circumstances change all the time, though. Unexpected things happen, you know. Stephen and his family fancy living here for a bit before selling on, and raising a few cattle, I think. Or ponies. I can't quite remember, but I will mention you and Pete to him, as you just never know, do you?'

'So, did you sell the ten acres off separately or not?'

'No,' Drew says, somewhat impatiently. 'The new owner wanted it, even though I've let the land grow rough. It's worthless; nothing but nettles and thistles now.'

'A family is moving in then?' Hannah asks.

'Yes. It's a family home. I would go mad living here on my own. It pains me to sell something at this underdeveloped stage; it's got such potential. It would sell for a couple of million all done up, but I'm here to say goodbye to the place for good.'

AJ can't help but quietly gloat that Drew didn't max out on this property.

'Are you prepared to travel, to stay away, AJ? It's not ideal, I appreciate,' Drew says, looking directly at Hannah, 'but I have contacts further afield who'll have work for you, if you are.'

AJ looks Hannah in the eye, relieved when she smiles at him and not at Drew. 'If the money's right, I will. Short-term, like. Hannah's got a good job as a trainee accountant, so we want to stay put.'

'I'll text you. There's a good chap I know up near Hexham. An old friend who's doing up another barn into several catering cottages. He's gone into tourism in quite a big way. We stayed there last year for a family break one bank holiday. It's a beautiful spot, a few miles out of town, overlooking the River Tyne. We walked a section of Hadrian's Wall with James on my back in a carrier.' He pauses for a second. 'Seems like a decade ago now.'

Hannah looks at her feet.

'Well, good luck.'

'Catch you again, Drew,' AJ says, heading towards the grubby van and waiting for Hannah to follow.

'Bye!' Hannah calls and waves. Inside the van she says, 'I feel sorry for him. He really misses his son. I can tell.'

'Hmph,' he grunts at Hannah, disliking the sympathy she is showing for his ex-boss, who has happily dropped him like a stone and driven off into the sunset.

'I know he was unfaithful to his wife, but anyway, he's a decent bloke really, isn't he? Helping you out with contacts, I mean.'

'If I cheated on you, would I still be "a decent bloke"?'

'No, that's different.'

'How? They were married. We're not, but I still wouldn't cheat on you because I know it would hurt you.'

She reaches for his hand and squeezes it. 'I bet he knows plenty of people with cash needing people like you. Everything is going to work out fine.'

*People like me*, he thinks, and accelerates out of the drive. The wheels of the grubby white van spin and churn up gravel like a whirlpool of dirt and debris. His toolbox slams into one side of the van in a metallic punch.

Even if the new owner of the farmhouse contacts him about labouring in the outbuildings, he has no intention of going back there. Not ever. He'd sooner beg on the streets of Shrewsbury and pray Hannah didn't walk by on her lunch hour in that smart suit of hers that cost a month's salary.

They drive in silence for several minutes, his knuckles white on the steering wheel, Hannah oblivious to his frustration.

# 24

The cat flap rattles.

Emma-Jane could open her eyes, or she could count sheep and hope to go back to sleep. Her eyes don't need to be open for her to know what the room looks like. Its antique wallpaper and grubby, grey carpet. Her muscles ache, but she doesn't move.

If only a cat would walk in and wrap itself around her legs, purr a little to remind her of what it sounds like to be happy, contented. Bring in the cold and the dew of early morning on its fur.

She remains still while Drew sleeps beside her on the mattress. The silence in the room is profound and heavy. It feels different today. It feels like the seeds of Evie and James, watered so frequently, have taken root while their bones move beneath the carpet. His spoken memories of them float like dandelion seeds, to land and settle wherever they please.

Drew's body is in the sleeping bag, curled into a ball like a dormouse in hibernation. She doesn't move, afraid that she isn't scared of the man beside her. It isn't just gravity that is tethering her to this man, this moment, this house. If she begged, would he let her go? If she tried, could she escape?

Did she really want to escape?

*I can help him.*

As each day goes by, the pull on her past, the clarity of memories, and the signposts she's carefully constructed to navigate the days and the evenings are fading. More than the sight of him, it is this which frightens her the most. If he were cruel, nailed her palms to a cross, made her gaunt from lack of food or water, the suffering would occupy her mind and senses. The immorality would remind her of who and what she is.

To be civilised to one another—a new torture. The mind is her dungeon this time.

Drew's breathing is deep and slow. Then he stirs a little in his sleep and she feels the imprint of his breath on her neck. Emma-Jane licks her bottom lip. Her face appears as if it's been stung by a rogue insect. The tears start quietly, trickling. She softly turns to look at his sleeping face.

*Why can't I hate you?*

As time goes on, it is becoming increasingly difficult for Emma-Jane to imagine petrol stations, supermarkets, bars and shops, office buildings opening and closing at defined times, people moving in and out of them talking on phones, smiling at the first hints of summer in planted hanging baskets.

How ordinary things are slipping away. The known and familiar. A world she understands. The way streetlights, the asphalt and puddles once spoke to her, and cars splashed. Those things made sense.

The fruit bowl is on the carpet, beside the mattress. He regularly adds plums and cherries to it. Only once or twice has she seen him take something from the bowl and eat it. She's watched juice from the plum squirt down his chin and found her own tongue wiping her lips. The fruit is spoiled now. Time goes on. Perhaps that's why he leaves them there, these dying reminders of supermarkets, fields, trees—alien places to her.

Will she grow fur the way the plum has? Or shrink, the way a plum becomes a prune?

Suddenly, he moans. A dream, or perhaps a nightmare, stirs him. Should she crawl on her hands and knees to the kitchen to hunt for the key? No; he will only wake up and the trust between them will be over. Drew's grief is the only real thing she can think about right now. His life must be a constant bleed, waking up each day to the ugly ending Evie chose.

She hears his grief, like ghosts playing in an orchestra. It's snowflakes, it's an avalanche, and it's a light bulb popping. His grief is fierce. Its hue is coloured by the nature of the deaths, premature: one suicide, one murder. Like a season stopped prematurely, from summer to autumn. Like a tree that has disrobed itself of leaves and colour having been in full life, full bloom, the sap rising. Rising.

She squeezes her eyes shut so she doesn't cry.

He takes a while to come round, as though he is resisting waking up. Emma-Jane knows that, wherever he's been diving in his dreams, it was dark and frightening. This troubled man perplexes her; a man who likes to watch her, a millionaire who sleeps on a mattress in a dirty, stuffy room.

Drew suddenly sits up and looks at Emma-Jane. His eyes open like a camera clicking a long-anticipated shot. He wipes his mouth with the back of his hand and blinks several times.

'I haven't slept that deeply in a long time. You are good therapy for me, Dr Glass.' He swallows and rubs at his face. 'Did something happen to you? Something frightening?'

'Why do you ask?' she says, moving away.

'You have nightmares.'

'Well, this isn't exactly my idea of a holiday.'

They both stare at each other, neither wanting to give in.

'So, you are as damaged and deformed as I am, aren't you, Dr Glass? We are both used goods with trauma in our past. In our present. We each have a heart of stone; nothing but emotional leftovers to give to the opposite sex. It is sad.'

'No, Drew. I am not angry, and I am not bitter.'

'And I am?' He moves closer. She flinches.

'I've been here for over a week now, Drew, and my clients need me. Some are very vulnerable. I need to contact them, please.' He doesn't respond. 'Drew?'

'That isn't possible.' He strides into the kitchen, where he takes two pasties and a bottle of water from the fridge. 'Breakfast is served.'

The plate is outstretched. She grasps it, still wearing the handcuffs. He removes a keyring from his trouser pocket and uses a small key to unlock them. 'Eat those.' He puts the bottle of water in her lap. 'Drink that. Don't even try to move from that spot.'

'You can trust me,' she says, with more conviction than she was expecting, like she is carving the words into the bark of a sycamore tree.

Drew removes a make-up bag from his rucksack. It is pink, with *Lancôme* written on one side. 'Your fingernails are all chipped.' He dabs nail polish remover on a tissue and begins to remove the residual colour. 'Do you have a man in your life, Dr Glass? Someone who loves you?'

'I'm single,' she states, not wanting to be drawn into talking about her private life. She is beginning to struggle to comprehend his strange moods and actions.

'So, who loves you, Dr Glass? Your patients might think they love you when you make them feel better. Ah, Lucy; she is fond of you. But what about family?'

'Don't you already know my family tree? Somehow, I thought you did.'

'I'm flattered. No, I don't know. Enlighten me.'

The nail polish remover stings where the cuticle is raw, and she flinches again. 'There isn't a great deal to tell. I was an only child. My father disappeared before I was two. My mum raised me until I was eighteen, and then I left home for university on a scholarship. Mum passed away the year before I graduated. Breast cancer.'

'I see. So, no one heroic to rescue you.'

'You will let me go. I am sure of it. This situation isn't what you want. It's not you, Drew. It's a reaction to a terrible event, but you aren't that terrible event; you are just a man. A man who was a good father.'

'Done.' He puts the nail polish remover away. 'You haven't suffered yourself, Dr Glass, that's the thing. You've done well for yourself—a credit to your mother, to have a doctor as a daughter. While you might know the right answer, the right thing to say to people who are suffering, you yourself have never felt your chin go under the water . . . perhaps till now.'

'My role as a psychologist requires me to keep some emotional distance in order to help my clients. Sympathy isn't involved; that is personal. Empathy, however, which I do have, allows the person to talk and be understood without being judged or enticed down a certain path. I am good at my job. If you want therapy, you don't have to kidnap me.'

'Defensive, aren't we? And by God, do you flatter yourself. Talk, talk, talk. Evie was the same. On the phone, text. God only knows what she found to talk about, except complaining about me.'

'You must have been very dear to her for you to be the centre of Evie's universe. Only a good, kind man could be that.'

'You know nothing about me.'

'Then tell me.'

He watches her a moment, glaring deep into her eyes. Trying to read her. Then, he sighs.

'I left school at sixteen. Worked as an apprentice for a builder. Saved by living in my car so that, by the time I was twenty, I could put a deposit down on my first house. Between work in London and Surrey, I did it up. That's how it was for ten years or so, and then the property boom gave me a fair wind and I was away. Moneyed, married, a son. Three properties to my name before I was thirty.'

'I miss my home,' she confides in him. 'I miss—'

'The Glass House. Yes, quite a statement to live inside so much glass. It did not surprise me to find you lived in a sparkling palace. Our homes are our castles, aren't they? I mean, all that glass. A name and a job meant to be squeaky clean. It's a cliché. When I dropped that letter off, saw your blinds and that fancy one-way glass, I knew your conscience wasn't so clean.'

She frowns and wipes her sticky mouth with her sleeve. 'My conscience is clean, Drew. I have nothing to hide.'

His eyes flash. The mood change is swift.

'Of course, you do!' he yells. 'Everyone does, unless they're living in a cave! That's why I'm here, to help you see it's not clear. A degree and a doctorate mean nothing in this world, Dr Glass. You'd be better off getting some bloody life experience, if you want to help people and understand what drives them to do the unthinkable. An ignoramus wrote that article.'

Drew removes a handheld mirror from his rucksack. Judging by the dainty design, it must have been Evie's. He holds it in front of her face, hand shaky from all the wine he drank yesterday. He peers into her face like it's a deep well. The man is a narcissist, yes, but she's still a little surprised he has a mirror with him. There's a smell of body odour and something else. Something sour.

Fear. Sadness, perhaps.

'Look! Take a good, long look at yourself, Dr Glass.'

The hairs on the back of her neck stand up. The bleached blonde short hair shouts at her.

'If I cut you, would your blood be blue? Do you see a female, a woman born to nurture, protect, procreate? Or do you see a supporter of child-killers? Which one are you?!'

Frustrated that she can't bat the mirror away, she closes her eyes.

'Look! Are you just like Evie, like all those other women who killed themselves and their offspring to spite their husbands? Are you? Because I think you pity those monstrous women. Do you like what you see?'

'No,' she confesses, seeing a warped version of herself. A painting edited to the point of deformity. Words from his hate letter return with a vengeance.

*How many more are going to die before you stop meddling? One, two, ten, Dr Death?*

*I hope you're listening. Can you hear glass smashing? Those sharp little pieces will be your only legacy. No family. Just shards of glass.*

'Fucking woman.' His anger slides from him in waves. 'How can you live with yourself?

'As a man, you don't understand. You never will,' she states. 'Much of what a woman experiences during pregnancy, childbirth, and then into motherhood is taboo, which is why I wrote that article about Angela Lamb. Yes, in your mirror I see a woman's face—a doctor, a therapist, a friend—and I will live the rest of my life protecting the things I believe in.'

The room is still and silent. Her voice suddenly cracks, as does her confidence. She longs to be alone, to be at home, to breathe fresh, clean air and to feel nothing.

Drew's face bobs in front of her like an ugly misshaped balloon. God, she wants to pop it. Make it shrivel away and flop on the carpet.

'Woman, you are evil!' He thrusts the mirror closer still to her face. His eyes are red and wild with fury. 'Where is your shame for defending monsters? I see none etched on your face or in your eyes.'

Her head falls. Is he right in what he's saying about women? It is a thought so misshapen it could only grow in a dark, damp place.

But no. She can't think that way.

'You don't need to do this to me; to anyone, for that matter. What Evie did to James and what Angela Lamb did to Teddy was terrible, tragic. I never said it wasn't! And I never said I was perfect. By God, I know I'm far from it.'

'You defended those actions and lived with your own thoughts while sitting in an office with "Dr Glass" etched on the door, comfortably telling other people how to live their lives.'

He throws the mirror across the room and it smashes.

The crash makes Emma-Jane shiver. Not with surprise, but the knowledge of the foresight he'd put into those horrible hate letters.

'Those evil, unspeakable words you wrote. You are as rotten as them.' Drew falls onto his knees and his head drops suddenly, like a broken sun. She sees wetness on his cheeks.

'Yes I am,' she replies. 'And that's why I do my job.' She begins to breathe more easily and closes her eyes to the horror of this broken man. She watches as he crawls on his hands and knees to retrieve the smashed mirror. Its glass is shattered, but the wooden handle is intact.

He peers at his own broken reflection like he hasn't seen himself before.

A knot of emotion forms in her throat. Astonishingly, it is pity she feels for him. Not hate.

Seeing him lying there on the carpet, like he's in a deep dark trance, staring into another time. She can imagine what he might see: a wreckage of James's toys, a rusty scooter, a spoiled chocolate Easter egg. The ruins of his family life must keep rising, because his mood changes so starkly. He moans and rocks as if those ruins are up to his shoulders, his mouth. She wishes she could exhale a strong wind and blow it all away.

But she can only count the seconds she has left to live while he stares at the carpet.

'It wasn't your fault,' she says softly, and the tears fall. Her head feels heavy, so she lets it fall too. To have conversed so intensely has exhausted her completely. Like some catharsis, a sense of calm and peace washes over her, almost to the point of detachment from the situation. There can be no judgement from him or her in this quicksand, in this bizarre reversal of roles from therapist to client.

She begins to sob so loudly that she does not hear

Drew move towards her.

'You're crying!' Drew says as he kneels beside her.

She sniffs to stem the flow of snot and raises a shoulder to wipe one side of her face. By looking away she avoids looking at him, avoids feeling exposed and vulnerable.

Drew scrutinises her face.

'How much longer must I stay here?' she asks.

Gently, he holds her chin to tilt her blotchy face towards him. First, he applies red lipstick to her lips.

'Did you know no two lip prints are the same?' he says.

Not expecting an answer, he then inexpertly drags blue eyeshadow across her eyelids. His fingers rummage through the make-up bag, unsure of which item he needs next. He chooses a blusher, and gently sweeps the brush against each cheek.

Lastly, he removes a hairbrush from the bag. There are knots in the ends of her hair. Having been bleached, it is dry and brittle, ready to snap . . .

Just like her.

# 25

The red-haired woman she met last time had hydrated, unblemished skin and a waterfall of hair.

This version has a different appearance. A different aura. Perhaps it's the eyeliner that hasn't been scrubbed from her face, or the yoga pants hanging off her hips that shout, I don't give a damn. From the items of furniture on the lawn, and the piles of rubbish strewn around the bins, it looks like the woman is leaving at any moment.

'You'll have to come in if you want to talk to me,' she barks. 'I'm busy. What's your name again?'

'Lucy. Yours?'

'Kat.'

Lucy reluctantly follows Kat into the kitchen. A stray sock, unopened post, and a bra are on the lounge floor. The sofa has a creased look about it, like it's only just been vacated after a lot of use. A blue throw is scrunched up at one end. A wall calendar depicting an enormous snake catches her eye.

They move toward the sound of a washing machine whirring its way through a cycle and the smell of greasy bacon. There are enough wine bottles on the kitchen counters to open a shop, with stained glasses and a crusty frying pan in the sink. Kat heats a mug of coffee in the microwave. It's hard not to wonder how old and stale the coffee tastes.

'What do you want this time? I ain't got another phone number for Drew, if that's what you're here for,' she says, stuffing a saucepan into the open cardboard box. 'The bastard wants me out tomorrow.'

'So, have you spoken to Drew Rogers? That's why I'm here.'

'No, he won't speak to me.' She sighs, and her shoulders drop. 'The solicitor or the estate communicate with me. Drew doesn't.'

'Oh, well—'

Kat aggressively points to a plastic bag on the kitchen counter.

'That's his stuff in there. Expensive shaving stuff, mainly. Take it, will you?'

Lucy nods.

She takes a peek inside the bag. The Drew she knew sautéed potatoes, cooked with garlic and seasonings, took his time shopping, preparing, cooking. Seeing a bottle of aftershave and his shaving gear in the plastic bag unsettles her some more. He is less and less the man she thought he was. A man who had an affair with his tenant and then disappeared.

'The telephone number you gave me, it only goes to voicemail. I mean, I've left messages, but Drew hasn't called back. Do you have any idea where he might be?' There's an open bottle of milk on the kitchen counter, which looks to have curdled. The kitchen has an air of sadness about it. Lucy can't wait to get out of there and back on the road.

'I don't know, and he won't call back, unless you've got something he wants. Not that long ago, he had one of his labourers round here doing the house up. I had a new shower, as the old one leaked. There was me thinking what a great guy Drew is. The bloke wanted a power shower after we—'

She takes a slurp of coffee and Lucy gets a whiff of body odour from her unwashed body.

'Anyway, since then, Drew's changed his business, changed his whole bloody life probably, 'cos of grief—or running from something—and I'm not in the picture. He's made that loud and clear. Are you in the picture?' She attempts to smile, but the muscles quickly give way like it's too much effort. She tosses a cheese grater into the box, and it makes a loud clatter.

'No, I'm not. It's my friend who's missing. She was Drew's therapist. I'm worried about her.'

'She? I thought last time you said—oh, never mind. Was she seeing Drew or something?' she asks sharply. 'I mean, I don't know who he is seeing anymore,' Kat says bitterly.

Lucy looks at her shoes on the linoleum floor and blushes, remembering how attracted she had been to him. The troubled look on Kat's face suggests she also still has feelings for Drew, and perhaps she has invited Lucy into her house only to investigate Drew's habits now that he is on the brink of a new life.

Something about the woman unnerves Lucy.

'Emma-Jane is a professional therapist and, Drew being her client, they wouldn't have a relationship. She is a person of routine, and her disappearance is out of character.'

'So, like being married, only without the ceremony? Is that the kind of relationship you mean? Well, I'm sorry to disappoint you, but marriage meant nothing to Drew. I can say that, hand on heart. Of all the women in the world, why do you think your friend is with him?'

'I'm not sure she is, but I want to check. That's all. Listen, do you know the addresses of his other properties?

I can see you're very busy.'

'Well,' she grins, 'the farmhouse is sold. He owns another terrace like this just round the corner opposite the bus stop, but I know the couple who live there.' She scratches her chin. 'The name of his business is Amver. That might turn up something if you Google it. I dunno, love. Look, I need to crack on.'

'Sure, sorry to hold you up, but one more thing. It's important. Did you know Drew's wife, Evie?'

She stops reaching inside the cupboard and turns to glare at Lucy.

'Why would I?' Her voice is thick, as if she were drunk. The tilt of her head and the fix of her eye hold a portentous interest.

Lucy shrugs, sensing her time is up. Something irrevocable has happened. She isn't there to judge. 'I . . . Thanks, anyway.'

'Take the bag, please, in case you see him. I know I won't. I was gonna chuck it, but now you're here you might as well take it. See yourself out.'

Lucy takes the bag and leaves, finally happy to get away.

Back in the car, Lucy puts on her seat belt and rummages through the plastic bag. It feels like an invasion of Drew's privacy but, right now, that's not her priority; knowing that Emma-Jane is safe and well is.

Inside the bag, there's an electric toothbrush, aftershave, a shaving kit from The White Lemon, and a round tin of aftershave balm scented with lemongrass.

Something clicks into place . . .

The White Lemon is on the high street in Shrewsbury. The familiar name gives her a trickle of hope. The shop is not one she normally goes to; the products are fancy and out of her price range.

Lucy turns her car round and speeds off toward the high street.

*Trust your hunch. Trust your judgement.*
*You're not a fool.*

# 26

Drew's empty wine bottles catch the sunlight coming through the gap in the curtain. There are more and more of them strewn on the carpet, taunting Emma-Jane with the idea of a message in a bottle, thrown straight through the window and onto the sea of asphalt outside.

She tries to remember the song about empty bottles to divert her mind from the hope of being found and rescued. Those veins and arteries of his must be drunk on red wine because he is drunk night after night, and now sometimes during the day.

Drew forever seeks obscurity, vacancy, but can't seem to find it.

The wine doesn't make him laugh or smile. Sometimes he lifts a limp, heavy hand to wave at her. He always sits opposite her: his version of the sessions in her office, only now the roles are reversed. Metal shadows spill onto the carpet. Light will nose its way inside. It's a Sunday or a Monday, she thinks, but she can't be sure. Perhaps, elsewhere, church bells ring. She keeps still and quiet, not wanting to antagonise him or to see those purple veins rise in his throat, like angry snakes from a pit. His past lingers in the doorway and the four corners of the lounge.

All she wants to feel is close to him. To help him. To help herself.

He's going to cut himself. She knows it because he's bare-chested and the bag where he keeps the knife is beside him.

She wishes that a rebirth of each day would heal him and that the bustling of life would banish the lethargy and staleness from this house. Not a sanctuary; his tomb. If he were an ant, she'd lift whatever was in his way so he could let go of his past.

'My wife's magazines say yellow is in fashion this season,' he says, tossing a glossy magazine back into the rucksack with force. He throws Emma-Jane a look. The tiny threads of reddened capillaries in his eyes, like shafts of electricity, make her tense.

He digs out his knife and starts to cut.

The room is silent as he carves into himself. What is it he is trying to cut out of his flesh? The cutting seems to give him peace. Or fatigue. The undoing of his seams. Lately, he never speaks when he cuts and cuts, but she has to watch. His head nods and his eyes move around his body as slow as an ache. He looks at her and sobs, and each sob is like a fist in her stomach. The criss-cross pattern of cuts and welts are a vivid confession of sorts.

She sees pain expanding in his eyes as he makes a deep incision into his bicep.

Slick wet blood trickles into his clenched hand and a waft of iron permeates the room. Sweat glistens on his temple. Perhaps he hopes to be reborn when he cuts, because there is anger living under his skin. Something he wants to remove to undo himself.

'You are not bad, Drew. You are not bad. Can you hear me?'

His face is flushed from the pain, the heat. A sadness sneaks up over her shoulder and a hollowness opens in her stomach as the wound of him fills the stark room. This man is no longer a stranger to her. He flinches as a chunk of skin is lifted from where it belonged on his forearm.

His chest flushes as the pain grows. The blotches form like watercolour on paper.

His hypnotised face is far away from her now. She cannot call him back. All she can do is keep her mind toward logic; for him, and for her.

Her throat closes up when he moans in pain. To him, his organs are black. His insides are rotten and wretched. His wounds give him relief. A shimmering sky of stars. The routine of making her watch is eating away at them both. It's a relief to see his stone eyes staring back, his face like a deserted chapel. He hates it when she turns to look the other way.

'I'm here, Drew.'

She imagines gently closing his eyes with her finger and thumb, those dark eyes that seek clemency which only he can give to himself. His mouth is open, and a line of dribble works its way down his chin. Blood has run to the gutters of his nails and cuticles, where it dries.

Then, his eyes snap open unexpectedly and he swallows several times, lubricating his throat and mouth, never once taking his eyes off her face.

'You,' he says, his head lolling to one side.

She watches a spider slowly crawl across the ceiling and onto the lampshade, sprinkling dust like dandruff. All that ceiling, all those walls, they're like acres, countries, to a spider. Such freedom. Here she sits, trapped in a web. The spider's unhurried movement stirs the mounting hysteria building inside her.

An hour later, Drew gets to his feet and staggers into the kitchen to wash his hands and prepare something to eat. He returns with a bowl of chicken soup, which he feeds her, spoon by spoon. It is delicious, a comfort food she might choose to eat herself. It's his way to leave it a long time between meals, so she suffers with hunger and thinks about all the food she can't eat in the meantime.

'You can trust me to feed myself,' she says, between spoonfuls.

'I enjoy feeding you.'

'You don't trust me.'

She wonders if he sees her as a child or a sick patient. He doesn't hurry her. As he kneels beside her, she savours his familiar scent and the shape of his long fingers. Nearness to him is a strange comfort and discomfort. The movement of that spoon reminds her of how much she needs him to stay alive. It reminds her of how far away from normality they are.

She has a flash of self-consciousness about her unbrushed teeth, bad breath, body odour. It is good that she knows these things about herself, that the weird isn't acceptable. There is more of her than just a husk of her old self. Civilisation is still within reach.

The bowl is almost empty. 'Is there more?' she asks. She hates herself for wanting him beside her, looking at her while the sustenance floods her hollow insides.

He gets up and returns with a bowl of ice cream. He makes a show of placing a lump of vanilla on her tongue, which she lets sit there for as long as possible. It's like taking communion.

'Mmm,' she groans.

Ice cream has never tasted so good. If only she could stick her fingers in the tub. Part of her wishes she could grab the tub and deposit the lot in her mouth; the other part likes this slow, sensual eating.

'No one is looking for you, are they?' he asks. 'You are more of a workaholic recluse than I thought.'

'You don't know that for sure.'

'I do. We are so alike.' Perhaps Drew is right. Perhaps no one is looking for her.

Drew disappears into the kitchen. She hears the lazy drone of a fly. Helpless to defend her skin, her nostrils, from it, she listens to its hypnotic sound. She must look like a lost soul to it, squinting like that. The fly rushes towards her—a fuzz of static and indecision making it hang in the air like a light aircraft, stalled above her—and then it lands near her left eye.

The tiny insect makes her feel so horribly helpless.

She violently shakes her head, sending the fly's fuselage and wings off into the air, only for it to land in almost exactly the same spot again. It's not just the tickle of its tiny legs on her face that bothers her; it's the helplessness it writes all over her face. She surrenders to its message and imagines herself as a carcass with flies crawling over her, swarming her oily, bloated corpse.

Drew reappears in the lounge, holding a half-full bottle of white wine in one hand. He takes a swig straight from it.

'Tell me, doctor, why do women kill their children? All that longing to be a mother and to nurture, the goddamn awful pregnancy that they suffer through, then childbirth, the sleepless nights. Is it the complete and utter loss of their separate selves—complete absorption into the child?' He leans against the door frame. 'How can it happen?'

'Mental illness, for one, which underlines pretty much all reasons. Mothers may suffer from post-partum depression without knowing it. It can manifest and gradually become psychosis. The mother of a dead child receives a great deal of attention. That is desirable for some women who are mentally ill. Sometimes, it's caused by mental illness combined with something else.'

'Like what?'

'Some mothers believe their child is ill or evil, or that the world is cruel, and then it's a kind of mercy killing, born of altruistic intentions. Others do it because the child is unwanted. Emilia Fray, for example, killed her stepchild because she just wanted to have a relationship with the child's father. Accidental deaths also occur, from abuse or anger.'

'Anything else?'

'Spousal revenge, perhaps, because of infidelity or abandonment.'

Drew remains still, leaning heavily on the door frame to hold himself up. He seems to absorb the information very gradually.

'A jealous rage, perhaps. Or divorce. There was a Canadian woman who drowned her two children because she feared her ex-husband would gain custody of them.'

'Poor man.'

'Poor children, and poor woman. She was ill, desperate. Still is, as she serves a lengthy prison sentence. Life, probably. A human has to be ill to go to such an extreme, but is not necessarily insane.'

'Don't you dare talk about pitying those monsters.'

'I'm aware of the science and the social taboo around the act. It's not about pity.'

'Abhorrent acts.' He takes a long swig. 'Abhorrent.'

'Did Evie take drugs or abuse alcohol?' she asks, enjoying the irony of the question in the face of his own alcohol abuse and mental instability. 'That can be a factor in a tragedy.'

'No more than the rest of us,' he says, holding up the wine bottle to toast her, smiling sarcastically. 'The woman starved herself, probably to fit into her pre-pregnancy clothes, which I'd paid through the nose for. But she wasn't mentally ill. Evie was completely sane when she killed James and herself. There was a thought process behind what and where. Evil. Plain evil.'

'How do you know there was a thought process and that it was not a spontaneous decision?'

He stares at the bottle for a time, as if it were a piece of unusual art.

'The house was perfect. She looked great, as usual, doing yoga, and James was always immaculate. We had a meal out over the weekend and shared a bottle of wine back at home, listening to Leonard Cohen. She was fine. Moody and needy, but that's how she was. We had sex on the sofa; first time for a while.'

'So, everything was good between you?'

'Don't put words in my mouth. You're not married. You're not a mother. She was never satisfied with me. Always wanted more and more. That meal, the drunken sex, the music. She cried afterwards. I didn't understand.' He strokes the wine bottle. A finger traces its curve as if it were a woman's body.

'Did something happen? Like, I don't know, a trigger, like a loved one falling ill. Something to make her desperate, to snap like that?'

'Reasons. I mean, does a reason even matter? When people kill each other, it's bad enough, but a child . . . *my* child.' He looks down at the floor and speaks in barely a whisper. 'I'm done talking.'

He slams the front door behind him. The click is like a bite. It is the first time he has left in an angry mood, leaving her without water. What if he forgets about her? Her death would be slow, painful. She hears his car speed away. He's driving over the limit. What if he crashes?

She swallows down her rising panic. Urine trickles down her leg. She winces at the unpleasant smell and the unwelcome warmth.

# 27

Drew returns around two hours later, drunker than when he'd left. He immediately falls asleep on the mattress, snoring loudly. Emma-Jane is so dehydrated she has a coughing fit, and the sound wakes him up.

'What the . . .' He wipes his mouth with his hand and gets up from the mattress. A deep frown etches on his forehead when he looks up at the ceiling for several minutes. He staggers a little and stops to listen once more. 'I heard footsteps upstairs.' Drew's eyes bat open and closed and then he stares directly at Emma-Jane, as if she has an answer for the footsteps. 'Didn't you hear them?'

Emma-Jane could cry. He looks insane. 'No. I don't think so, Drew.'

'And giggling. A ball bounced down the stairs: bump, bump, bumpety-bump.' Drew cocks his head, expecting to hear just that. He covers his face with his hands. 'It was so real. James was playing with a football.' Thin sadness leaks from her heart for him. 'I was never there when he needed me.'

Rocking an imaginary baby in his arms, he quiets down. The room is as silent and dead as an empty shell. Drew, as if cradling James, leans forward and tilts his head to one side to admire his baby, listening for a heartbeat. Then, he feels for a pulse in an imaginary neck and wrist.

'Nothing. Nothing. Nothing.'

She thinks Drew's body looks shipwrecked. The tide has come in and taken his reason away. He is a hull on the bottom of the seabed. With light fingertips, he makes to close James's imaginary eyelids and strokes his imaginary hair so gently, and with so much love, it should bring James back to life if there was any goodness left in the world.

Crying with jerking spasms, he hugs himself, still standing in the middle of the room. An actor in the warped theatre of his mind. She winces when he drops to the floor. His body is slumped at an angle and she cannot console him, touch him. One arm, like a rag doll's, remains limp underneath him.

'My baby boy. I'm so sorry. My baby boy!'

Snot runs down his face and his cheeks shine with tears. How pitiful he looks, wearing stained tracksuit bottoms and one flat brown shoe.

Suddenly, he crawls into a ball and bangs his head on the carpet over and over. He is breathing hard. When he puts one hand to his brow, she finds the gesture unspeakably touching.

'Drew?' She shivers, frightened for herself, and for him. He is so horribly uncomfortable inside his own skin, his own head.

Drew uncurls his body and stands up tall, with one hand on the wall. He looks around the room like he hasn't seen it before and staggers out of the lounge.

Emma-Jane stares at the carpet. And there it is . . .

In all his movements, Drew has accidentally dropped the keyring holding the key to her cuffs within inches of her feet. She could escape. The fear, the control, would end. And so would their closeness.

She hears the interior door to the kitchen fly open and Drew's feet ascending the stairs—at surprising speed, for a drunken man. The room has never felt hotter. She hears him play a game of something upstairs, perhaps hide and seek, or snakes and ladders, only it sounds like there are too many snakes and not enough ladders.

'James! I'm coming! It's Daddy! I'm here for you!'

His torment reverberates around the house. The shouting and running beat a tuneless sound above her head. She has to get away, get help, for her and for him.

The key is right bloody there.

*Run.*

As usual, the radio is left on in the kitchen on low. He likes to untune it, leaving them to listen to loud crackles and sizzles, like she's in space and losing contact with ground control. Perhaps it echoes the sounds in his brain?

'Here I come!'

His world is spilling out upstairs, like a party popper pulled in two. She imagines the inside of his mind, where white doves fall, covered in soot. The flute of Evie's voice or the harp of his son's is all he hears. He runs along the landing, trying to catch the words in nets, like moths and butterflies, to preserve them behind glass.

*Save yourself. Save yourself,* she chants, willing herself to find the strength to act. To leave.

She lifts one leg and turns her foot at a ninety-degree angle. The key is only millimetres away. She flexes her foot backwards and forwards, then makes little circles with it to loosen the muscles. The sound of Drew crying disrupts her movements and thoughts.

*Focus on yourself. Remember, Drew's peace of mind flickers on and off like a light switch. The gentle, calm Drew who feeds you, pours cool water into your mouth, is invisible, and only a red outline of rage and a silhouette of grief are left.*

Her foot reaches the keyring, and she drags it— slowly, slowly, catchy monkey—towards her. It is hers, but she has no way of picking it up and using the key to unlock the handcuffs unless she can fall forwards. She pushes it under one shoe.

The slightest movement brings a fresh burst of perspiration to her forehead and upper lip. Whether Drew enjoys living in a tropical house or the radiators are broken and can't be switched off, she's not sure, but in weak moments she's let herself think about how a cool breeze on her skin feels, how it would move through her hair in waves and ruffle her clothes. He mustn't see signs of effort on her face should he return.

'I can't find you, James!' His voice cracks. 'Where are you, James? It's Daddy! I'm here now. I am.'

Drew is laughing and giggling one minute then crying hysterically the next, at the mercy of the broken synapses in his brain. Upstairs, doors creak open and then close. Some are banged shut.

Drew's anger, back again.

He runs down the stairs and she braces herself. Drew is in the kitchen. He opens the front door. He is walking around the house. She imagines him out there, moving around, like a lost plastic bag in the wind. Alone in his own absence.

Moments later, the door slams, and Drew's malignant presence fills the lounge. He is ashen. It looks like he's aged ten years in less than ten minutes. He continually runs one hand through his hair, the other at his collar, which is now open and gaping. The sweat stains under his armpits are almost down to his waist. The buttons on his cuffs have come off, so they gape and flap.

'It was so real. James was here.'

Emma-Jane doesn't answer at first. Part of her wants to reach for his hand and help tether him to reality. But when she moves her hand, the metal click of the cuffs makes her decide against that. She feels herself balancing on a tightrope of saving herself or pushing Drew over the edge, sticking one finger at a time through the lacework of his mind.

'It's over now,' she whispers.

'No,' he wails. 'It's not. She killed James out of spite! How could she do that?' Saliva dribbles from his mouth as it opens and closes. 'I want to dig up his little body and hold him in my arms and stroke his hair. His poor little throat.' He touches his neck where he imagines the rope and the ligature marks would have been. 'Evie knew I didn't love her. I didn't even like her. Why would I care if she starved herself? James, though!' He moans. 'Poor James.' His voice croaks. 'I never thought she'd do what she did.'

'Did you hurt Evie?'

'Yes, I hurt her.' He snaps. 'By screwing other women. I didn't bother hiding it. Why pretend?'

He removes a camera from his rucksack and looks at it like a child holding a new toy in their hands, feeling its weight, absorbing its colour and shape. 'This is hers.' The black strap dangles in the air like it's looking for its owner. It's lost its muscle memory; its owner isn't alive to hold it.

'Smile,' he orders.

Emma-Jane spits at him. He grabs her face and forces it into a smile.

Suddenly, he lobs the camera through the window. Crash! It takes the curtain out into the fresh air through the smashed glass. She screams.

Was there something in her smile that sent him over the edge? Or was it something else he'd seen through the lens?

Most of the smashed glass is outside, but some splinters on the carpet catch the light when the curtain billows. The movement of air is like a person coming back to life, like a broken bird growing new wings, fresh feathers. That movement, a fresh flutter. It's so difficult not to watch it ripple; *as fresh as water*, she thinks. The sound of ravishing wind comes, the rustle of fabric.

Freedom.

'Fucking hell!'

He kicks her chair, picks up the porcelain fruit bowl, and smashes it against the wall like the breaking of difficult words into single letters. His gnashing eyeballs look for something else to break.

A single shard of glass, shaped like a teardrop, catches her attention. Her chair wobbles slightly, so she steadies it with her planted feet.

Emma-Jane opens her mouth and closes her eyes to feel the breeze finger her face and hair. She could shout or scream and someone might hear, now that the window is broken. The world outside takes a step closer, peeks in. It comes to life, like a magic mirror inviting her into another dimension. Soon, she will step through the looking glass. She will. How merciful of his rage to take out the leg of her chair.

She waits as his anger burns and his wild, carnivorous eyes search the room for more opportunities of menace. Not seeing any suitable prey, he flies into the kitchen, opens and slams cupboard doors, throws a saucepan, kicks the door.

'Bastard! You fuck—'

The glass from the broken window twinkles and winks on the carpet. The hole the camera left is a bit small, but she can smell freedom beyond. The shards of glass remind her of the letter he'd sent to her, telling her she would shatter into tiny pieces of glass. The curtain flutters and the breeze licks her neck. She leans forwards and the broken chair topples over, winding her and squashing her face against the carpet.

Plates continue to smash in the kitchen as she uses the keys to unlock the wrist and ankle cuffs. The click is painstakingly quiet and beautiful.

She turns, takes a deep breath. Then, there is an ear-splitting shattering of glass as she throws the chair and then herself through the window.

The shock of being outside brings her to.

*Air! Sky!*

She quickly gets up from the ground and runs along a plain road lined with trees. In her wake, she leaves two peculiar objects: an old, broken kitchen chair and a camera, its long, black strap coiled like a serpent. The sky is vast and wide above, and even the trees look strange and threatening.

Emma-Jane runs as fast as she can in the direction she thinks leads to a main road, where a faint hum of traffic gives her hope. She is oblivious to the bleeding cuts on her face, limbs, and hands.

'Help!' she shouts breathlessly as she runs and staggers. 'Help me!'

When she sees the first vehicle, she waves wildly at it, but they accelerate away. A second, blue car slows down and the face behind the wheel gradually comes into focus.

Familiar.

'Stop! Please! Help!' she screams, still running, now on the main road, prepared to stay in the middle of it if she has to, to make the car stop. Her patchy bleached hair and filthy clothes work better than any stop sign. 'Help!'

The blue car comes to a halt and Lucy gets out.

'Bloody hell!'

She opens her arms, just in time for Emma-Jane to collapse into them.

# 28

'Turn back!' Emma-Jane shrieks as she stares out of the back window.

Blood drips down onto her nose from a cut on her forehead. When it reaches her mouth, she licks it and swallows the copper taste without flinching.

'Lucy!' she shouts again. 'Did you hear me? Turn around! Go back to Drew's house! Now!'

Lucy speeds up as her now bleached blonde friend sobs unconsolably. The woman is a wild animal, released from its cage, violent and scared.

'Now! I mean it!'

'Emma-Jane! For God's sake!' Lucy child-locks the doors.

Emma-Jane flares the whole way home. A human firework, sparks flying, spraying the windows and roof. The plastic bag Kat had given Lucy is now on the back seat, sliding from one end to the other as she swerves bends in the road at speed, her nerves tight as a wire.

'Calm down. You're safe now.'

'Listen. Go back!'

Something plastic drops into the footwell. Drew's shower gel, perhaps.

'No.'

The air freshener dangling from the rear-view mirror suddenly irritates Emma-Jane for some reason, and she yanks it down and tosses it onto the floor. Lucy doesn't pull over until they are outside Emma-Jane's house.

'You have to go back to help him! He's sick, Lucy. Drew! He can't be left there alone. He's not well!' she wails.

'I will get help, but first we are going inside your house.' Lucy stares at her friend in horror, still unable to find the right words at this vision of savagery. 'It's important you listen to me.'

Emma-Jane's head drops. The adrenaline has got her this far. Now shock, pain, and exhaustion are taking hold.

'I'll get the spare key and let us in.'

Inside, the house is cool and unaired and there is so much space and light around Emma-Jane that she is disorientated for a moment. Her gaze travels from one wall to another, from floor to ceiling.

'You're home now.'

She collapses onto the bottom stair in the hall and wipes her face, like a child with a runny nose. Blood stains her hand and creased blouse. It trickles down her neck and between her cleavage as she sobs and gasps. Lucy puts a hand on Emma-Jane's shoulder. The weeping goes on uncontrollably until she is gasping for breath.

'It's over now,' Lucy says in little more than a whisper. She is surprised by the motherly instincts she feels towards another adult, but the childlike behaviour of her dear friend demands it. Somehow, she knows that intuitively. 'I've been looking for you for days. I need to make a few phone calls so that people know you are alright. I need you to stay here while I do that. I'll get you a glass of water and tissues. Please, just stay here.'

She runs into the kitchen and returns moments later, afraid her friend will disappear again. While Emma-Jane wipes her face, Lucy puts the chain on the front door, making it more difficult to escape. It feels like a bizarre action in her friend's home, but very little has been ordinary or predictable for quite some time.

She's spent the last few days driving around housing estates near every Co-op in the vicinity. Thank goodness she hadn't given up. The Co-op only 400 metres from where she'd found Emma-Jane was the second to last on her list, and her hope had been fading.

From her pocket, Lucy removes her phone.

'Who are you ringing? I'm fine,' Emma-Jane says, wiping her eyes. 'It's Drew who needs help.'

'Has he hurt you? Touched you?'

'It wasn't like that!' Emma-Jane yells, her hands twisting her blouse. Her eyes fall on Lucy like a cold sun. 'No! He's not a monster! Please, just send a doctor round there for him. Quickly.'

'A doctor? You have to mean the police!'

'A doctor, Lucy! He hasn't got much time!'

Lucy goes into the kitchen and calls the police and a local doctor. She locks the back door and hides the key in her jeans, stroking its shape in disbelief that she is doing this.

Emma-Jane's home is carpeted, so it cushions footsteps like the soft pink pads on a cat's paw. It is a sanctuary, decorated throughout in neutral tones of beige or white without stain, chosen windows wearing white wooden horizontal blinds. Sunlight peeks through the slats as if the sun is tilting its head and peering inside at the spectacle.

The sky out there is flawless, but it shouldn't be. It should be dark and windy. The rain should deluge the streets and the wind should wreak havoc. Buildings should be uniformly covered in black and white newspaper print, reporting the crime of abduction and ... What else? Lucy doesn't know, but every fibre in her body tells her there is a great deal of small print to get to.

She returns to the hall with a mug of black sweet tea and a warm full-length coat from the hall to drape over Emma-Jane. It's wool, one of the coats she wears for work.

'He told me about what happened to his wife and child. Listening to Drew talk about Evie and James—and being with him—I started to feel differently.'

'What do you mean?' Lucy asks, sharply. 'You know she killed herself and her son, don't you?'

'I know that now. I failed him.'

'How can you fail someone who keeps secrets? He pretended to be someone he's not, to you and me. Oh my God. Has he given you drugs?'

'No.' Emma-Jane pulls up her legs to her chest, her torso leant forward to cuddle herself. The childlike behaviour calms Lucy's frustration.

'Did something happen between you two?'

'That depends on what you mean. Did he frighten me? Did he strap me to a chair and make me shit and piss myself? Did he leave me alone for hours in the stifling heat, not knowing if he was coming back or whether I was going to die of thirst or starvation? Yes, those things happened, and yet, eventually I wanted him to touch me. I wanted to be found too, but—'

'I can't believe what I'm hearing.' The shock of this eclipses everything: all the worry, the trek in the dark, the fear. 'We need to get you to a doctor. Never mind him.'

'When he got angry, he didn't slam his fist into me, but at the door or a wall. This isn't for the police. It's between Drew and me.'

'You have to report him. If he wasn't dangerous, you wouldn't have jumped through a bloody window to escape! Have you seen your cuts? You have been through a terrible ordeal, Emma-Jane. Please, just let us take care of things.'

Emma-Jane slowly gets up from the stair and looks at her reflection in the mirror. 'Can you get me a wet cloth, or a wet wipe, something to clean this blood off?'

By the time Lucy returns with a wet towel, Emma-Jane is wearing burgundy lipstick. With dyed blonde hair, she looks like a vampire. She has sprayed on perfume and has brushed her straw-like hair.

'Let me do it,' Lucy says, taking over gently cleaning the cuts and gashes on Emma-Jane's face and hands. 'You're shaking.'

Together, they look at their reflections. Is the tautness in Emma-Jane's expression a hint at the silver barbed wire around the red muscle of her heart? Same clothes, same shoes. The elasticity of her skin seems to have gone because she stares, unblinking.

Blank.

# 29

When the door opens to Drew's room in Brayley Psychiatric Hospital, he doesn't need to look up to know who it is. He can smell her.

Reclining in the soft chair, *The Daily Telegraph* in his lap, he sees red in his peripheral vision. Red hair, a red top. He knows there is a red sports car parked outside.

Kat.

'I wasn't expecting to see you here,' Drew says with a sideways glance. It seems like the temperature of the room rises. When her strong perfume reaches him again, he eyes her with suspicion and shifts in his seat.

'You weren't expecting to see me, full stop.' Kat says with a smile, then gestures to the broadsheet newspaper. 'You didn't make it to the nationals, but you've been in the local paper, though.'

'Oh, I see. So, you've heard and tracked me down. Bravo. What brings you here, Kat? I'm assuming it's not to talk about the local economy. But I'm afraid this place isn't doing a lot for my libido.'

'I missed you,' she says. 'I'm twenty next week. Did it slip your mind?'

'Happy birthday,' he says sarcastically.

'Silly me. I should have brought grapes and a "get well" card for the sick man.'

'Not really. Here I am, still alive and kicking. What do you want? Money? A roof over your head?'

'There's no need to be nasty. Play nice. You kicked me

out of my place to make your money, but now I have a new base for Stan. Thanks for asking.'

'I didn't.'

'Well, I'm glad you are alive. "Alive and kicking" as you put it, with your neck fully intact at least.' She steps back from his chair, sensing his intense hostility. She perches on the side of the bed and crosses her legs. One ankle boot patterned in leopard skin flicks up and down, like she's counting to a beat before moving closer still to her kill. 'Nice room,' she comments, looking around like she's in a hotel suite with a punter for a night of sex and champagne. 'Very minimalist.'

'Is interior décor a strength of yours?' Drew picks up the newspaper again. 'I hadn't thought so, somehow.'

'Look, you've made it clear you don't want to see me, but I want to know before I head off for good if AJ gave you the letter. The letter I took all that trouble to write? Best handwriting and everything. You were never at home, never answered my calls. I had no choice but to give it to that bloke. That's why I'm here.'

'No, he didn't give your letter to me. I'm a bit old for love letters with kisses and cursive hearts.' He sneers. 'He mentioned it, though. Why?'

'I thought as much.' Her eyes flash with intense fury. 'When AJ was round at my place fixing that new shower, he told me you were completely in love with me, that I was unlike anyone you'd ever met, and that you were going to leave Evie for me—you were just waiting for the right moment. I went round to see Evie; I know, it was wrong of me, but I was fired up. Jealous, I suppose, so I went round there to the farmhouse.'

He looks at her now, like he's seeing her for the very first time. The sight of her is a siren sounding in his head.

'You spoke to Evie?' he manages through clenched teeth.

She nods, trying to snare him in her gaze.

A shiver works its way down his spine, all the way to his toes.

'Yeah. It surprised me that she invited me in. We stood in that lovely farmhouse kitchen of yours with that huge table and the Aga. I could see myself there, I thought. It wasn't long after lunch; she was washing up, and she'd taken her engagement and wedding rings off. Your son had thrown tomato pasta all over the floor. That's when I told her you were going to leave her for me.'

His face pales.

She stares at him, saying nothing, her nostrils flared like she's smelling him. Tears prickle in the corner of his eyes. He senses her waiting, watching. The blow of her words makes him crumple a little into the chair of the mental hospital he's a captive in.

Eventually, he collects himself, puts the newspaper on the floor beside him, and meets her gaze like a silent collision.

'And you're here to gloat?'

'No,' she says, putting a hand on her hip. 'I thought you should know, that's all. We were fuck buddies for quite a while and, in my book, I thought I owed it to you.'

'When was this? When did you go round to the farmhouse, Kat?'

'The same day she . . .'

He puts his head in his hands. 'Oh my God.'

'It's AJ's fault,' she interrupts. 'He convinced me I was something special to you, so I was just moving things along.'

'Moving things . . . Jesus Christ.' He stares at her,

crushed, unable to find the words. He stammers. 'Within hours of your visit, Evie and my son were hanging from a tree.'

'I didn't know she'd do that! She just stood there when I told her. Her face didn't change or anything; it was weird how she didn't react. I told her to pack her things. She just stood there, and then James came running in and she came back to life. Whisked him into her arms, like I was going to steal him.' She shakes her head. 'It annoyed me, seeing her do that. So, I said that James would stay with you and me.'

She looks at Drew, waiting for a reaction.

'She kicked me out then. Screamed at me. It was funny, really, after her being so calm before.'

'You are poison, Kat. As venomous as that stupid snake of yours.'

'Stan isn't venomous, you fool.'

A coldness creeps over him as she shrugs. His anger inflates. The trance-like state is replaced with white knuckles and a look of revulsion as she reaches for his arm and lightly squeezes it, her nails painted in that signature red.

'I know you well enough to think you aren't here to say sorry or to pass on your condolences,' he growls. 'Say what you've got to say, then get the fuck away from me. For good. Before I fucking kill you.'

She rolls her eyes. 'No, I'm not here to say sorry. You can thank me for telling the truth,' she says, swishing her hair. 'Besides, I didn't know the woman, did I? I'm here because of AJ. I did what I did because of him. Because of the lie he told me. I don't enjoy being played by a little prick like him.' She smiles. 'Do you want me to get even with him before I leave this place? He could find a snake in his van. Or are you going to see to him?'

'Leave him to me,' he says bitterly. 'You've done plenty.'

'You're stuck in this place,' she says with hardened eyes. 'I'm not.'

'I won't be in here forever. I'll get even with AJ. You can be sure of that.'

'If you say so, but you'd better do a good job of it, or I'll finish him off. The rat. I don't like his game.' She rolls her eyes. 'You look like a beaten dog. I almost feel sorry for you.' She opens her arms, expecting a hug.

'Get the fuck out, Kat.'

'It's your loss,' she replies, and flicks her hair in the face of his agony. 'Do you want a blanket? You look like you're cold. Very cold . . . and old.'

His voice is little more than a whisper. 'Get away from me before I do something I regret.'

Her laughter travels down the corridor long after the door is slammed. It pierces his eardrums. He imagines her animal eyes heading towards the exit, a smile on that red, dirty mouth of hers, home to a pierced tongue—the sexiest, most despicable woman he has ever seen lick and bite his dick.

He puts his hands over his groin, ashamed now, and thankful she hadn't eaten him alive.

*Poor Evie. Poor, poor Evie. She didn't stand a chance.*

After she has gone, Drew touches his head, expecting his hair to be standing on end. From under his mattress, he removes the pen knife. His hands shake. Shivering, he makes it out of the chair and into the privacy of the bathroom, where cutting for contrition is his only release, until he is a free man.

Until he can get to AJ.

His only wish is that he never sees Kat again, for as long as he is lucky enough to live.

# 30

'Are you here?' Lucy calls from the bottom of the stairs, presumably because she expects Emma-Jane to be in bed, like a sick patient.

Lucy must have kept the spare key to Emma-Jane's house when she had been here two days ago, because she let herself in. It's not exactly uninvited, but it still feels a little like an invasion.

'I'm in the lounge.' Emma-Jane sighs, knowing Lucy wants to discuss bringing charges against Drew, which she resolutely refuses to do.

*Please don't ask me how I am. If one more person does, I will scream!*

'How are you?' Lucy asks cheerfully, plonking herself and a Tesco bag on the sofa.

'I'm fine.'

Lucy leans forward to take a better look at her. 'Your hair looks great. And you look more rested. I bought us some cakes and a few other things I thought you might need. Just milk and stuff.'

'I can walk to the shops, you know. I'm not an invalid.'

'How are the cuts healing up?'

Emma-Jane self-consciously touches her face. Her leap through the window has left its temporary mark on her face and limbs. Nothing which won't heal soon, though.

'Still looks sore,' Lucy says. 'Have the police been back in touch?'

'No, they're satisfied I've told them everything they need to know.'

Lucy bristles. 'How did you explain throwing yourself through a window if you weren't in danger?'

'Everyone has a temper. It was a one-off argument, understandable . . . They've got far more serious cases to deal with.'

'So, no charges. They're not pursuing it?'

'No.' Emma-Jane looks at her friend and smiles. 'I'm fine. Everything is fine. Please, stop worrying about me. Drew is in a mental hospital, getting the care and attention he needs. I'm at home and have no immediate plans to go into the office.'

'That's something, I suppose.'

She breathes a deep sigh of relief that Lucy has stopped pressing the matter. She hopes Lucy's perpetual and well-meaning inquiries about her health, her sleeping habits, her appetite, will be truly over. In a short space of solicitude, she has consumed a lot of sweet tea with friends and colleagues. She has telephoned clients to reassure them that she is fine.

*Everything is bloody fine.*

Drew is fine too, as far as the word goes—safe, at least—and in a place where he can get better. There is so much she can tell no one, and barely accepts herself.

Is it in a casket, a coffin, a safe where she must lock away what she feels for her captor?

Some details of the traumatic event have changed in her memory. Not Drew's face, his quiet aura, his cool look, the lounge in that house, or the hours spent staring at that curtained window. Some details in the short-term memory get lost, others added. But then, trauma and memory coagulate like egg whites over heat. Memory is the wooden spoon in a mixing bowl of cake batter, choosing what it clings to and what it leaves around the rim.

If she were asked to describe Drew to a police sketch artist, the details she recalls—the curve of his lips, the shape of his eyebrows, the fan of his dark eyelashes— might betray her. The memory of him makes her want to hop into her car and drive at speed with the windows down. She needs air, the sound of tyres on gravel. She feels self-conscious just thinking his name.

'Do you fancy an éclair or some kind of cupcake?'

'Mmm. Cupcake, please.'

'I'll make us a brew.'

'No, stay there. I'll do it. Make yourself at home.'

Earlier, an enormous bouquet of flowers had been delivered to Emma-Jane and the signature on the card was simply *D*. Beneath it, a date, which she assumes is his release date. Anticipating Lucy's arrival, she put the beautiful flowers in her bedroom, out of sight.

Returning to the lounge with two mugs of tea, she finds Lucy has eaten her cake and is already on her second slice.

'Are you stress-eating?'

'No.' She gives Emma-Jane a sideways glance. 'Well, I might be. I do have something I want to tell you.'

'Okay, fire away.' Emma-Jane takes a sip of tea. A memory of Drew holding a water bottle to her lips returns.

Once, he'd caressed her cheek with a finger as she drank. The memory of that touch, so rare and delicate and so pleasant, catches her unaware. She knows pieces of her have been lost. The fragments are stitched together with alcohol, hope, distraction, make-up. Drew is a thief who has stolen parts of her that haven't been returned. Will they ever be? *But that doesn't make him bad,* she thinks, and blushes at the guilty thoughts when her friend is in the same room.

'Listen, it's not just because of Drew, but I'm thinking about returning to Carlisle. I love it up there, and my parents are getting on.'

Emma-Jane stares at her mug of tea.

'What happened with Ross and Jennifer really shattered my confidence. I need to get more experience working for someone else before I run my own business. When you weren't there and Vanessa turned up and read her stories, I'd never felt so helpless. Even before that, I never felt in control of my work with Jennifer.'

'I'm sorry that happened. In every way,' says Emma-Jane. 'You know what happened to Ross has nothing to do with you, don't you? I can understand why it's troubling, early on in your career, but don't let it derail your plans. I could blame myself for Vanessa's suicide, for not being there when she needed me, but that won't change what happened.'

'If anyone is to blame for Vanessa's death, it's Drew. You would have been there if he hadn't—'

'Don't,' she says, her voice clogged with sadness. 'It can't be undone.'

'You are not thinking right, Emma-Jane. I won't waste my breath telling you to report Drew. Your mind isn't sending the right signals to your brain. I have no idea what you've been through, but I went through a fair amount of shit myself with Ross dying, and then being stuck in the arse end of nowhere with no one to help me, and then Vanessa desperately needing you, and—'

'I don't—'

Lucy gives her a hard stare. 'Mate, you're not getting it.'

'I am. I'm listening.'

'Yeah, but you're not understanding! I was out there in the middle of fucking nowhere sitting under Sycamore Gap with a dead mobile and no food or water for hours, and no one could save me except me. The only thing that motivated me to get to my car safely was fear for your safety.'

'We've both suffered in different ways. Is this a contest?'

'Of course not. All I know is that adjusting is difficult, and you have come back home a different person than you were. Just, maybe, you're affected by what happened more than you realise. I mean, have you seen your supervisor, Celia, lately?'

'We have chatted on the phone and Zoomed.'

'I mean, have you seen her in person? Please, for me! I think Celia can help you work through a few things. You need help! You can't expect to just carry on as normal, as if nothing has happened.'

'It is still me! I am well, and I want to move on with my life. You talk like I'm sick and I have just been discharged from hospital. I don't need help and I don't appreciate being told what to do! Please, let me heal in my own way and in my own time.'

'I didn't want the conversation to go this way,' Lucy says morosely.

Emma-Jane looks at her friend sadly. The thought of not working side-by-side with Lucy fills her with a strange mixture of relief and disappointment. They have shared so much laughter and mutual interest.

But people change.

'Me neither. I'm so grateful for you helping me. Thank you. I mean it. You were there when I needed you most.'

Lucy takes a deep breath. 'So, enough gratitude. How do you feel about getting back to work?'

Glad to be on safe territory, Emma-Jane makes herself more comfortable on the sofa. 'I've been thinking about that. I'll be better as a therapist than I was before.'

Lucy raises her eyebrows.

'I used to treat clients suffering with trauma. I can hear myself use the word "trauma", like *"losing a loved one so suddenly is traumatic . . ."*. It was a noun plucked from a textbook, a diagnostic term, a word from a dictionary. Not anymore. I used to say surviving trauma is to live with a violated self, but it's so much more. The trauma recycles. It's a different animal from the original beast, one which mutates, and keeps on changing.'

'Is that because of *your* trauma?' Lucy asks gingerly. 'Is this post-traumatic stress disorder?'

'My trauma, yes—and Drew's. The thing is that, after the trauma, there's rarely anything visible to explain the irrational behaviour.'

'What do you mean?'

'Imagine you feel fear. When you see a killer beast in the same room, the fear is explained, justified. It's "normalised." But what if the fear is there, but the killer beast isn't?'

'I see.'

'With trauma, there's nothing and no one to run away from. A door bangs. A rumble of thunder. Heavy rain tapping on a window. These ordinary things can turn the most intelligent, educated adult into a child afraid of a monster. So, what do you think they do?'

'They take it out on somebody else. The very person who was trying to help them.'

'Exactly,' Emma-Jane says. 'And now I understand why.'

'But that doesn't justify what Drew did to you.'

'No,' she says quietly.

Night-time darkness, which tells your body clock to go to bed, used to be a familiar velvet comfort, enjoyed under a duvet. It's morphed since spending countless hours with Drew into lonely hours in the groin of night. For a time, their proximity on that single mattress had been like a hand over her mouth, but after a while, the softness and scent of him around her had eased her into sweet sleep.

Last night, Emma-Jane had slept with the light on. Despite the warmth, the light, the soft mattress, her eyes moved from left to right and up and down, her skin prickled, and her thoughts tripped over themselves. She saw everything was normal. Normal, except for her, in the bed, under the covers, trembling, a different person to who she was before because she slept soundly beside a madman. Stirred by the muffled whispers in his sleep and waking to his voice in the morning.

To his breath on her neck

But Lucy can't know these things.

As soon as Lucy has gone, Emma-Jane takes a large bite out of a peach and relishes its soft flesh and juice. With sticky fingers, she wolfs the peach and immediately starts on a second one. Then a third. After the fourth stone rolls towards her on the floor, she stops eating, spits a mouthful into the palm of her hand and stares at it, seeing Drew's mutilated flesh. She sees his and her failure in the torn flesh, the bite-marks, the sticky mess on her fingers. In the quiet digestion in the pit of her stomach, she hears Drew's voice wanting a piece of her to fill the emptiness.

The hunger pangs.

A noose of light.

The voice of her education answers when she disposes of the stones and washes her hands; it knows that the fissure in her eating habits isn't healthy. It isn't just that her appetite is returning, flourishing. Even her hair is back to its original colour.

And yet, how can she still feel this obsession for Drew? The question returns again and again, only bigger each time, like a Russian doll.

Lucy calls him a monster, but that means Emma-Jane's mind belongs to one. It is a monstrous obsession fed by everything, and she will not have her stomach stapled or deny herself a moment longer.

She wants her fill of him.

Every inch of his skin, his every word a morsel to be savoured.

*I know what I have to do.*

# 31

She took pains to dress in a new silk blouse, tailored trousers, and a suede jacket. Pains to style her luscious black hair.

The mirror in the hall greets her favourably, it seems, as she applies plum lipstick. The cuts to her face and hands have healed nicely. It's nine-fifteen, and she would normally be at the office by now. At least she isn't still in her dressing gown. At least she is taking control. Doing something to feel better. To define day from night, night from day. There's no need to feel such a failure. At one time, her name frosted on the door and piles of neatly arrange paperwork would have given her all the self-assurance she needed.

It hadn't been possible to eat a decent breakfast. She had stared into a cup of tea, still stirring, stirring—even though she had forgotten to add sugar. She stirred for so long the tea went cold. A little later, a pang of hunger hit. She made a plate of toast and raspberry jam, but only ate one bite.

Today, she is seeing Drew. A victim wouldn't choose to do that. Only a woman in control. A woman who knows her own mind.

It will most likely be one of those days with no end, which means tomorrow will be dream-like, hazy, and she won't remember very much. Perhaps it's a good thing to not sleep well at night. Tiredness is a version of numbness that will help her through the meeting. She checks herself in the hall mirror again. She looks healthy, almost pretty.

*Am I behaving as I should?*

She checks her actions as often as her appearance, no longer sure of either. The truth of her obsession with helping Drew clings to her like wet clothes. How can she have feelings for her captor, a patient in an acute psychiatric ward who has been sectioned under the Mental Health Act? Other men have shown her their vulnerable side, so why is Drew different? She touches her ear lobe and tilts her face to one side, then cups it in one hand. The surge of emotion with tears pricking her eyes comes as a shock.

She slaps herself across the face. Hard. Pain sears across her cheek, stamped in her own handprint.

She heads out through the front door and climbs into the Golf, immediately checking her appearance again in the rear-view mirror.

*He frightened me, he made me squirm and suffer, yet I felt more than compassion when he shared his story with me. Understanding. Pity. Never dislike. When he touched my hand or curled his body around mine at night, I didn't recoil.*

*I enjoyed living with a madman. So, what does that make me?*

Neither the situation nor her thoughts make sense to her. If she were driving through this moment, her windscreen wipers would be on full. The radio would be switched on, but the music would be drowned out by the torrential rain on the roof of the car and slapping the glass. She would keep driving at a slow speed—thirty, twenty, then ten miles an hour—a little afraid of what was discernible in the headlights. Disorientated, she would pull over, park up. Sit and wait for the storm to be over.

Thinking. Too much.

It is time to catch hold of her thoughts and feelings

so she can look them in the eye, define them. Words and phrases from the time of her captivity circulate on repeat. Her words, and his. The track is getting scratched. Repetitive.

*'Ruminating' is the term*, she tells herself, like she should know better, as she pulls the Golf onto the road.

She thinks about Lucy and her words of warning as she drives towards the hospital. The rift between them is something sharp and new; never before has there been an undercurrent of secrets and bitterness. Shouldn't she be driving to see Lucy, instead, to sort out their differences?

At some point during the journey a decision was made. She parks outside the hospital, walks into reception to sign in, then through the double doors and into his private room.

'You look well,' Drew says, like he's greeting her in the French Riviera and about to air kiss both her cheeks. 'Your hair—black again.'

'I am well,' she says, lost for words.

'Your perfume—is it different?'

'Yes,' she says, unsure of where to sit in the pristine room. Its furniture consists of a bed, chair, and a desk. He pulls the stool over for her. She leans towards him. He's clean-shaven, pale. 'It's called Poison.'

His eyebrows move upwards. It is a faint but unmistakable gesture that his senses are working. Whatever medication they have given him, he still smells, hears, sees, perhaps feels.

'I've been thinking about you,' he says, hunger in his dark, wolfish eyes. Or is it hatred? 'About very little else, to be honest, as weak as that sounds.'

'Weak?'

'I've been starving for you, Dr Glass.'

'For me?'

'Starving for your guidance. Our conversations. There's nothing I wanted more than to see you.'

'How are you?'

'Bored. Restless.' Suddenly his look is appraising. 'You haven't come here to tell me what to do, I hope?'

She shakes her head.

'Good.'

'I came to thank you for the flowers.'

'How were they?'

'Oh, beautiful. Unexpected, so thank you.'

'Are they on the kitchen windowsill?'

She frowns.

'I know your house. You do know I liked watching you. I mean, not just in that house, but before. Leaving you those letters. Choosing my moment, seeing you through your kitchen window, it was so intimate. I saw you, and I saw the ghost of my wife and son, too.'

He smiles at her and some of the tension in the room fades.

'All this glass . . . It's only what I deserve. Here I am. My lack of transparency. Locked away behind glass windows and doors. A nice twist of irony, don't you think, Dr Glass? This is all your doing.'

'My doing? No. But the glass . . . It's for your own safety.'

'Glass,' he continues wistfully. 'Glass in the morning, afternoon, and evening. What chance do I have to forget you?'

'You can rest here, get stronger.'

'I've missed you,' he says, lightly touching her arm. She pulls away. 'I don't understand my own feelings. Tell me what you've been doing. Please.'

He smiles and shifts his tense shoulders. The austere personality of the place pales for a moment in those gestures. She flicks her black, shoulder-length hair over one shoulder.

'My hair had some TLC at my regular hairdressers, and I've been shopping. A few new clothes to fit my frame. I've been trying to make the most of my free time before returning to work. I have clients who need to see me, who won't accept my referrals. The office is being painted—a facelift—so it's a natural break. Time to recharge before getting back into the chair, so to speak.'

'Like New Year's Eve,' he says bitterly. 'Starting afresh. Out with the old and—'

'In with the new,' she says with a smile. 'You know how much my work means to me.'

'I do.'

'Have you had many visitors lately, to keep you company?'

'An associate of AJ's, someone who works for me, came to see me. You may remember AJ phoning me a few times. There's some business or other to take care of.' He looks down, as if seeing a smashed object on the floor. Seeing fragments of something she doesn't understand.

'It's good to keep your mind occupied while you receive your treatment, Drew. It won't be for that long in the grand scheme of things if you make the progress that's expected. Perhaps we could discuss using hypnosis once you're ready?'

He shakes his head and his eyes flash in anger.

'You won't be controlling my mind.'

A turn in mood, a sudden transformation from a domestic into a wildcat. It takes her back to captivity, to the times thunder boomed in his brain and she felt fear, brittle and sharp, to the periods of sobriety and reflection, when there was a rainbow hanging in the room.

'So, I will see you again when I'm out of this place by your own choice?' he asks, looking straight into her eyes. She nods. 'I have harsh critics, Dr Glass, and I need to prove to them that I am safe outside. If I do, in a month they'll let me go. Unless, of course, you change your mind and press charges.'

'I won't do that, but a month is too soon to leave the hospital.'

'I'm sorry?'

She puts her hand up to signal there's no need to say any more. 'You must toe the line here, Drew. Please. Engage with the therapy. Be kind to yourself. I want you to get better. I mean that sincerely, because—'

'Because?'

'I'm your therapist.'

He lowers his head. She sees from the movement of his Adam's apple that he is conflicted. The edges of his face, the pencil-drawn lines of his cheekbones, nose, and forehead almost soften.

'You're a remarkable woman,' he says, leaning forward, making her aware of the rustling of his clean shirt. 'Emma-Jane.'

'Dr Glass,' she corrects him. 'But no. Ordinary. A very ordinary woman who wants to help someone who isn't well, someone who was a good father to his son.'

'We aren't talking about my boy. You and me, that's what we're talking about. I feel something, and I think you do too. My farmhouse is sold, so I will live at the house we stayed in. Perhaps you'll visit me there, by choice this time?'

An image of the chair facing the curtained window

flashes before her. She recalls the longing she'd felt for him to pour water into her mouth, to feel the wetness dribbling down her chin and down her blouse, marking the contours of her breasts.

'I want to help you, and I will.'

'You said that once before.'

'But you need to spend longer here before stepping outside these walls and engaging in therapy with me.'

'Are you saying I need to stay here because you're afraid of me?'

She smiles warmly. 'You hurt me, abused me, but I am well and healthy. Those terrible things you did to me don't change the fact that I want to help you.'

'You know me better than anyone, as I do you.' He grins like the devil. 'I know you, Dr Glass.'

She knows it's true, and the thought frightens her.

She makes a swift exit from the hospital, glad to be back in her car and with a seat belt on. The leather steering wheel is firm and secure in her hands.

*I know you.*

---

As she drives to Corbet Hill, the road narrows and the hedges grow tall and thick, until she finds a lay-by to pull into and parks at a spot with a wonderful view of Shropshire and into Wales.

At one time, she had never dreamt of obsessing over a client, let alone her captor. Her image of herself is now entirely altered. A car drives past and, as the wheels turn, Emma-Jane thinks she sees her friend Lucy's concerned face in the hubcaps dulled by dirt, smeared on the black rubber, turning round and round. Lucy's warnings about Drew, her pleas for Emma-Jane to seek professional help, echo in her ears. But Lucy isn't around to make her question her feelings and thoughts. She closes her eyes and blinks hard.

*You know me better than anyone, as I do you.*

The sky is like an artist's palette of pink, orange, and blue worked in vast swathes, with only the distant black outlines of trees to provide perspective. She has never seen such vivid colours in the sky; it is ablaze. The remaining hues of pink deepen to purple, and the trees and the hedgerows resemble a child's scribbles in black ink. After seeing Drew again, she decides now is the time to book a holiday and take time out from work. Ever since she started treating Vanessa, the work-life equilibrium has been completely off balance. It will be good to reset.

From the sharp rise of Corbet Hill, with the wind playing with her hair, the steeple rising below from the Shropshire landscape is shaped like two hands perched together in perfect thought or prayer.

She thinks of Vanessa, now buried beside Avril, and of Evie and James. The shape of the steeple reminds her of the rhyme she used to recite at primary school.

*Here's the church and there's the steeple.*
*Open the door and see all the people.*

The church bells chime. She imagines the voice of the choir inside, gently reaching inside the hearts of the congregation and squeezing, squeezing.

From her vantage point on the hill, she imagines the vicar beginning a sermon with 'We are blessed,' and then the congregation bowing their heads, or kneeling on prayer mats. 'We are one,' they say.

*We are one.*

*Am I right to want to help him, after everything he's done?*

She closes her eyes, like a red admiral closes its wings tight when the wind is playing rough. It waits for the gust to pass before fluttering away. The impulse is to pull his wings together. Shut. She had been brave before, though.

She can do it again.

With the sun behind her, the glass woman on the hill has a lonely shadow, which is long and thin like the pine trees she stands above.

Can she trust her feelings, or is she suffering from post-traumatic stress, or Stockholm syndrome? From below, she might look like a distorted person, a foolish giant. Is she? The thought sends her arms to the sides to embrace the surrounding space, clawing the energy of pure nature into her, like a hibernating creature foraging for feed, for sustenance and reassurance in all its forms.

She feeds on the view and that vision inside the church. Eventually, when ant-like figures file out of its mouth, she steps away back to her car. The giant with its arms wide shrinks to nothing. Only the trees see her.

*Ave Maria, farewell, we are one* echoes in her ears as she pushes the accelerator to the floor and smiles at the dust in her wake and the narrowing road ahead.

# 32

The sun through Celia's office window is like smashed glass, winking menacingly at Emma-Jane. The unsettled feeling grows in the pit of her stomach, like an ulcer growing on the gastric juices of stress and anxiety.

'Emma-Jane?' Celia asks softly.

She shuffles in the soft chair and pushes her hair behind one ear. 'Sorry. My mind wandered.'

'Are you alright?'

'I've been thinking about taking a break.'

'A holiday?'

'Maybe. You used to say that I needed to find an equilibrium between work and life. There are so many places I haven't seen yet. America, Canada, Europe. The Golden Gate Bridge. The Red Sea.'

'I did say that. You're a driven woman and whatever you do, you pursue your goals with an unwavering commitment. I am curious why you want to find a work balance now.'

'You know why.'

'I'd like you to tell me.' Dr Glass looks down at her hands clenched in her lap. 'You've talked about eating too much and wanting to lose weight. I sense you are unhappy with yourself?'

'It seems like my face should look different after what happened, but outwardly I look unchanged. It feels like a lie, somehow. I'm not explaining myself well. I'm a stranger to myself, to the truth, so how can I expect my clients to be honest with me? My history is all different but here I am,' she says, surprised by the lump forming in her throat, 'still looking the same, only with a few extra pounds!'

Celia nods encouragingly for her to continue.

'I thought the meaning of my life was all about my job, but I don't know anymore if I'm truly good at it.'

'Why do you say that?'

'Some days I loathe myself for thinking about Drew Rogers. I look at my face in horror. I think to be true to myself, I have to see Drew again. I have to help. He was a good father, Celia.'

'No man is all bad, and I understand that not all of your experience was bad. Think of it as being in exile, though. You got used to a frightening and intense arrangement, so it became the norm. In time, you will be sure of yourself again and your routines.'

'But how can I be a good psychologist when my own thinking is impaired? When I am not sure of my own mind?'

'Humour me. Remind me, why did you start practicing in the first place?'

'Because the mind and its potential fascinate me.'

'Is that all?'

'Because I want to help people whose thoughts and thinking patterns are damaged by negative experiences.'

Celia nods and Emma-Jane's face breaks into a smile of understanding. 'That is the beginning: knowing when we aren't in control of our thoughts and feelings.'

Tears prick her eyes. 'I see something of myself in him. What does that make me? I must be a wolf in sheep's clothing.'

'You don't mean that. You're catastrophising.'

'You're right, but it's unsettled me.'

'We grow by being unsettled. Our mind and thought process develops. Just because we reach adulthood and professional maturity, we don't remain static. Despite what you think right now, you will be a better psychologist for the experience—provided you give yourself time before practising again and think carefully about who you treat.'

'I just don't know if I can do this job when I am just like many of the clients I treat.'

'In what way?'

'Coloured thinking. Pixelated, if you like.'

'And you are aware of it.' Celia smiles. 'Emma-Jane. Dr Glass. What would you be saying to you?'

She laughs a little. 'To listen to my thoughts. To be aware of when my thinking is faulty, obsessive even, "off." To have faith in the power of my own mind. To know I am in control of my own thoughts and feelings.'

'Exactly,' Celia smiles. 'Tell me, do you have romantic feelings for Drew Rogers?'

'No, I don't.'

'You were abducted and held against your will by an ill, frightening man. Like I said, give yourself time to think whether you are the best person to help Drew with accurate empathy after what he put you through.'

'I think I might have to see him to know either way. He's still so unwell. Lucy thinks I'm suffering with post-traumatic stress disorder. I've never felt so observed at every angle by Lucy. It's pathetic, but I have been avoiding her company and her phone calls.'

'It's not my place to tell you what to do, but I think it is too soon for you to return to work in any capacity. Lucy has your best interests at heart. Come back in a couple of weeks' time after resting at home. Or, do some travelling. Do things that make you feel good about yourself and who you are.'

*No*, Emma-Jane thinks. *Who I was.*

# 33

The hospital confirmed they had released Drew a week early. It's been a long time since she saw him, but he is often in her thoughts.

Dressed in a winter coat and boots to keep warm on a breezy afternoon in early September, she parks her Golf at the bottom of the no-through road and walks towards the house where Drew held her captive. By four o'clock, the light is subdued and mellow. She thinks rain is threatening, and pulls her coat around her a little tighter, wishing she'd brought an umbrella.

Clouds hang low, but she is still fizzing with the nervous kind of energy you get before an interview for a job you really want. She wills the sun to push through the clouds and for the rain to pour on another part of the country. Her palms are sweaty as she walks in the direction of the house.

To be here of her own volition makes her feel powerful—and a little afraid.

How strange it is to have been forced to live here, not knowing where the house was. To now have driven and parked at the bottom of the lane, knowing it takes less than twenty minutes by car from her own house, and even less from her office. She hears a lorry thundering past and a horn beeping. A pigeon takes sudden flight from the telephone pole as the wind blows, and a strand of hair obscures her vision.

Will he be ready to see her? She had asked herself that question repeatedly, at all hours of the day and night.

Lucy has made it clear what she thinks, but Emma-Jane keeps walking towards the house.

In the maze of time at that house, she had sat through those rambling memories of his family, like he was turning a page in a photograph album until the pictures faded from colour to sepia. When she thinks about those days here, it is one heartbeat after another: hers, Drew's, Evie's, and James's. True, some days the beating hearts were too loud to bear, but she'd listened. She did. That's what she'd been trained to do. And she was good at what she did.

As she approaches the house, Emma-Jane remembers the drab curtains permanently drawn, the lounge almost entirely free of furniture, which gave the few objects in the room—the two chairs, the mattress—prominence in an otherwise bland space. The house was deserted, like a ship at port, its decks swept clean with no one aboard, except her, Drew, the chair, the mattress, and the ghosts of Evie and James.

It is an ordinary house, and yet what went on inside was anything but. Her whole life has changed because she has changed. Not because of a wedding, a birth, or even a bereavement. She tries to imagine what the house is like now that Drew is living there, having moved all his furniture and belongings inside. Perhaps antiques, a king-sized bed, decorative mirrors, tasteful artwork, and a plush sofa perfect for hypnosis. The TV aerial protrudes from the roof into the slate sky, which hangs low and heavy.

His Range Rover is parked outside, recently washed and polished. There is no mistaking that he is at home, perhaps relaxing with a book. She gazes at the house and car, metres away now, standing still as the rain pours down.

The cool droplets fall to the ground like an unexpected baptism.

Nervously, she glances at an upstairs window, Drew's voice echoing in her ears.

*If I fail, you fail.*

She self-consciously touches her cheek, hoping her mascara won't run. Yes, she recognises herself, despite what Lucy says. Her hair clings to her head. There are curtains and blinds at the various windows which weren't there before.

How will she feel when she sees him? She knows things about him no one else does.

She moves with purpose towards the lounge window, drawn to it, having stared from the other side of the room at the curtained pane of glass for hour after hour. To be on the other side of the glass, looking in, gives her an immense sense of power.

She has beaten him. But there is still something else . . .

A hollow exists in her tummy, like a hunger. Will he smile when he sees her?

She feels the rain like she hasn't felt it before: in sheets, dense and impatient. It douses her from head to toe, and the feeling of apprehension and pleasure is like blotting paper. She steps into a deep, brown puddle.

*It's a good thing to revisit places where you've experienced fear or terror. This is my therapy. I tell my clients this. Look. Look through the window.*

*Look through the damn glass.*

She does a double take when she sees the curtain to the lounge window hasn't been drawn. A sound makes her stop in her tracks. She peers inside and her eyes fix onto the middle of the lounge. The light is switched on. The bulb is dressed with a lampshade this time, and directly beneath it is the very chair Emma-Jane had spent her days on.

Her mouth opens. No sound comes. A throttling overcomes her, like a gag pushed hard into her mouth. There's no chloroform this time.

Drew, the thief. Has he stolen her voice too?

Drew's eyes are closed but Emma-Jane can clearly see a young, naked woman writhing on top of him. The bones in her spine move as she wriggles, screwing him hard, moving one way, then the other. The hairs on his bare legs are dark and thick, so dark against the pink flush of the woman's skin. The chair and the two entwined bodies cast a shadow on the new beige carpet as this strange woman is born into Emma-Jane's universe.

Ignorance ends, like a collision of planets.

This terrible shop window she has chosen to peer into seems to grow larger. Inside, that girl-doll tilts her head back with abandon and his hands search through her hair.

The familiar chair. The humiliation.

Emma-Jane is a voyeur looking in, a peeping Tom. She collapses onto the ground and puts her head in her hands. There is no unwinding of this moment. Her shame feels like thrown stones are bouncing off her skin. What is she doing here? This isn't professional. This is obsession.

Out of control.

This version of herself—who, what, and why for this man? She puts her hands over her ears because she can hear the moaning and the thumping and the grinding.

The pleasure grows louder as they head towards a climax. It sounds like pain. It sounds . . .

'Hannah!' Drew cries in a crashing of syllables. 'Hannah!'

His voice saying that strange name cuts like a knife through her skin, writing a foreign name in blood across her chest. Emma-Jane takes in air like she's been half-strangled by a lanyard with the name DR GLASS written across it. If only she could pull her coat a little tighter and make herself invisible.

A white van speeds towards the house.

From the way it is being driven, she senses urgency, and then, from the way the man gets out of the van and slams the door, she senses fury. He is muttering as he charges towards the house.

Emma-Jane leans closer to the wall. He isn't a man she recognises. Whether or not he has seen her, she doesn't know. Concealing her professional identity matters now more than anything. She realises how cold it is, and how chilled she feels being wet through. Her back and knees are aching from the awkward position she is crouched in.

He strides into the house, leaving the front door open, and then there's a muffled sound before a sudden, scuffling movement. She rests her head against the wall, hidden out of sight under the window, and jumps when she hears crashing and thumping. Afraid, she remains motionless, imagining blood, thinking she can smell it, and semen.

'Bastard! I'm gonna fucking kill you!'

Hannah shrieks. 'Stop! Stop it!' Her voice is pulled hoarse, desperate. 'Get! Off! Me!'

'You fucking bastard, Drew!'

Something close to the window breaks; perhaps the wooden chair. Her pulse peaks as the rain thuds against the windowpane. The sounds of fighting—of banging, bodies falling, objects being thrown—resumes.

'Revenge is a dish best served cold, you cunt,' Drew shouts between pants. 'Kat told me what you said, what you did. Making her think I would leave Evie and James for her. If you hadn't fed Kat that sack of lies, she wouldn't have had the gall to confront Evie, and my fucking wife and son wouldn't be dead! You're welcome to Hannah now; she's used goods to me. Now fuck off.'

'You complete and utter bastard!' Hannah spits, frantically grabbing her clothes. 'You sick fuck!' The vowels unravel like a spool.

AJ shouts, 'Don't you fucking come near me or her ever again or I'll—'

'I'm getting the fuck out of here!' Hannah shrieks at AJ, sobbing and sounding desperate to get away from Drew and the humiliation of being used.

Emma-Jane ducks at the sound of punching and air expelled from lungs, thumps, and bangs. Then it stops. The motionlessness and quietness are just as frightening.

'You fucking deserve it, Drew!' AJ pants. 'I hope you fuckin' bleed to death!'

Inside, Hannah screams.

Emma-Jane's stare at the wall is empty, like she's looking out at an ocean without a horizon. She clamps a hand to her mouth.

*Is Drew dead?*

The front door slams.

Emma-Jane cowers against the wall at the sound of hurried footsteps, Hannah sobbing, and AJ mumbling. She glimpses a scantily clad Hannah and blood on AJ's shirt. AJ's boots thunder on the gravel and the puddles splash as the van speeds back the way it came.

She slowly rises to her feet, keeping her hand against the wall to steady herself. Her nose is running, and she doesn't have a tissue, but it is raining so hard it doesn't matter. She takes a tentative step around the side of the building and staggers away from the window, not looking, not trying to think, just focusing on walking, getting away, listening to the sound of her feet urgently moving on the gravel.

Away.

Then she turns back towards the house and the open door. Hurrying now, every second matters if she can save him.

'Drew!' she shouts, splashing through puddles back towards the house.

'Emma-Jane,' Drew whimpers as he appears in the doorway, his nose and mouth oozing blood. 'What—why are you—?' He looks panicked at the sight of her.

She stops running and stands still in the rain. She can see all of him so clearly. She knows the real him now.

The ties are finally cut.

'I said I'd help you. That's why I'm here.'

'Is it?'

'It was wrong of me to come here, though.' She wipes the rain from her cheeks. 'I guess this was more for me, than for you. To see this place. This hell. You. I think it would be better if you saw another therapist.'

'How selfish, Dr Glass.'

'You know I care, Drew. I've always cared.'

'Or is it you're a dog, beaten so often it is obedient to its owner's heel, not knowing anything different?' At that moment, the candle of his face melts into a smirk and the dirt on her shoes says everything. 'If I fail, you fail.'

She shakes her head and raindrops fly off and drip down her cheeks. Whatever they had shared, the fabric is now torn and tattered. She has never been more grateful that the flimsy curtains at the lounge window were not drawn. She turns to leave.

'Wait,' he screams. 'Don't do this!' And for all his words, she knows he needs her.

He needs Dr Glass.

'Goodbye, Drew,' she says, holding her palm up like a mirror to him, then letting it fall to her side. 'Get help.'

He screams louder as she walks away.

A part of her wants to cry, to break, but she is still a doctor. Again a whole person. Still Dr Glass, a good woman, with her own integrity in place, like a pane of glass in a window battered by a storm. She matters to herself and to her clients, to her friends.

Then, she pauses and rubs her hands through her hair, blinking at the enormity of what has just happened. Her knees quiver.

*Keep walking,* she tells herself.

If she stays there a moment longer, Drew might come for revenge. She looks up at the sky, hearing the wind and the rattle of branches, the rustle of leaves, the dismantling of twigs to the ground and their final snap in half as they finger the soil and the insects. She feels a cold, long finger of light stroking her hair and shoulders, her neck and chin. The sound of the wind increases, rattling branch arms, more urgent and persistent, like the incessant clicking from a camera.

When she turns on the ignition in her car, the engine sounds like it is crying.

As she drives, the windscreen wipers keep the glass clear. It seems like the radio signal improves as the wheels turn, like the static fades and the wavelengths of sound connect with her senses and her intellect, at long last.

As she drives, she gains fortitude by imagining her front door, stepping inside, and then closing it.

Shut. For good.

# 34

The last things for Lucy to pack away in the large cardboard box are the framed posters on the wall of her old office.

BE THE PERSON YOU WANT TO BE.
EAT TO BE WELL.
LOVE YOUR BODY.

She won't be sad to leave the chairs where Jennifer and Ross had sat side-by-side, holding hands. The chairs will stay put, along with the desk and office chair, for whomever moves in.

Emma-Jane has been inundated with enquiries from all manner of businesses, including ones performing treatments such as acupuncture, homeopathy, and massage therapy. Lucy puts the potted plant in the box, closes the flaps, and then slides her laptop into a rucksack. When she hears footsteps, she opens the door to greet Dr Glass.

'I'm almost done!'

'Coming to work won't be the same without you. I shall keep the door to your office closed.' She hugs Lucy. 'It will feel horribly lonely. Who am I going to drink tea with and moan about my workday to?'

'I thought you'd found someone suitable to move in here.'

'It's not the same. You and I have known each other a long time and been through a lot. I will miss you, that's what I'm making a mess of saying. Don't be a stranger!'

'I won't. I'm only a few hours' drive away. You could have a mini break with me and walk some of Hadrian's Wall—avoiding certain sections, obviously.'

'Obviously,' she says, with raised eyebrows, not wanting to mention what happened to Evie and James at Sycamore Gap or Drew Rogers, before or since.

They both need to escape. And that, sadly, means putting distance between them after so many years and memories, working side by side in the office, sharing simple routines, chatting as they waited for the electric kettle to boil. Emma-Jane knows she will think of Lucy when she switches the kettle on and reaches inside the cupboard for a mug.

Like prisoners who have been incarcerated for a long time, they both have to navigate new worlds and learn to trust, to live a free life without the stigma of their past.

Punishment. Emma-Jane recalls it spoken from Drew's mouth as she watches her friend make her last preparations before leaving the office and Shrewsbury for good. They are all connected in one way or another, through suffering.

The lives of Ross and Vanessa, in different ways, had ended here: a good place—not a dungeon, but a business, to help people.

'If there's anything you need, or if you change your mind and want to come back, you only have to say the word.'

'I'll remember that, but let's hope you won't need rescuing again.'

'Look,' Emma-Jane says, opening the lid to a square, scarlet cake box. 'I hope you've got a good appetite. I know I have.'

After tea and cake and a last hug, Emma-Jane kisses

her friend goodbye and, feeling bloated from the food, she flops onto the soft chair in her office and picks up the local paper.

The story about the suicide of a local millionaire is on page two. It's not a story that makes her feel much at all.

Not anymore.

It happened in an outbuilding at a farm, in the shippon. Drew Rogers had tossed a rope over one beam and hanged himself. He'd left a note, the article said, confirming the suicide. There was nothing suspicious about the death except there was a cryptic line in the note, which said:

*If I fail, you fail.*

She imagines his body there, dangling like a silenced bell from a deserted church to punish her. A kind of execution, a death row of his own making—without an audience, save for the owls and the stars.

And perhaps a ghost or two.

# ACKNOWLEDGEMENTS

Many thanks to the terrific team at TCK Publishing/ Quilla Books, especially Nicholas Holloway, who championed *Doctor Glass* and made it a better book. He is a wonderful editor to work with. Most of all, thank you to the people who read my books. I hope you continue to enjoy my stories.

# ABOUT THE AUTHOR

Louise Worthington was born in Cheshire, England. She graduated from the University of Essex with a degree in literature. Formerly an English teacher, Louise studied psychology before taking up writing as a full-time career. She lives with her family in Shropshire in the UK. *Doctor Glass* is her sixth novel and the first in the *Glass Minds* series.

# CONNECT WITH LOUISE WORTHINGTON

Sign up for Louise's newsletter at
**www.louiseworthington.co.uk/newsletter**

To find out more information visit her website:
**www.louiseworthington.co.uk**

Social Media
**@louiseworthington9**
**@louise.worthington.714**

# BOOK DISCOUNTS AND SPECIAL DEALS

Sign up for free to get discounts and special deals
on our bestselling books at

**www.TCKpublishing.com/bookdeals**

Made in the USA
Columbia, SC
19 April 2022

59109741R00159